KANE

A Small Town, Friends to Lovers, Hidden Identity,
Military Protector Romance

Ghost Ops
Book 4

LYNN RAYE HARRIS

All Rights Reserved. This book or any portion thereof
may not be reproduced or used in any manner whatsoever without the
express written permission of the publisher except for the use of brief
quotations in a book review.

This is a work of fiction. Names, characters, places, and incidents either
are the products of the author's imagination or are used fictitiously. Any
resemblance to actual persons, living or dead, businesses, companies,
events, or locales is entirely coincidental.

The Hostile Operations Team® and Lynn Raye Harris® are trademarks
of H.O.T. Publishing, LLC.

Printed in the United States of America

First Printing, 2025

For rights inquires, visit www.LynnRayeHarris.com

KANE
Copyright © 2025 by Lynn Raye Harris
Cover Design Copyright © 2025 Croco Designs

ISBN: 979-8-89117-051-3

Chapter One

THE BELL ON THE FRONT DOOR TINKLED AS A PATRON entered One Shot Tactical. The building was arranged with the store in front, where guns and ammunition were displayed in glass cases. Holsters, targets, concealed carry purses, and other items were on racks in the center or shelves against the wall.

"Welcome to One Shot Tactical," Daphne Bryant said with a sunny smile as she stood to greet the newcomer.

Her desk sat behind one of the counters. She was the receptionist during business hours, but she did so much more. She also took care of scheduling self-defense classes for the six men who owned the range, and she booked security consultations with other businesses in town and over in Huntsville where most of the defense contractors were located. She also did the ordering for supplies that weren't guns or ammo, and Alex had recently let her start working on the books.

Not all the books, since the gun ordering and weapons inventory was separate, and that was fine with her. She had a line item for those orders when they happened, but the actual details were up to the One Shot guys.

Alex hadn't blinked when she said she had accounting experience. It was maybe too close to the life she'd left behind, but the truth was that no matter how rewarding it was to work for these guys and live in gorgeous Sutton's Creek, her skills were a little wasted taking calls and booking appointments. He'd asked her to go over the spreadsheets and give her conclusions. Next thing she knew, she was handling the business expenses. Which she did carefully and diligently.

The man walked over to her counter. He had a range bag slung over one shoulder, hands in his jeans pockets, and a look of concentration on his face. "Hey. You got any open bays?"

"We do." Daphne stood. "We have a class in two hours, but you can shoot until then if you want. It's twenty-five an hour if you aren't a member. We also rent guns. Ten for one or twenty for up to five. You have to purchase the ammunition from us."

"Got anything interesting?"

Daphne shrugged. "A Desert Eagle. Most guys like to give that one a try."

His eyes narrowed. She got the feeling he was studying her more than thinking about the weapon. A coil of unease unwound itself in her stomach.

"You know much about guns? Or are you here for decoration?"

The question was rude and misogynistic, but that wasn't why it bothered her. A narrow line of sweat beaded beneath her breasts, across her lip. She wasn't about to tell him she could disassemble that Desert Eagle and reassemble it in under five minutes. She didn't tell anyone that kind of information.

Not even the men she worked for.

"I work here. Bound to know a little. Why do you ask?"

He nodded and the truth came out. "You look familiar. Not sure why."

Fear crawled up her throat and wrapped icy fingers around her neck. "I've heard that before. They say everybody's got a double somewhere, don't they?" She smiled to sell it. "You want to try that Desert Eagle or you good?"

"I'm good. Got my own gear."

"All righty then. You want one hour or two?"

"Just one is fine."

Daphne's fingers trembled as she reached for the paperwork. "Need you to fill this out and I'll need ID. Driver's license, military ID, pistol permit, etcetera. Take your pick," she said as she pushed the clipboard toward him. "We take cash, credit, PayPal and Venmo."

The man took the clipboard, turned it. But he didn't stop looking at her. "I never forget a face. It'll come to me eventually."

Daphne forced a laugh. "Some people think I look like a younger version of the actress on Yellowstone. You know, the crazy one?"

She was talking too much. She needed to stop. But fear had her in its grip. She didn't recognize the man, but if he knew her father and brother, then he wasn't anybody she wanted to spend time with.

"Don't watch that show so I can't say."

"Well, she's kinda famous and her face is everywhere so that might be it."

He shrugged. "Could be." He finished the paperwork and pushed it toward her with ID and cash. When she'd processed everything, she gave him a pass and targets, then explained the procedures for entering and exiting the range.

"Bay Five," she said. "Your range safety officer is Chance."

"Thanks." The man hefted his bag, grabbed the targets, and headed for the entrance to the shooting bays.

Daphne waited until he was inside before she sank onto her chair and let out a shaky breath. She'd been in Sutton's Creek for six months. She'd told herself it was too remote, too hidden, for her family to find her. It was a risk working in a gun range, but what were the chances some criminal associate of her dad's would show up in a tiny town in a tiny corner of Alabama?

Besides, she hadn't started out working at One Shot Tactical. She'd been cleaning rooms at the Wheeler Inn, figuring that was lowkey enough, but then she'd lost her job and ended up squatting in the Sutton building where the guys found her one night. They'd taken her in, offered her a job, shelter, and safety. It'd been a risk, but she'd had no other options at the time.

She didn't know for sure this man was somebody from her old life. She focused on the paperwork again, studied the details.

Nathan Fader.

He wasn't from New Orleans, which was good. Destin, Florida. Self-employed. She hadn't asked why he was in town, but that would've been a red flag if she had. Or an invitation.

Her stomach twisted into knots. She told herself he might have been flirting, that his idea of a pick-up line was to say she looked familiar. That was usually followed with the comparison to a celebrity, which he had not done. But maybe he was just bad at it.

Daphne chewed her lip and glanced at her phone. Another fifty-five minutes before she was out of here. The range closed at six but she was leaving early because it was book club night. She'd be gone before he finished shooting, thank God.

Maybe by then he'd have forgotten about her anyway. Chance was charming when he was on RSO duty and he'd get the guy talking, find out more about him. Maybe even tell him about the Dawg and direct him there for dinner.

Thankfully, the Bookalicious Besties Book Club was meeting at the library tonight. There was a new librarian in town and everyone wanted to welcome her. Miss Hettie had finally retired after sixty years, though she was still planning to work part-time as needed.

When she wasn't lounging around in Orange Beach, Alabama, where her son had a holiday condo, that is.

The Besties were having a potluck dinner as well, which meant Daphne needed to head home and pop her casserole—bought from Miss Mary's Diner, of course—in the oven before walking over to the library. The main reason why she was leaving an hour early. Most of One Shot's clients were range members anyway. Whenever anyone came in, one of the guys would come from the back to check them in. They got the alerts for the door, and there were cameras. Nobody entered the building without everyone knowing.

In fact, she'd thought when Alex first hired her that it was out of pity—and it probably was—but she'd set out to make herself indispensable and prove she could be an asset to the business.

Which she'd done.

Daphne stared at her computer screen, not really seeing the inventory sheet she'd been working on. Maybe she should have moved on a couple of months ago, once she'd saved up enough money to travel, but she liked her apartment, dammit. And she liked Sutton's Creek. Not to mention she'd found friends, not just in the guys, but in the women who'd trickled into their lives. Emma and Rory had been a package set even before Chance and Rory got together, but now there was Callie and her teenage sister, Nikki, too.

Not to be confused with Waitress Nikki at The Salty Dawg Tavern, who was older and had a raspy smoker's voice. Whenever they all went to the Dawg, the two Nikkis joked with each other about being twins—Big Nikki and Little Nikki. Sometimes Little Nikki followed Big Nikki around the restaurant and took orders with her like they were a matched set. It was silly fun for both of them, and the patrons never seemed to mind.

God, she'd miss these people if she had to leave.

Daphne put her head in her hands. She didn't want to go. Sutton's Creek was home, even if the people in it would be horrified if they knew where she'd come from. The kind of shit her family was involved in. She was tainted by association—and she was tainted by participation. That was the worst of it.

"What's wrong?"

Daphne jerked her head up to find Kane watching her. He'd emerged from the hallway that led to the offices and she hadn't even noticed. Kane Fox was the last man she'd want to know about her past. She sniffed and straightened her spine.

"Nothing at all. I'm just thinking about the book club tonight and what I need to do."

He rolled toward her with that easy gait he had that spoke of confidence and power. All the men of One Shot Tactical were gorgeous, but Kane did something to her insides that none of the rest of them did. Then again, he had that effect on women. So many women who came for classes and then kept coming back, asking for Kane, sighing and giggling when he emerged to talk to them about their bullshit excuses for returning.

It fired her up and made her determined not to be one of them. Which would have been difficult anyway since Kane insisted on treating her like the little sister he'd never had. He was thirty-five and she was twenty-eight—though her fake ID said she was younger—but he treated her like she was fifteen.

He'd been helping her look for a car for months now, but none of them ever met his exacting standards. She still had Warren's old beater that he'd loaned her, but she needed to either buy it or give it back. Warren Trigg was the nicest man she knew. Even though he'd broken up with her recently, he was still her friend and he'd told her she could keep using the car as long as she needed.

She'd been upset over the breakup, not because she loved Warren or anything, but because his decency had made her feel like she was decent too. So when he told her she wasn't the kind of woman he wanted to marry, it'd crushed her for a different reason than anyone knew.

She'd told everyone he thought she wasn't smart enough, that she was too vain. Warren was too kind to say either of those things, but she'd been drinking that night around the fire when she'd told her friends and she'd let her feelings of self-loathing pour out. She *had* been vain at one time, though she wasn't so much now. Her old self wouldn't recognize this version.

"You look like it's more than the book club. You still upset about Trigg?"

Daphne sniffed and turned her attention to the computer screen again. "None of your business."

"Just looking out for you, Daph."

She liked when he called her Daph. She'd never thought of herself as a Daph, or a Daffy, but when these people gave her those nicknames, she liked it. She'd only started going by Daphne when she'd fled New Orleans, but it felt more right than her old name did anymore.

"I need a car, Kane. If you haven't found one you think is good by the end of the week, I'm buying Warren's. It feels wrong to keep driving it after we've broken up."

He folded his arms over his chest. She very deliberately did *not* look at the way it made the muscles of his chest and arms pop. "I've been busy. We can go tonight. Or tomorrow."

"I told you book club is tonight. It needs to be tomorrow."

"How long does book club last?"

"A couple of hours. We're starting at six-thirty, and we'll be at the library tonight, so it'll be too late when we're done."

"Why the library?"

"Paisley Allen. She's the new librarian since Miss Hettie retired. We're having a potluck and we've invited her to talk about the book with us."

"So tomorrow then. After work."

"Works for me."

"What's the book?"

She glanced up at him, startled. "The book?"

"That you're discussing tonight."

"Why?"

He frowned. "Just being friendly. Don't friends ask each other questions about the things they're interested in?"

"Uh, sure. But you've never asked before so forgive me for being surprised."

"I'm asking now. What's the difference?"

Daphne sucked in a calming breath. "Nothing, I guess. We're reading a romance novel about dragons and Fae warriors. Nikki picked it."

"Title?"

She told him. Then she frowned. "Wait a minute—are you asking so you can use this book as one of your flirty pick up lines on the next hot babe to cross your path?"

He scowled. "Why would I do that? I could do a Google search and find a popular romance to talk about if I wanted to. I'm just making conversation here and it's like pulling teeth from you. Since when did you get so uptight?"

"I'm not uptight," she said, her ears growing hot. "But I've got work to do and you're distracting me."

"Didn't look like you were working. Looked like you were worried about something."

Daphne made herself smile. "I'm not worried, Kane. Just preoccupied. I'm leaving at five so I need to finish up this inventory sheet and prepare the time cards for the new part-timers Alex hired before I go. That's all."

His frown didn't abate. "Okay. But you know you can tell me anything, right? I'm in your corner, Daph. You wanna talk about Limp Dick Trigg dumping you, I'll listen. I'll pat you on the back and tell you he made a huge mistake because he did."

She thought she should be mad at him calling Warren names, but it felt good that he wanted to defend her and be a friend.

Always a friend. Only a friend.

Probably for the best, really. She didn't need to get involved with a man like Kane. A charmer. A man with deep secrets of his own if her instincts were right. *All* the One Shot guys had secrets, and all of them could've worked for her brother and father they were so similar to the men who had done so over the years.

Except for the integrity thing. That was something the O'Malley family enforcers didn't have. They were plenty scary, and they were loyal to her family, but they didn't have the kind of morals she was pretty certain governed Kane and his friends. Her father's people would kill anyone without question so long as they got paid for it.

"I hear you, Kane. Thanks. But I'm not talking about Warren with you. He's a good man and he wants different things from life than I do. That's all it is."

Kane jerked his chin up in an affirmation. "Gotcha, babe. Here if you need me, though."

"Did you come out here for a reason or was this visit spontaneous?"

He blinked. "Uh, yeah. I was, uh, coming to grab that new Sig from the case. Got a dude who wants to come in later and try it out."

Daphne was too rattled to figure out why he was making up a lie. And what would be the point anyway? He'd have another bullshit excuse lined up if she called him on this one.

He headed behind one of the glass cases that lined the wall and took out a key to open the sliding doors, reaching in for the weapon and pulling it out. Then he sauntered back the way he'd come, giving her a salute before he disappeared down the hall.

Daphne leaned back in her chair, her heart pounding like she'd run a marathon, her bones melting into her skin with no one there to talk to her and keep the panic at bay.

Trouble was the word that echoed through her mind.

But whether it was about Kane—or Nathan Fader— she had no idea.

Chapter Two

Kane sauntered into the Salty Dawg Tavern, and six chicks made eye contact and smiled. He smiled back, knowing he could take any one of them home for a marathon in the sheets if he wanted to.

Which he didn't. Hadn't for a while now, though he kept up the pretense since everybody expected him to chase tail like a man ten years younger. His own fault, really. What people saw was what they believed, and he was an expert at making them see what he wanted them to see.

"Dude," Chance said as he walked over and took a seat at the usual table.

"What?" Kane reached for a chicken wing from one of the baskets in the middle of the table. Theo Harper, co-owner and chef of the Dawg, made some damn fine wings. Even Ethan agreed, and he was from New York. Not that NYC was Buffalo, where chicken wings in hot sauce originated, but it was a lot closer than small-town Alabama.

"Heard you're taking Daphne car hunting again

tomorrow. Are you gonna stop jerking around and pick a fucking car or what?"

He should have known the news would get around when he'd mentioned it to Ethan before he'd left the range for the day. "Yeah, I'm gonna pick a fucking car. What's wrong with taking my time to find the right one, huh? Daphne's got a budget."

Alex snorted. "Yeah, but it's been, what, four months now? She's probably got a bigger budget by now."

Kane shrugged his shoulders, shaking off the teasing. "Car shopping is better now. More used cars in her price range on the market than there were before. We'll find something good."

Seth arched an eyebrow. "You should just tell her to buy Trigg's car and call it a day."

"That car's a piece of shit."

"Yeah, but it works and he'd sell it to her cheap. She doesn't go anywhere except to work and things around town. She doesn't need to be able to drive to the other side of Huntsville, for fuck's sake."

"Would you want Callie driving around in an old rust bucket with no anti-lock brakes or modern crumple zones?"

"Not the same thing. Cal drives to Huntsville every day. And Daph's been driving that beater for the past few months, so what's your point?"

Kane eyed his teammates. They were all there except Ethan, who was on the way.

"Is there a reason y'all are busting my balls tonight?"

Blaze shook his head while Chance may have grimaced. Seth remained blank.

Kane studied them. And then it dawned.

"Wait. It's your women. They're turning the thumb-screws, right?"

Chance groaned. "Dude, Rory is filled to the brim with fucking pregnancy hormones—"

"Emma, too," Blaze added, because that was a new development he and Emma had announced recently. Apparently, despite her parents being pillars of the community and regular church goers, they weren't scandalized at all by their unmarried daughter having a baby with her fiancé. No, they were thrilled and making huge plans for baby showers and shit.

"Yeah," Chance continued. "Two women in nesting mode, who've known Daphne for a while now, and who feel protective. They've got that book club and they talk, and one of the things they talk about is Daphne's relationship status, her car situation, and God knows what else. But they've chosen to focus on the car for the moment. Girl needs a functional, decent car, STAT."

"Yeah, yeah, I know," Kane said, dropping the wing he'd cleaned and grabbing another one. "I'll get it solved, promise."

"This week?" Blaze asked.

A shot of temper flared. "Sure, man, I'll poof up a magic car that fits the bill and she'll be all set."

Alex intervened. "I realize your feelings about Daphne are complicated, but either solve this shit by the end of the week or one of us will help her instead."

Chance dropped a wing in the empties basket. "Or let her solve it herself. Daphne isn't helpless. She'll find a car, take a mechanic to look at it, and make a decision."

"What mechanic?" Kane fired back, ignoring the part about complicated feelings. He didn't have complicated feelings. He was protective because Daphne was young and sweet and she didn't need some asshole taking advantage of her. How was this so hard to understand?

"Hell if I know. But Emma and Rory know everybody in this town. They'll make a recommendation."

Kane held up both hands in surrender. "I've got this. You dickheads act like I've purposely avoided finding a car, but everything we've looked at has either been overpriced or a death trap. And let's not forget the drama around here when we've all been doing other things because the women some of you love were in trouble and needed our help. Not exactly prime car shopping opportunities, 'specially when she had Trigg's car to drive. But she wants to give it back, and we're solving this ASAP."

"Good. Glad to hear it," Alex said.

"Thank God," Chance said.

Blaze nodded. "Agreed."

Kane swung his gaze over to Seth. "What? You aren't getting shit from your woman too?"

Seth shrugged. "I am, but I'd say it's a normal level of shit, not a pregnant level." He shot a glance at Blaze and Chance. "Gotta admit, that level seems kinda terrifying."

"You have no idea," Chance muttered into his beer.

Blaze squeezed Chance's shoulder and sighed.

Ethan swaggered in, the last to arrive, and took the chair next to Kane. "What'd I miss?"

"Me getting my ass grilled over a hot fire about Daphne's car search. Thanks for telling everyone we're on the hunt again."

Ethan shrugged. "You didn't say it was a secret."

"It's not."

Waitress Nikki strolled over to take orders and the conversation moved on. Thank fuck. Kane kept his eye on his surroundings, same as they all did, looking for things that weren't right. They weren't the kind of men who sat in restaurants, oblivious to the people around them. Sutton's Creek was typically safe, except for a few notable exceptions involving his teammates' women, but letting down your guard was the kind of shit that could get you killed on operations when the location wasn't as secure.

For Kane, no matter where he was, he stayed on high alert. He knew how badly things could go wrong in an instant, even in the most seemingly normal of places. Hell, Blaze had met Emma when he'd walked in on a robbery at the Gas-n-Go outside of town. If he hadn't gotten there when he did, who knows what might have happened?

All it took was a single moment in time and your life changed forever.

His life changed forever.

Shit.

He focused on the conversation, not really paying attention as memories of that time in his life pushed against the barrier he kept them locked behind.

Fortunately, Theo Harper arrived with Kane's cheeseburger. "Just the way you like it with smoked gouda instead of cheddar," he said, setting it down in front of Kane. "The rest is coming. Y'all good tonight?"

"Yeah, man," Kane said. "You?"

Theo grinned. "Doing great, my man."

"How hard was it to get Rory to take the night off?" Chance asked with an arched eyebrow.

"Duuuude," Theo groaned. "So hard. But we've got it. Amber has the bar, Nikki and Keisha have the floor, and I've got my guys in there rustling up the grub. If it was Friday or Saturday, different story. But we've got this, which I had to stress over and over again. Rory worries it'll get busy or somebody will ask for a drink only she knows, but I promised to call her if it happened. Don't worry," he added. "Even if it did, I'm not calling her."

"Good man," Chance said.

"She texted once," Theo said. "But that was over an

hour ago. Think she's probably too engaged with the book club to care by now."

"That's my hope," Chance said. "If she's having fun, she won't worry about this place."

"I'm doing my part to make sure she knows we've got this. Once she has the baby, I expect her to take some time off. Which I've told her," Theo said.

Chance snorted. "Lemme guess—she told you to fuck yourself, right?"

"Pretty much. I know she'll be in here just as soon as she feels up to it, probably with an infant strapped to her chest in one of those sling things, but I'd like her to take a couple of weeks off at least. Preferably more."

"Rory knows what she needs and what she can handle," Chance said. "But I'm with you on taking some time off before she jumps back in with both feet."

Waitress Nikki showed up with their food, Theo helped her deliver it, and then he returned to the kitchen while they dived in. The conversation shifted to things that didn't piss anybody off for a while, and then one of the women who'd smiled at Kane earlier accosted him on the way to take a piss.

He managed to disentangle her arms from around his neck, politely turn her down, and continue on his way. He'd no sooner returned to the table than the book clubbers came strolling into the Dawg.

Chance was on his feet in an instant, grabbing the bag Rory carried, setting it on the table as he kissed her forehead. Emma went into Blaze's arms for a hug and kiss. Seth and Callie looked soulfully at each other and tangled their fingers together.

Kane deliberately looked away, ignoring the pinch of anger in his gut that always flared whenever he watched his teammates with their women. It pissed him off that he felt that way, because they were his brothers and he wanted them happy, but it reminded him how unpredictable life was.

As if he didn't live with that knowledge every moment of every day. It got easier with time, like people said it would, but it didn't make it fair. Hannah had only been twenty-three, like Daphne was now. So much life left to live. So fucking unfair.

Nikki went to high-five her 'twin' while Emma took a step to the side to reveal another woman who'd followed them over to the table.

She was short, probably five-one or two, with black hair that was cut short against her head. It was a masculine cut, but on her it looked feminine and flattering. Took a well-shaped head and a pretty face to pull that one off, but she had those things. She was curvy and pretty, with a slender neck and big blue eyes. She wore a black sheath dress that wasn't tight but somehow emphasized all her curves.

"This is Paisley," Emma said. "She's the new librarian."

Paisley waved, revealing a small tattoo heart on her wrist. "Hi."

When her gaze reached Ethan, she looked puzzled for a second. But then it was gone and everyone welcomed her, including Ethan. Though he looked like he'd just got hit by acid reflux or something. Maybe he was knocked flat by her beauty, or he'd been hit by the love lightning. Who knew?

Kane would have thought his teammate was about to offer her a chair, but instead he shoved to his feet and said he had to go. He threw a few bills on the table, made polite excuses, and walked out like he hadn't just been sitting there laughing about Dorothy Jones's review of the range.

The sixty-eight-year old grandmother of two had used the words *meemaw* and *action hero*, which now had a prominent spot on their homepage.

It'd been Daphne's idea to solicit reviews, and the ones from older women were often hilarious.

"Where's Daphne?" Kane asked. He'd thought she'd stopped by the restroom and she'd be here any second, but she still hadn't appeared.

"She said it'd been a long day and she wanted to go home and get ready for bed," Callie told him.

Kane didn't like the sound of that. At all. Daphne usually showed up at the Dawg when they all did, unless she was with Limp Dick. But since they weren't dating anymore, she should be here with the gang, kicking back and having a few laughs. Besides, it wasn't even nine o'clock.

"Is she sick?"

Callie seemed to consider it. Then she shook her head. "No, she didn't seem sick. She ate everything, didn't seem off or anything. And we laughed a lot while discussing, uh, stuff. Book stuff. I think she's just tired, like she said."

"You could go check on her," Rory said, showing a surprising ability to overhear conversations she hadn't been a part of. "It's a short walk to the Sutton building."

Rory grinned and Kane stomped down on the urge to do as she said. Everybody thought he and Daphne needed to be a thing, but that was impossible. She was too nice for the likes of him. And she was too young. Twenty-three was just starting out in life whereas he'd lost that rosy outlook of youth. Left it in the rearview miles ago.

Sweet, innocent Daphne Bryant didn't need his brand of darkness in her life.

"Nah, if she's tired, let her be," he drawled, grabbing a few pretzels and tossing them back for something to do.

What he really wanted to do was walk out the way Ethan had. Then he'd make that trip to the Sutton building, head up three flights of stairs, and knock on her door. Just to make sure she was really okay.

He'd seen her talking to the guy on the camera today when he'd glanced at the feed on the monitors. Something about her body language had made the hairs on his neck prickle. He'd been about to storm out there and make himself known when Ghost asked him a question. By the time he made it to the front, the man was inside the range and Daphne was sitting at her desk with her head in her hands.

Of course she'd denied there was anything wrong. And really, it didn't have to be anything the dude might have said to her. It could be fucking Trigg. She'd gotten drunk and cried the night she'd told them about how Trigg had dumped her. That was a month ago.

Had she really cared for the scrawny guy that much? They were still friends, she said, but maybe she was hoping for more. Hoping to get back together.

Whenever Kane thought of Warren Trigg putting his hands on Daphne, his gut twisted. He'd imagined them kissing, imagined Trigg touching Daphne's soft skin, making her moan his name, and it'd made him ragey in a way few things had in a long time.

He shook his head. Not his business. Not his problem.

Daphne was a friend, and he cared about her. That's all. He didn't want some guy to hurt her, and he didn't want her upset by anything some asshole said at the front desk. He'd be there for her, just like the night they'd found her squatting in one of the unfinished apartments in the Sutton building. He'd taken one look at her and known he had to help.

Known *they* had to help.

And they had. Gave her a job, which helped her afford the apartment she'd hidden in, and gave her a friend group she could count on. He'd be there for her if she needed him. They all would.

Daphne was family, same as his guys, same as their women. That's all it was. All it would ever be.

Chapter Three

A good night's sleep always did wonders for a body, or so they said.

Daphne wouldn't know since she'd slept like shit. She dragged herself from bed around five-thirty, showered, and washed her hair. She'd been tired when she'd parted ways with the Besties on the sidewalk. The library was only two blocks from the square, so they'd walked over together and walked back when it was over.

It'd been a great time, but she'd known if she went inside the Dawg, Kane would be there, probably flirting with a woman who'd either taken a course from him at the range or who just liked his rugged good looks. It wasn't usually a problem for her, because she knew her crush was silly and not in the least bit reciprocated. Besides, the more she inoculated herself by watching him flirt with other women, the better.

It reminded her like nothing else could that he wasn't the man for her. She wanted an ordinary man like Warren. Somebody kind, sweet, and steady. A man who didn't inspire awe or envy from other women, who was devoted to her only.

A man who could give her a normal life.

Assuming she ever got to a point where she could consider settling down with anyone.

That's why she'd tossed and turned. That and the man from the range who'd stared at her with such intent, asking if he knew her.

Would she always be looking over her shoulder? Always be wondering if her brother was there, ready to strike? Her father wouldn't be the one she had to watch for. He'd send Jackson to find her and drag her back home where she'd have to answer for what she'd done.

And maybe pay for it, too.

Daphne shuddered as she stood on the bath mat and dried herself off. Her gaze landed on her face in the mirror. Her hair was dark, red, nothing like it'd been before she'd fled. She'd spent money on expensive salons because she'd liked herself as a blond. She'd never liked the O'Malley red. It was too deep, too dark, not sun-kissed enough for her.

For someone who'd run away with the intention to disappear, she looked more like her real self than she ever had. Before, she'd been blond and she'd worn contacts that enhanced her green eyes and made them bright emerald with a ring of black around the iris.

Her true color was a much lighter shade of green. Pale, uninteresting. Almost ghostly.

She'd also gained weight. Before, she'd worked hard to be thin, willowy, to wear whatever she wanted and look perfect in it.

Her hips were fuller, her chest too. Instead of a rail thin body, she had curves now.

She'd thought her appearance different enough to fool

anyone who didn't look too closely, but now she doubted. Maybe she should have gone brunette, gotten blue contacts, and put on another twenty pounds.

She still could.

Or she could pull up stakes and run somewhere else.

But then what? She'd be Daphne Bryant with no references because she wouldn't be able to let the guys know where she'd gone. She'd be back to cleaning motels and being miserable because she had no friends and no life.

But did that really matter?

Daphne had learned from an early age not to feel sorry for herself. Worse, not to try and invoke her father's sympathy.

Because he had none.

If her brother hit her and she cried, she got in trouble. If Jackson terrorized her with a bug or took her dolls away, or any number of mean things an older brother could do, she got in trouble for telling on him. For crying. For not toughening up and taking care of herself.

She'd learned the lesson well. When she was twelve and he'd put a snake on her bed, she'd gone to her dad's study, taken as big a book as she could find, and then she'd walked up to Jackson's smirking face and swung the book at his head before he realized what she was about.

She'd dropped him like a shot. Then she'd had to run hide so he didn't kill her when he came to. But when her dad got home that night, she hadn't gotten in trouble. He'd been proud, and he'd told Jackson to get over it when her brother complained about the bruise darkening his cheek and temple.

Not to mention the headache she'd given him.

Daphne dragged on jeans and a One Shot Tactical polo. She knew that raising kids that way was abusive, but she hadn't known it then. She and Jackson had spent years taking shots at each other, but they'd also learned not to be too cruel because their dad would be pissed at them both. He wanted them tough and unemotional, not maimed or dead.

Their mother hadn't had any say in the shit their dad put them through. She was damaged enough herself that she hardly noticed what her children were up to. Maisy O'Malley spent most of her days drugged up on Xanax or Valium, a glass of bourbon in her manicured fingers. She'd OD'ed when Daphne was eighteen, and all Daphne had felt was a vague numbness.

Her mother had never been very motherly. That honor fell to their housekeeper, who'd had a heart attack last year after thirty-five years taking care of the O'Malleys.

That death had hit Daphne like a load of bricks. Any slice of normal life she'd ever had was due to Grace Donovan and her kind heart. Sympathy and kisses when she was small, warm cookies after school, a fierce protector when Jackson was being rough. Though Mrs. Donovan couldn't stop all their fights, she'd stopped her fair share.

Daphne dried her hair, put it into a ponytail, and looked wistfully at her reflection for a moment. She didn't wear makeup anymore because the old her had done so. She'd never left the house without a perfect cat's eye and false eyelashes. She didn't miss the fuss of the lashes, but she missed that cat's eye. And lipstick. She missed that, too.

She went into the living room and opened the curtains, then she grabbed a yogurt from the fridge and stabbed her spoon in. She had a front apartment that looked onto the square. She never got tired of how quaint Sutton's Creek was. Like somebody's idea of the perfect Southern town, meant to grace postcards and make people think of slow drawls and sweet tea.

She would have never thought she could afford this

apartment, but the Suttons were kind people who said she'd be doing them a favor by saving them the trouble of advertising the place. She wasn't sure she believed them, but Emma Sutton, who was their daughter, assured her it was true.

"Besides," Emma had said, "What makes you think they could ask much more than you're paying? We're way out in the middle of the sticks, girlfriend!"

Sutton's Creek could hardly be called the sticks anymore with the way Madison and Huntsville were growing in its direction, but who was she to argue? She got the apartment, she could afford it on her salary—which was generous, in her opinion—and she loved living there.

She finished the yogurt, threw away the container, and made sure she had her purse, keys, and phone before she stepped out the door. It was early and the range didn't open until ten, but she'd feel better there than she would staying where she had nothing to do but think. At least at work she could find things to do.

She didn't have keys to the building, but one or more of the guys would be there early. They always were.

Out of habit, she glanced both ways down the hall. There was a staircase in the front of the building and one in the back so a person could come from either direction. If she was going to the park or the library, she went out the front. If she was headed for her car—Warren's car—or even the Kiss My Grits Café, she went out the back because it was shorter to go through the parking lot for bakery treats.

This morning, it was the back entrance. She locked the door and made her way toward the stairs. They were wide, with worn treads from years of traffic, but the stairwell was also darker than the hall this early in the morning. The back of the building faced west, which meant they weren't getting a ton of light yet.

She was halfway down the stairs when she stopped. Her heart kicked up and she sniffed the air, breathing deep. Was that a hint of cinnamon and mint she smelled? And not just any cinnamon and mint, but the kind that came from a certain blend of vape favored by her brother.

She dragged in another breath, her heart hammering now. And again.

But no, there was nothing. It was her imagination, egged on no doubt by her dark thoughts this morning. And by the lack of sleep last night.

She was tired, stressed, and letting her memories drag her into thinking she smelled familiar odors. Not to mention that *anybody* could vape the same blend, so it wasn't a sign that Jackson was lurking in dark corners.

Daphne took another step, and another, until she was on the landing. There was no smell here, no cinnamon or mint, nothing but the smells of old wood and wax.

"Nobody's there," she muttered as she continued down the steps and out into the daylight. "You've been thinking way too hard and you're scaring yourself."

She headed for the car, breathing deeply of the morning air, and telling herself not to let her imagination run away with her. Her father had always emphasized that a cool head was vital to survival in their world. It was a cool head that'd gotten her this far. It would get her farther.

Across the parking lot, Colleen Wright stood in the little back garden area of her shop, eyes closed and head tilted back, arms raised, her caftan—turquoise today— wafting in the morning breeze.

She looked to be chanting, her arms raising and lowering. Then she turned in a circle and did the whole thing again.

The tension in Daphne's chest eased a fraction as she got in the car and started it up. All was normal—and kooky—in Sutton's Creek. Colleen was still chanting and turning circles when Daphne drove out of the lot. Now that was a woman who wasn't afraid of anything. Demons in the wardrobe, aliens in the night sky, mysterious things that went bump in the night.

Daphne shook her head. Maybe she should go for a reading, get a crystal or two for protection. The thought made her laugh.

By the time she reached the range, her heart was lighter and she could breathe again.

She went to the back door and rang the bell since it wouldn't be unlocked this early. A few seconds later, the door opened and Kane stood there. Shirtless.

Daphne's tongue got in the way of speech for a long moment. When she found her voice, she resorted to sarcasm.

"Damn, Kane, you turning the range into your bachelor pad now? Do I need to worry about used condoms and lube lying around? Should I get a tetanus shot first?"

Kane only gave her an exaggerated frown as he stepped back so she could walk inside. "Very funny. I'm working out. Not a lady in sight. Except for you, but you don't count."

Now why did that hurt? "No, I definitely count. I've got all the right bits and everything. Just saw 'em this morning in the shower."

Kane locked the door and frowned harder. "Don't want to talk about your bits, kid."

Kid. As if she were a child. He did that sometimes and it annoyed the ever-loving piss out of her.

"Listen, dude. Twenty-three is not a kid."

She wished she'd had Kenny make her older instead of younger. But he'd told her she wouldn't pass for older and that would cause people to ask questions. Better to go with younger.

He'd been right, of course. Kenny was someone she'd met while running The Diamond Queen. He was an expert at creating new identification and the backgrounds to go with it. He wasn't on the O'Malley payroll, and he liked her because she'd gotten his baby sister out of a bad situation a couple of months before she'd needed to leave town. He'd never set foot in her club, so there was no obvious connection between them. That was the only way she would have asked him to help her.

"Twenty-three is a kid to me. I'm ancient compared to you."

He didn't look ancient. He looked delicious. Kane was the very definition of ripped. Glistening muscles that flowed like a river over rock whenever he moved. He had scars, which surprised her. One in particular, a round puckered scar in his side, caught her attention.

"Have you been shot?"

He glanced down and then back at her, eyes intense. "How'd you know?"

Daphne folded her arms and shrugged. "It's round. I assumed."

"Yeah, got shot years ago when I was still a young Army grunt. It healed, obviously."

"Obviously."

He turned away from her and headed toward the room where they kept the gym equipment. She didn't know why, but she followed him, stopping in the doorway while he went over to the bench where he had an array of dumb-bells lying on the floor. He sat and picked one up, curled it eight times while she slouched against the door jamb and pretended to be uninterested.

"Why're you here so early anyway?" he asked.

"Couldn't sleep any longer."

Or *at all*, but she wasn't telling him that.

"You went home early last night."

"I was tired. When I got in bed with a book and started reading, I woke up more than I would've liked."

He eyed her as he transferred the weight to his other hand. "What kind of book this time?"

"A thriller."

"Huh."

"You don't like to read?"

"Who said that?"

"Well, you haven't exactly started talking books with me, so I figured you didn't read much."

"I read. Just don't have a lot of time for it. I like Jack Reacher. Alex Cross. Walt Longmire. Dudes like that."

"Detectives and badasses."

"Yep. I need action. Romance is too boring."

Daphne arched an eyebrow. "Oh, I don't know. They've got action. Different kind of action. More fun, less deadly."

He finished his set and dropped the weight. "Did Trigg read those things with you?"

"None of your business," she said with a tight smile. "But you might want to try it with one of your dates sometime. Might learn something new."

He grabbed the towel he'd lain on the bench and wiped it across his brow. "Yeah, got no problem in that department, so I don't think so."

Daphne had a vision of pushing him back on that bench, straddling his lap, and letting him show her what he was capable of. Not that she'd do it. She was too much of a coward to even try.

But, damn, it'd been a long time since she'd had any kind of activity down there that wasn't her own fingers. The Besties didn't talk about sex when Nikki was around, but when she wasn't, whoa. They didn't go into detail, but it was clear those women were satisfied. Seriously satisfied.

"I'll take your word on it," she said. "Unless you want to demonstrate? I'm in a bit of a dry spell at the moment."

Oh, Jesus, Mary, and Joseph. Where had that *come from?*

Kane stared at her. Hard. The air between them crackled, or maybe it was her imagination. Maybe he was disgusted with her. Or the idea made him sick and he was trying to think how to respond.

"Don't say shit like that," he finally growled.

"Why not? Does it bother you?"

"Yeah, it fucking bothers me."

She didn't know what devil got into her brain as she sauntered toward the bench. Maybe it was the conversation with the Besties last night where they'd asked her why she didn't just grab Kane by his sexy collar and plant a kiss on his utterly sexy lips. She'd insisted she had no thoughts of doing any such thing, that he wasn't her type, yet here she was.

There was a part of her somewhere—up on the ceiling, maybe—staring down at her and telling her this was a very bad idea.

Unless she wanted to embarrass herself so badly she'd never recover her dignity. A very real possibility if she didn't stop what she was doing.

Kane tilted his head back as she approached. His nostrils flared as she stopped in front of him, close enough to touch him if she reached out. She wasn't that brave, though.

Still, she bent at the waist, lowered her torso until her face was on a level with his. Until he could see down her shirt if he looked—

And he looked because his gaze darted there before fixing on her face again. It almost made her smile.

He wasn't immune to her, no matter how much he insisted on treating her like his annoying little sister.

"What are you doing?" His voice was strangled. She could smell the sweat on him, the iron from the weights he'd been lifting.

She moved her face closer to his. He didn't flinch, didn't back away. She had a wild thought to kiss him. To do what the Besties told her and take charge.

"What's the worst that could happen?" Rory had said. "He says ew, no, I don't think of you that way? Newsflash, Daph, that man is hot for you no matter how hard he tries to pretend he isn't."

Daphne didn't kiss him, though. What if Rory was wrong?

Instead she dropped her gaze down his chest, those ridged abs, the waistband of his shorts—and the hint of a hard-on that was beginning to show.

Shock—and longing—blazed a path through her nerve endings. Still wasn't enough to make her take action, though. But the devil in her brain? That one had things to say.

"Listen up, Kane. I. Am. Not. A. Child. I'm a woman. I've had sex. Lots of sex. I know how to suck your dick so good you'd see stars. Stop calling me *kid*, stop infantilizing me, and I won't make you uncomfortable anymore, 'kay?"

His eyes widened a fraction, his gaze settling on her mouth. Tension vibrated in the air between them. Her heart hammered. Hot embarrassment sizzled into her the longer the silence stretched.

Daphne straightened, her face heated as she whirled,

intent on going to the front desk and burying herself in work for a while. Kane's hand closed around her wrist, stopping her. She turned, watched him rise like a mountain from the ocean floor.

His face was a study in contrasts. He looked confused, pained, and angry at the same time. And like he was probably thinking about his dick in her mouth. It ought to thrill her she'd gotten through his indifference, and yet she had the feeling she'd poked the bear.

"I'll repeat, don't say shit like that to me. You work here, you're under our protection. I don't fuck around with people I care about, you feel me? I have meaningless sex with faceless women because that's who I am. You don't want a piece of me because I've got nothing to give. You get what I'm saying, sweetheart, or do I need to say it a different way?"

Shame crawled through her. She jerked her wrist from his grip. "I heard you, Kane. I'm not a child *or* an idiot. And who the hell said I wanted a piece of you, huh? Maybe meaningless sex is all I'm capable of, too. You ever think of that?"

She saw the doubt flare in his eyes.

"No, of course you didn't. Because I'm a woman— excuse me, a *kid*—and females don't think that way. We're all looking for a ring and a house, right? We couldn't possibly want a hard dick and a hot tongue to take us to heaven, could we?"

His nostrils flared. Dark emotion colored his expression. But he didn't say a word, didn't apologize, didn't do one thing to make her believe her feelings mattered.

"Go fuck yourself, Kane."

This time when she turned and stalked away, he didn't stop her.

Chapter Four

It took Kane a full ten minutes after Daphne strode away to get his wayward dick under control. He kept thinking about her tits in the pale pink lace bra he'd glimpsed beneath her shirt, the way those creamy swells pressed together and looked like they might spill free if she just bent over a little farther.

He'd wanted them to spill free. He'd found himself stuck on the idea, on reaching up to cup them in his hands, on how soft they'd feel in his palms. What would her nipples look like? Were they big or little? Did they bud up tight or point enticingly?

He'd been transfixed by her tits, his dick throbbing to life, his brain conjuring up the picture she'd painted for him.

Her mouth wrapped around his cock, his hands in her hair as she made hot sounds in her throat. Him losing control and shooting his semen into the back of her throat while she drank him down.

Yeah, the thought had made him hot and it'd made him angry. She was Daphne. *Daphne.* Sweet Daphne

Bryant, the kid they'd rescued from a cold building that winter. The pretty, red-headed, innocent girl who smiled with her whole face and put everything she had into being the best assistant they could ever have.

She was kind. A hard worker. A good person. A kid in this game of life.

Except Daphne wasn't a kid at all. He knew it objectively but thinking of her that way kept her in the safe zone. If he ever took her out of it, made her an object of desire and pursued her, then he didn't know what he'd do or how badly he'd fuck things up.

He wasn't capable of the kind of relationships that his teammates were engaged in. He wasn't the kind of guy who dated the same woman and got close enough to care.

He'd been that guy once and it hurt too much so he wasn't ever doing it again. Which meant Daphne was off limits because she was too important to their lives in Sutton's Creek. Not that they couldn't hire a new range assistant, but Ghost would be pissed if they had to start over with someone new because he, Kane Fox, couldn't keep his dick in his pants.

A pissed off commanding officer was the last thing Kane wanted or needed in his life. Three of his teammates had already tested Ghost's patience by going against orders and getting involved with local women. They'd survived the experience, but Kane had a feeling that choosing Daphne would be crossing the line in a big way.

Best not go there, no matter how much a part of him might want to.

Kane finished his workout, showered, and put on his work clothes. It was still a couple of hours until the range opened, but there was always work to be done before that happened. He'd very deliberately avoided going anywhere near Daphne. Let her be pissed at him. It was better than having her lean over so he could see her cleavage.

Not literally better, because nothing was better than soft breasts in his face, but better in the sense he didn't need Daphne's to be the ones he fantasized about.

"What's wrong with Daphne?" Ethan asked as he walked in a little while later with a bag that Kane hoped contained breakfast sandwiches from the Gas-n-Go. Clarence layered smoked sausage on a homemade biscuit with egg and cheese, and it was amazing.

Kane was sitting at one of the desks in the shared office-slash-breakroom space the team occupied when they weren't on range duty or engaging in training classes. Ghost often joined them, but he had his own office if he didn't want to hang out with them. His was the official range office, though all the guys knew it was Ghost's even if they tried to pretend they were equal partners in this business.

Kane's coffee was halfway to his lips. "Why are you asking me? And do you have sandwiches from the gas station in there?"

Ethan laughed. Whatever had been bothering him last night seemed to have passed. "Yeah, man. I grabbed one for everybody since we've got a meeting this morning."

"You're my favorite, Dragon."

"Bet that's what you say to all the ladies. And you didn't answer the question about Daph."

"Because I don't know what kind of bee she's got up her ass today. Could be anything. I was working out, then showered and came in here. We spoke when I let her in earlier, then she went to her desk. Maybe she's annoyed at something she read online. Doomscrolling the Internet. It's enough to piss anyone off."

"Ain't that the truth?"

Ghost rolled in a few minutes later and got coffee. "You went to the Gas-n-Go?" he asked, eyes lighting on the bag sitting on the desk near Ethan's elbow.

"Yep. Figured we needed something happy once we get going."

By 'get going' he meant they were headed into the SCIF for a meeting before the range opened. It was only a month since they'd apprehended Dima Smirnov at Callie's place, and they still didn't have all the information they wanted on the Dashevsky Group or what the fuckers were up to.

If they were up to anything. Smirnov could have been working a double agent op, pretending to work for Dashevsky but still answering to the spymasters in the Russian Foreign Intelligence Agency, or SVR. Anything was possible at this point.

The rest of the guys arrived and everyone grabbed a coffee. They were about to head to the SCIF when Daphne popped in. A woman followed on her heels, but it was Daphne that Kane couldn't drag his gaze from. She looked normal enough, but she didn't make eye contact with him. Her cheeks were slightly flushed and he wondered if she was still angry.

"Agent Corbin to see you," Daphne said, her mouth twisting slightly. "I asked her to wait but she didn't want to."

"It's okay, Daphne," Ghost said. "I was expecting her."

That jolted Kane out of his contemplation of Daphne. He exchanged a look with his teammates. News to all of them.

Diana Corbin had her blond hair scraped into a low ponytail as usual. Instead of the black suit, she wore navy today. It looked expensive, or maybe he just thought so because they knew she came from money. Ghost had thought he'd gotten rid of her when he'd had her posted to Kentucky, but she was back like a rash.

Which is how they'd learned that her uncle, Stephen Adler, was the Deputy Director of the CIA.

It got better—or worse, depending on your perspective. Don Lewis, the FBI director, was a personal friend of the family. Agent Diana Corbin was Washington insider royalty with connections like that, and she'd used them to not only return to the FBI in Huntsville, but also to learn about their mission and get herself inserted into their business.

Seth had done a little covert digging after her surprise return. Diana Corbin was Diana Standish Adler. Standish was a family name, and it was her middle name in the tradition of hoity-toity people who did that kind of thing. Corbin was her mother's maiden name and the name she chose to use when she'd joined the FBI. Presumably so she wouldn't get special treatment. Or maybe questions about her last name and her connection to the powerbrokers at the top.

The Adlers were generationally wealthy, and they'd been a part of the Washington scene for at least a century. They boasted ambassadors, political appointees, a couple of Congressmen, and even a princess when a cousin married into a royal family in Europe.

Why Diana had chosen police work—and the FBI— when she'd gone to Harvard and majored in international affairs was anyone's guess. She'd seemed to be on the fast track to a political career of her own. Until she wasn't.

"Good morning, gentlemen," Diana said. "I hope I'm not late."

"You're not," Ghost said. "Daphne, we'll be in the private meeting room for a while. Call in if you need us."

"Got it. Y'all need anything before you go? Waters? Sodas?"

"I'm good," Ethan said. He held up the bag. "You sure you don't want a sandwich from Clarence's? I got extra."

"Thanks, but I'm fine." She gave Ethan the kind of smile she was not about to give Kane after their encounter. "Anybody else?"

Nobody wanted anything so Daphne returned to the front of the building. The range didn't open for more than an hour and the meeting would be done by then. Daphne wouldn't have to handle customers alone. Not that she couldn't, but some of the men who frequented gun ranges weren't the kind you'd trust alone with a beautiful woman —or any woman. She didn't get harassed often at the desk, but it'd happened.

And he, or one of the other guys, corrected it. Swiftly. Brutally. They'd barred a couple of guys from the range for shitty behavior to women, and they wouldn't hesitate to bar more. Man didn't respect a woman, he wasn't worth the trouble in Kane's opinion.

He shrugged his shoulders as uncomfortable thoughts filtered into his brain.

'Raped her before he shot her.' 'Obsessed with her.' 'Targeted her.'

Fucking hell. Didn't matter how many years had passed, thinking about Hannah's last moments on this earth, when he was deployed overseas and couldn't do a damned thing about it, drove him crazy with anger and guilt. He wasn't there when she needed him and he'd never get over it. Never.

By the time they'd entered the SCIF and took their seats, Kane had pushed those thoughts deep. Ethan passed the sandwiches around and the guys dug in. Diana declined. Ghost took a bite of his and indicated to Diana that she had the floor.

She wasted no time.

"Dima Smirnov is now a part of the prisoner exchange with Russia that I mentioned before," she began. "He'll likely be free in a month, once it's all arranged."

"You're fucking kidding me," Seth growled. "What about Callie?"

Diana turned cool eyes on him. Kane knew because Seth was siting beside him.

"I honestly don't believe Dima Smirnov will live much beyond the moment he sets foot on Russian soil. He's been playing both sides, and he's angered not only Viktor Dashevsky but the powers that be in Russia as well. If Putin doesn't have him executed, Dashevsky will. He won't be a threat to Ms. Crowell ever again."

"But they know about her."

Her expression remained unconcerned. "What they know is that Smirnov is incompetent. He targeted someone who didn't have the access required, a woman he was personally interested in, because this is what men do. He wanted to sleep with her, so he groomed her and he assured his bosses he'd found a way in. Maybe he thought he did, but he was wrong."

Kane could feel Seth's anger radiating from him. "That's not what happened. She didn't—. They did *not*—" He scraped a hand over his face. "Christ."

Kane wouldn't have believed Diana could feel sympathy if he hadn't been looking at her face. She actually cared that Seth was upset over what she'd implied.

"I know that's not what happened," she said gently. "I said it's what his handlers believe. That's an important distinction, right?"

"I think what Agent Corbin is saying," Ghost added, glancing at her, "is that our side has pushed that narrative. When Smirnov is released, and if our counterintelligence has done its job right, nothing he says in his own defense will penetrate the disinformation we've planted."

"That's correct." She actually looked serene. How did the woman do that?

Seth growled. "If you're wrong, if anyone comes for Callie—I'll fucking blow this shit sky high if anything happens to her. Unless you kill me first."

"Well, if that's what—" Diana began.

"No," Ghost said, his voice a chainsaw slicing through the tension. "We're all in danger until this is done, but we're on the same side here. And just so you know, Agent Corbin, the six of us are a unit. A team. You hurt one of us, you hurt us all. And that extends to the people we love. You keep those motherfuckers out of this country and away from Callie Crowell or you'll lose every single one of us. And I don't think you want that. I really don't."

"Noted," she said with a regal tilt of her head. "And yes, we're on the same side. You're here for a reason, the president trusts you, and I'm just trying to do my job. I came to tell you about Smirnov so you'd know." She reached for the messenger bag she'd set at her feet. "I've brought the gun he used when he took Nikki Crowell hostage. We can't trace it. I thought maybe you could."

She took a Glock 19 from the bag and placed it on the table.

"You're the FBI," Ghost said. "Of course you can trace the fucking gun."

She huffed a breath. "Okay, let me put it another way. We *can* and we have. To a point. A large shipment of weapons was reported as never received by the dealer about a year ago. The container was shipped via cargo vessel and there was a storm. The shipping company reported that several containers went overboard and were unrecoverable. That happens with sea transport sometimes, unfortunately. But the serial number on that gun matches one of the weapons from the manifest."

"And how does your boss feel about you bringing the gun to us?"

"He doesn't know because he's written it off as a typical weapons trafficker move. Claim lost shipments, sell the guns to criminals and terrorists. He sent this one to the evidence room to be stored. I borrowed it. I'll need it back, but I don't think anyone's going looking for it anytime soon."

"Noted. And why are you so intent upon this line of inquiry?"

"Dashevsky trades in weapons. His suppliers are global, hidden behind chains of shippers that go deep. I want to know where this gun came from once it reached this country because it could lead us to one of his suppliers."

Ghost shook his head. "I'm gonna assume the dealer checked out so it's not him or her you're interested in. But Smirnov could have bought that Glock on the street. It might not have anything to do with Dashevsky. We have plenty of homegrown criminals of our own that trade in illegal weapons."

"But what if he didn't? What if that shipment was meant for Dashevsky's people? His reach is global. Somebody received the weapons and sold them on again—and I want to know who that is, because you're right that the dealer checks out. His record is impeccable. It wasn't him. Someone with the shipper was probably paid a good deal of money to reroute the shipment."

Ghost looked annoyed. Never a good sign.

"You know, this sounds like a lot of work. Why don't you ask your fucking uncle? Or your good friend Mr. Lewis? Surely they have more access than a group of military operators on a secret mission do." Ghost flung his hands out. "Look around you, Agent Corbin. This isn't the fucking FBI headquarters. We have a limited capability, and we're focused on *one* thing. Saving this nation from a nuclear event by making sure Athena launches on time and successfully. There's nothing more important than that. You saw how close our enemies were to getting access to the command system. Is that what you really want?"

Diana forced out a breath, the first time Kane had seen her feathers ruffled today. "I can't ask them. It's not that easy." She sat with her lips tight and her brow furrowed. And then, as if she'd made a decision, the tension eased a fraction. "Smirnov isn't the only member of the Dashevsky Group we're watching. You have to know that. Viktor Dashevsky is amassing his own private army, because that's what psychopathic oligarchs with God complexes do. He's recruiting people everywhere, not just his home territory. There are followers here in north Alabama, and they're quietly gathering weapons and materials. We don't know for what yet. I want to know who's supplying them."

"Great," Seth said. "A fucking army."

"Exactly," Diana replied. "And they aren't all a bunch of redneck Bubbas, either. There are professional people who've bought into Dashevsky's vision. Military, law enforcement, people with experience and knowledge. It's a dangerous movement and we need to stop it. That starts with this gun, or so I hope."

Ghost picked up the weapon and turned it over in his hands. "I don't know what you think we can find, but we'll take it apart and study it. I have to assume your people did that already."

"They did. The trigger has been modified to allow for faster shooting, and there's a diamond pattern etched on the inside of the modification—"

Before she could finish what she was saying, Ghost

broke down the gun. Then he examined the trigger mechanism. "I'm not familiar with that marking. Surely your people have a list of these kinds of things."

"They do, but it's not on there. Could be a new player to the game. And they might not be the weapons supplier, but merely a cog in the wheel. I still want to know where this gun has been."

"There are a lot of aftermarket companies for Glock," Kane said. "It's an easy gun to swap out and customize. Could've happened at any point after the shipment landed in the US. Or, hell, Smirnov could have swapped the trigger himself."

"Did he strike you as the sort of man who would take the time to swap a trigger on a gun he intended to use for killing?" Diana shook her head. "I think it happened earlier, before the guns were distributed."

"I don't disagree," Kane said. "But the point is that swapping a trigger could happen at any time. What you need are more guns from the same shipment with this modification and the diamond etching."

Ghost reassembled the gun and handed it to Kane. "You're the Glock man. See what you can find about that trigger when we're done."

"On it, boss."

Ghost turned his attention to Diana again. "Anything else for us or you done making me into your errand boy?"

Her gaze darkened. "I thought you could help, Colonel Bishop. Excuse me, *Mister* Bishop. I thought you'd want to stop those terrorist assholes before they get a bigger toehold in this country than they already have."

"It's not that I don't, but like I said, we've got a job. So do you. The FBI, ATF, and Homeland Security should be handling this kind of shit, not us."

She got to her feet. "In an ideal world, true. But in case

you haven't noticed, there's a lot about this situation with your mission and Dashevsky's personal ambitions that intersect. I may have access to sources high above my pay grade, but that doesn't mean I want to go running to them every time I have a gut feeling. I can only take so many indulgent pats to the head before I start kneeing people in the balls."

None of the guys winced, but they probably all wanted to. Kane did anyway. Any man who'd ever taken a hit to the 'nads, which was pretty much all of them, didn't need a fucking reminder how much that shit hurt.

Diana shouldered her bag, the picture of unruffled elegance. Except for the tight lines at the corners of her mouth.

"I've read the secret reports about you," she said, aiming her gaze directly at Ghost. "You went rogue to help your commanding officer, ran military ops from a residential basement, and saved this country's future by preventing a presidential assassination and the dismantling of your unit, which was critical to national security. *That's* why I'm here with you and your handpicked team. Why I'm trusting you. Because you can't be bought, or corrupted, or diverted from the right path."

"I'd ask how you got access," Ghost growled. "But I imagine this is one time that you were happy to press the fam for a favor."

She didn't respond to the dig. "Thank you for your time. I'll see myself out."

Ghost was at the door before she was. He politely opened it for her and followed her through. The door sealed behind them. Kane looked at his teammates. They all wore varying expressions of surprise. And pride.

"Well, well," Chance said. "I think I like that woman,

despite her determination to be aloof. She's not really all bad, is she?"

"Probably not," Kane replied. "But she definitely has her own agenda."

He picked up the Glock and turned it over. The last time he'd seen it, Dima Smirnov had just used it to terrorize Nikki Crowell. Thank God Seth had been there, though apparently Nikki hadn't been entirely immobilized. Darn kid went limp and stomped the bad guy's instep. Nearly gave Seth a heart attack in the split second before he launched himself at Smirnov.

But she was alive and well, and that was the important thing.

"This job gets more and more fun, am I right?" Ethan grumbled. "First it's a simple job to surveil a warehouse, which almost gets Chance shot, then we've got fucking psychotic exes, a lady who talks to aliens and ghosts, murderous asshats, and then suddenly Russian spies arrive. But wait, there's more! They aren't Russian spies, or not only Russian spies, they're also terrorists who want to take over the world or some such shit. And now we've got gun traffickers, a homegrown army of assholes, and a nosy FBI agent with more access than God. Is that about right?"

"Yeah, but look on the bright side," Chance drawled.

"Which is?"

Chance ticked off his fingers. "Southern cooking. Theo Harper's special dishes. You don't wake up in your cozy bed in Bama and then find yourself sleeping on a desert floor twenty-four hours later, or humping through a jungle. Did I mention barbecue? Miss Mary's pies. Wendy Cochran's strawberry cake—"

"Dude, almost all of what you just said is food related," Ethan replied. "I'm from New York. We've got great food."

"Yeah, but you don't have Southern charm. Or The

Mystic Chick herself. Rory said Colleen's about to start writing a column for the Sutton's Creek Bee. Guess Judy Simpson's getting desperate to fill the pages. Or Colleen's got something on her. Not sure which."

"And why do I care if Colleen's writing a column?"

Chance shrugged. "Because it's bound to be hilarious?"

The door opened and Ghost walked in. He didn't look in any better of a mood than when he'd left. If anything, he looked more annoyed. Made Kane wonder what Diana had said between the door and the parking lot to put that look on the boss's face. Because she'd already said plenty before she'd walked out of the SCIF.

"Well, boys, looks like we've got us another unofficial team member. Because that woman isn't taking no for an answer. Seth, you find anything?"

Because of course Seth had been typing away on his computer from the moment Ghost and Diana left the room.

"Nothing on the diamond trigger. It'll take some time, but I'll get a list of the guns that went missing and the receiving dealer since she didn't bother to share either of those things."

Ghost tossed the pen he'd picked up onto the table and shook his head. "Fuck my life," he grumbled. "I could have been the HOT commander in another couple of years if I'd said no to this assignment. Washington could have sent somebody else, but no, I had to put duty before self, blah blah blah, and drag all of you with me. It seemed pretty straightforward at the time. Couldn't have predicted Diana Corbin—or you jaded fuckers falling in love."

"Sorry, boss," Blaze said with a grin. "But I'm glad you took the job and brought me along because I'd have never met Emma. Pretty sure Chance and Seth are with me on this one."

"Amen, brother," Chance said. Seth echoed with an amen of his own.

"I'm good," Kane said. "I like what we're doing with the range and the training. It's rewarding to help people learn how to defend themselves for a change."

It didn't help Hannah, didn't bring her back, but maybe it'd help some other woman defend herself if she got attacked. Daphne, for instance. It was time Kane pressed her into learning to shoot. Past time. She'd taken the self-defense course early on, when they'd wanted to test new material, and she'd been a star. But, to his knowledge, she didn't know how to shoot.

Ethan frowned. He looked torn, so what came out of his mouth wasn't quite what Kane had expected. "Not saying I love it here or anything, but I'm not complaining. The Dawg has great food, and the beer's good. Kinda like the change of pace, too. Beats sleeping in jungles and deserts, getting eaten up by bugs and digging sand out of your asscrack."

Ghost snorted. "Yeah, nothing like sand in your crack. It's almost as annoying as Agent Diana 'guess who my uncle is' Corbin. But at least you can wash the fucking sand away."

"You gotta admit she's pretty hot though," Kane said. "In a touch-me-and-I'll-break-your-fucking-arm way."

"No," Ghost said, pointing at him. "You can charm every woman who walks through those doors if you want, break hearts, fuck around, I don't care. But not that one. She's too dangerous and too unpredictable. Last thing I want is you getting tangled up with her."

He was almost offended. "Wasn't planning on it, boss. Pretty sure she's immune to my charm anyway. And I like my balls where they are, so not even trying. You or Ethan can have her."

"Not me," Ethan said, shaking his head. "Cold and deadly isn't my type."

"None of us," Ghost added. "It's bad enough she's inserted herself into our mission. I don't want to see any more of her than I have to. She gives me a fucking headache. We clear on that, Demon?"

Kane blinked. Seriously? Why did they all think he couldn't keep his dick in his pants? Like his brain wasn't the one in control? They'd be surprised if they had any idea he wasn't actually as much of a man-whore as they thought he was. Too fucking exhausting for one thing.

"As crystal. Like I said, I like my balls too much to tangle with that one."

"Good. Maybe we can get some work done then. Too much damned romance lately," Ghost grumbled. He cued up a slideshow on the overhead. "Let's get some work done."

Chapter Five

Nathan Fader was back. Daphne was busy inputting numbers at the computer when he walked into the range with his bag and his eerily intense focus. She forced a smile and prayed one of the guys would come out from the back. Blaze and Chance were RSOs, Alex and Ethan were checking in a shipment of weapons, Seth had gone to Research Park to consult with a defense contractor, and Kane was somewhere around.

Surely one of them would need to ask her for something.

Please, please ask.

"Welcome back, sir," she said politely.

"Hey, doll. You got any free bays? Just need an hour."

"I believe we have two." Daphne reached for the paperwork and slid it to him on the clipboard. "If you're new to town, or just new to us, you can join the range for unlimited usage. It'll be a lot cheaper than twenty-five an hour. Plus you get unlimited gun rentals."

Oh shit, had that sounded like prying? She'd tried to

keep her tone light, but she knew as well as she knew her own name there were some kinds of men you didn't ask for details. She'd been raised around those kind of men. Knew one when she saw one, which meant she should have kept her mouth shut.

Fader finished the paperwork, his oily gaze sliding to hers. Questioning, assessing. Daphne's heart skipped. Had he been this creepy yesterday? Or was her imagination running away because he made her uncomfortable?

"I don't expect to be around long. In the area for work, need to keep the skills sharp."

"Of course."

She took his money with a smile, retrieved the targets, and assigned him a bay. "Number four today. You get Chance again."

Fader took the targets but didn't walk away. "You ever been to New Orleans, doll?"

Daphne's stomach bottomed out. "Once or twice. In college. It's quite a party town."

"You from around here then?"

Oh shit. "Not Sutton's Creek, no. Tennessee. Little town up near Lynchburg. Came down here for work."

"Lynchburg. That's where Jack Daniels is made. What's the name of the town?"

"Oh, I don't expect it's one you've heard of. Just a little holler in the hills."

Her heart tapped a quick beat in her chest. She was certain he could smell her fear, but he didn't press her for more.

"Understood, doll."

"Happy shooting," she called as he headed for the range door.

He waved a hand over his head without turning

around. Then he entered the first door and Daphne sank into her chair.

She heard footsteps coming down the hall before she saw Kane. His expression was hard, like he was on a mission to bash some heads together.

"That guy bothering you, Daph?"

Not what she expected at all. If she said yes, would he bar Fader from the range? She wanted him gone, but that would be a suspicious move to a man like that. If he suspected she wasn't who she claimed to be, that would cement it for him. And then what? Better to have him where she could see him.

"What makes you say that? He's just a customer."

"Yeah, but you don't look like yourself. Same thing happened yesterday. Same guy."

Daphne didn't know what to say. He paid that much attention to her? To her moods and expressions?

"I told you I didn't sleep as well as I'd have liked. I'm just tired. And maybe still a little upset about Warren breaking up with me."

That was a lie, but maybe it was one he'd believe. She didn't miss the way he seemed to grow tense for a moment before he controlled it. "Or upset at me," he added. "I'm sorry I was a dick this morning."

Okay, shock. Not what she'd expected at all. "Well, I didn't make it any easier. I'm sorry for the things I said. Except for the part about treating me like a child. That needs to stop."

He gave her that grin that made her insides thrum. "I'm doing my best, babe. Thing is, you're one of us. These guys are my brothers. That makes you my sister. And since I never had one, I'm afraid I go overboard on the protective stuff. That's all it is, but I promise to do better."

Daphne sighed. "I know you mean well, but I'm not your sister, Kane. I can be your friend, and I can be part of the work family you've got going, but don't spend time torturing yourself over looking down my shirt, okay? You can look at my boobs and you can get a boner over them. Nobody's going to arrest you for it. And I'm not upset about it either, so don't go thinking I am."

He held up both hands in surrender. "Okay, fine. Can we move on from talking about your boobs and my dick?"

Daphne shuffled some papers on her desk. "You're as jumpy as a virgin on her wedding night, you know that? Such a prude. Fine, no more dick talk. No more boobs. Are we still going car shopping after work or do you plan to ghost me again? If you do, I'm going over to Warren's with a wad of cash and handing it to him. He's let me use that car long enough."

"Not ghosting you. I've got a couple of calls out on some cars I saw online, and I figured we'd hit up a few other places if there's time tonight."

"What time?"

"We can leave early, so let's say four. The rest of the guys will be here. I'll follow you home so you can leave Trigg's car, then we can grab something to eat at the Dawg and take off."

"Works for me."

He seemed to be thinking about something. "I'm teaching beginning shooting for ladies after lunch. You want to join?"

Daphne blinked. That was new. "Uh, who would check people into the range?"

"Alex. Ethan. Blaze. Chance. Seth. Whoever the fuck isn't on RSO duty at the time. They can handle it for an hour. It'd be good for you to learn to shoot."

A headache was forming in her temples. "What makes you think I don't know how?"

"You've never once stepped into a bay and taken shots at a target. Even if you've shot a gun, you're way out of practice by now. You could use a refresher."

"I'm good, Kane. Thanks anyway."

He didn't go away. Instead, he moved closer, studying her like he was trying to figure something out. "You afraid of guns?"

"Not in the least. I work here, don't I?"

"Yeah, but handling a new weapon that hasn't been shot, or the rentals that you know are cleared, is different from stepping into a bay and lifting a loaded gun. It can be scary for some people."

"I'm not afraid. I just don't need a beginner class."

"Then let's shoot some targets sometime. You and me. Just for fun."

Well, fuck. She didn't want to shoot targets because she didn't want questions. Sure, she could blow some shots, but what was the fun in that? And why did it matter anyway? For all she knew, he was right and she was rusty. She might blow shots without wanting to.

"Fine. Can I get back to work now?"

"Holding you to it, Daph."

"Yeah, yeah. I hear you. Go away."

Kane grinned again. "I'm going. But babe—that guy bothers you, he's gone. All you gotta do is say the word."

"He's not bothering me. But if he does, I'll handle it. Unless it's a banning offense, I don't need you to fight my battles. Thanks, though."

Kane shook his head. "You're a lot tougher than you look, you know that?"

"I've been told that a time or two."

"Just don't be afraid to ask for help if you need it,

okay? There's tough and there's stupid. Don't mistake one for the other. That kind of thing can get you hurt. Or worse."

He looked serious enough (and haunted enough?) that she didn't fire back at him for assuming she didn't know the difference. "I promise that I'm not afraid to ask for help if I need it. But I took the self-defense course, remember? I can deal with a guy trying to intimidate me. Not that he was, mind you. He's just a little creepy, that's all. But he's not the first creepy guy to cross the threshold and he won't be the last. It's the nature of working in a gun range, especially as a woman. Guys with too much testosterone frequent places like this, and they think they're charming alpha males who can get any woman they want." She made a show of looking down at the paperwork, as if the man's name wasn't seared into her brain. "Mr. Fader wasn't hitting on me, he didn't say anything inappropriate. He has creepy eyes and he might stare a little too intensely, but if you went around throwing out all the guys who stare, you'd lose about a third of your clientele. Maybe half. So don't worry about it until I tell you I need help, okay?"

He frowned. Then he nodded. "Okay."

They stared at each other without speaking, her heartbeat picking up with every moment of silence. Just as she was about to say something, anything, to end the awkwardness, he spun on his heel and disappeared down the hall.

Daphne let out a breath. She barely had time to wonder what the hell that had been about when he was back, carrying a tray with gun parts over to one of the work areas behind the counter. He plopped the tray on the desk, dragged the chair out, and sat.

"What are you doing?"

He slanted gorgeous hazel eyes her way, and Daphne's pulse thumped in places it did not need to be thumping.

"I'm looking for information on a modification. Figured I could do it here as well as anywhere."

"Kane," she began.

"I'm not going to say anything. I won't stand up or walk over or do anything to intimidate the guy with my size, okay? I'm just going to be here. Quietly working. As a friend who's got your back. That okay with you?"

She ought to tell him to go back to wherever he'd been, but she couldn't. Her throat was tight. A friend who had her back? She hadn't had any of those growing up. She'd had her family's enforcers, the weight of the O'Malley name, but nobody who would sit quietly nearby in case she needed them. Not without a paycheck or a threat from her father or brother.

"Thank you." Because there was nothing else to say. Those were the right words—the *only* words.

"You're welcome. And Daph?"

"Yes?"

"I know you aren't stupid. It's just… I've seen things. I know how easy it is to think people play by the same rules, but they don't. Some people are just… *not good.* And sometimes you don't know that's what you're facing until it's too late."

Her heart hammered. Some people are just *not good.*

Not good. Not good. Not good.

The words echoed in her head. But he wasn't saying it because he knew where she came from, what her family was. It wasn't about her. It was about him, the things he'd experienced. She knew these guys were former military, that they'd experienced some shit in their careers. She'd seen them in action a month ago when a man had attacked Nikki Crowell because he wanted something from Callie. She didn't know what that something was and she hadn't really cared. She'd been too focused on her own past, on escaping and staying hidden, to ask too many questions.

Questions got you noticed, and getting noticed got you caught. Maybe dead.

Daphne dragged in a breath. Forced a tight smile.

"I understand."

But she wasn't sure she did. At all.

Chapter Six

Daphne parked Warren's old Chevy sedan in the lot behind the Sutton building and got out. Kane parked beside her, his black Yukon with the tinted windows looking big and badass beside the old Chevy. When he rolled down the passenger-side window and peered at her, mirrored shades on his face, she had a visceral reaction.

He was masculine and gorgeous, every girl's wet dream of a bad boy. It was no wonder he attracted the attention he did, no wonder he had his pick of women whenever he stepped foot into the Dawg.

Hell, probably every single time he went anywhere in this town, he had his pick of women. The grocery store, the gas station, the drugstore. Anywhere. Even old ladies flirted with him. And married ones.

The guys teased him about his effect on women. She teased him, too. Like this morning when she'd asked if she needed a tetanus shot before she entered the building. But he'd been shirtless, glistening with perspiration, and her brain had been in danger of short circuiting.

Hell, it *had* short circuited if she thought about what

she'd done next. He'd called her a kid, which he'd done before, but this time she'd let go of the leash on her temper.

Probably shouldn't have done that.

But why did Kane Fox find every single woman in this town attractive except her? Why did he keep her at arm's length? He said he didn't fuck around with people he cared about. She was still thinking about that and wondering *how* he cared for her. Or if he'd just said it because it was an easy excuse.

"You want to eat at the Dawg? Or you got something else in mind?"

She didn't want the Dawg, not because she didn't love it, but she didn't want to sit through a meal with women coming over to talk to him. With him flirting back, his hazel eyes and long lashes that no man had a right to turning women stupid.

"We're going through Madison on the way to the car dealers, right?" she asked. "What about the new Indian place that just opened there?"

"Works for me."

Daphne hopped into the Yukon and belted herself in. Kane turned the music off. Gangsta rap, which she found amusing for some reason. Though she'd also heard him listen to Country, Top 40, Classic Rock, and Blues, among others. Those were just his top rotations.

"Thanks for doing this," she said when they'd left the parking lot and headed north. "I know there are probably other things you'd rather do on your off time."

"I'm happy to help. I always have been. The guys said I'm too picky about cars, so I'm going to try not to be this time. We'll find something."

"It's just a car, Kane. I don't care, so long as it's reliable."

The version of her that'd zipped around town in a cherry red Porsche 911 Carrera S would be horrified, but she'd buried that girl when she'd fled New Orleans.

"Like I said before, it needs good safety features and no mechanical issues. You willing to finance part of it or still insistent on cash?"

Her stomach lurched at the idea of filling out credit applications. "Cash only."

"Same budget?"

"I have a little more now. I'd go to six thousand. I hope that's enough."

They paid her well at the range. Since she'd determined she needed to live frugally in her new life, she'd been able to save money. Something she never did when she ran the club and lived in an apartment in the French Quarter. She'd lived high then, and she'd spent high.

"It's enough. I saw a couple of small SUVs for sale around that price. Is that all in, or can you afford a bit more for tax, tags, and title?"

"If the car is good enough, I could probably scrape together a little more to cover those things."

"If we find a really good car and you're short, I can help." He held up a hand to stop the protest he must have known was coming. "A loan, Daphne. That you can repay. I'm talking a small amount of money, because I know you won't accept more. I can probably even get Alex to give you an advance on your wages if that helps."

"I'll keep it in mind, but I really don't want to go more than a few hundred over, okay?"

"Yup."

The day was gorgeous, sunny and hot. Alabama in summer was stifling, but it wasn't as bad as New Orleans, so she didn't really mind it. So long as you dressed for the weather, it was tolerable. At work she wore jeans because of the air-conditioning, but she usually put on shorts or cotton dresses when she got home. Maybe she should have dashed upstairs to do just that before heading out, but she'd survive.

The town, despite being small, had a divided road that entered from the north and provided a grand entrance. There were trees in the center of the median, big ones hung with red, white, and blue paper stars from their branches. The Fourth of July was next week. Sutton's Creek would have fireworks as well as a big festival and picnic in the park at the center of town, which meant the town decorating committee was out in force with the stars, flags, and bunting.

Daphne was endlessly charmed by the pace of life there. She'd always thought she needed the tempo of New Orleans, the night life that never ended. The Diamond Queen closed at two in the morning and didn't open again until ten the next morning. Many bars stayed open around the clock, but not the Queen. When your club was as good as hers, you could afford to have the hours you wanted.

Not for the first time, she wondered how the club was doing without her. In truth, it was an O'Malley family venture, not her own, so her father would have sent someone in to run it as soon as he'd realized she wasn't coming back.

She pictured him in his office when he finally figured out she was gone, the rage and betrayal that would have crossed his face. It never failed to freeze her marrow in her bones. Especially when she envisioned Jackson there, begging to be allowed to track her down.

They would have both known that she hadn't gone empty-handed. That she would have taken evidence of their crimes with her. Finding her would be a top priority.

She'd never expected to get as far as she had, or to stay

hidden. It'd been a desperate, reckless move on her part. But she'd had no choice. She couldn't be a part of what they were doing. Not anymore.

It shamed her she'd ever been a part of it, but she'd compartmentalized that part of her life, telling herself that so long as she wasn't an active participant, it wasn't a problem.

She didn't believe that anymore, which was part of why she'd fled. The other part—well, that had been a hill she hadn't known she'd be willing to die on until she was confronted with the evidence.

"You okay?"

Daphne jerked her gaze to Kane. "Sure. Why?"

"You're rubbing your thighs like you're uncomfortable. Just wondered if you pulled a muscle or something."

She folded both hands in her lap. "I didn't realize. I'm fine. Just thinking." She searched around for something to say, to distract him from focusing too much attention on her lies. "I was wondering about the Fourth of July celebrations and how crowded the town will get."

Lame excuse.

"Don't know. I'm as new to town as you are. They don't have a big celebration where you're from?"

She wasn't sure how to answer. Kenny had created an identity for her that had her born in Florida, but he'd left the details vague. It was still possible to have a life that wasn't lived completely online, and she'd leaned into that. Her cell phone was pay-as-you-go. Her social security number was fake, so she could work. She had no social media as Daphne Bryant. No real history. Not typical for her generation, but also not impossible.

"I'm not from anywhere, really. My parents were… nomads. They had a deep mistrust of government and authority. We lived in an RV and traveled wherever the mood took them."

He nodded. "Got it. My dad was in the Navy. We moved a lot too. Two years at a base and we'd be moving on again."

That was the most he'd ever told her about where he came from. "So you don't have a hometown either?"

"Nope. I was born in Japan, in an American military hospital. My dad retired from the Navy when I was in high school. We were living in Virginia then, and he worked in Norfolk. I joined the Army when I was eighteen, so I don't think of Norfolk as home any more than I do Japan or the Philippines or Hawaii. All those are places we were stationed. California and Spain too, though I was a lot younger then and don't remember them as well."

"Wow. That sounds amazing. I've never been outside of the country."

"They were. I liked living overseas." He rolled up to a stop sign and flipped on his signal. "But you're young yet. You've got plenty of time to travel."

"You say that like you're old, Gramps."

He grinned. "Nah, not old. But I feel like it some days. The military can be hard on the body."

"Why did you join the Army if your dad was in the Navy?"

His fingers tightened on the wheel for a fraction of a second. "I didn't want to spend half a year at sea, away from family and friends. Saw what it did to my parents' relationship. I figured if I ever found somebody I wanted to be with, I didn't want to have to navigate the Navy and a wife, too."

Daphne gaped at him. He shot her a look.
"What?"
She shook her head. "I guess I never pictured you as

the kind of guy who'd even consider settling down, much less making life decisions based on the possibility."

He shrugged again, the nonchalance back. "Yeah, well it turns out the Army isn't much better. If they wanted you to have a wife, they'd have issued you one."

She wasn't sure if that meant he'd tried and failed, or he gave up the idea because one branch of service was no better for relationships than another. She wasn't going to ask at first, but then she decided why not? The worst he'd do was refuse to answer. Besides, it kept him from asking questions about her.

"So did you get married or not?"

He didn't answer at first, just continued to stare at the road. "I was married. She died."

"Oh my God, I'm so sorry, Kane. Forgive me for asking."

Mirrored sunglasses turned her way for a second before focusing on the road again. "It's okay. How could you know? It happened a long time ago. Not that you ever get over something like that, but you move on. I've moved on."

"Still. I'm sorry I blundered into it."

"I don't talk about that part of my life very often. And before you ask, I never use it to get sympathy from women. It's private. Hell, I don't know why I'm telling you, except my guys know so you might as well too since you work with us."

"I would never think you'd use such a thing for sympathy."

"Yes, you would. And I don't blame you for it. But I don't. Wanted you to know that."

She believed him. If he was the kind of man who used a dead wife to get into other women's panties, that would make him pretty fucking despicable in her mind. But Kane wasn't despicable. He was a good guy. They all were. She was certain of it, and there wasn't a lot she was certain of these days.

"What about you?" he said.

"What about me?"

"Ever been married?"

"What would make you ask that? I'm twenty-three. Thought I was a mere babe in your mind, far too young for that kind of thing."

"You are young, but believe me, I saw plenty of young grunts get married as soon as they were out of basic training. First assignment and a GI meet a girl, starts getting sex on the regular, and thinks that shit's golden so he marries her. Then they start having kids and before you know it, you've got twenty-three year old GIs with three or four kids to support. So, sure, you're a mere babe, but you could be running away from an ex."

"Not married, Kane. I've never been married. And there is no ex I'm running from. I was just passing through when I landed in Sutton's Creek. But I like it, so I'm staying for now. Also, that was an incredibly sexist line of thought about GIs meeting girls, etcetera. Women join the Army these days too, or didn't you know? Not to mention that if one gay soldier meets another and gets married, the kids probably take a bit more planning and thought."

"I'm aware, babe. But the majority is what I said, even if the female is in the Army too. Kids getting married and having kids, or not having kids, but fighting all the same because they didn't really know each other, just liked getting naked together. You could have been married and divorced by now, same as many of them."

"Did you marry the first woman you slept with, too?"

"I did. We didn't start popping out kids, though. We both wanted to wait. Wanted to enjoy each other first."

Imagining Kane married and thinking about a family

was completely foreign. She was sad for what he'd been through, and jealous of a woman she'd never met. Which made her feel like a jerk.

"I've never been serious enough with anyone to want to marry them," she said.

It was true. It was also true that she wouldn't have been allowed to marry someone she chose. Her father got to determine that, and he'd always intended her to marry for connections and to cement her family's position. Same for Jackson, so at least it wasn't a sexist maneuver on her dad's part. The O'Malley kids had a duty to the family, and they would do that duty when the time came.

That her father hadn't forced either of them into alliances yet was a surprise, but the time was at hand. That was something he'd started to talk more about lately, and she'd dreaded it.

Kane nodded. "You know, when we first found you squatting in the Sutton building, I thought you were running away from a relationship. A bad one, where the guy was abusive."

Not far from the truth, but not the truth either.

"I can understand that. But I wasn't running away from anyone. I just hit some bad luck and couldn't afford to pay my way out, especially once I lost the job at the inn. I was planning to look for work at the businesses in the square. But then you guys burst in, scared me half to death, and saved me at the same time. For which I am truly grateful."

She'd thanked them profusely over the first few weeks, but she hadn't as much lately because she'd settled into a routine. Maybe she should, though. When Kane, Blaze, and Seth found her in the empty apartment, she'd been cold, scared, and had no idea how she was going to get herself out of the mess she'd gotten into.

It was because of them she'd found her footing. Because of them she was still here. Maybe she should have moved on a couple of months ago, but then what? She'd be cleaning toilets again, probably, and she'd be miserable. She wouldn't have her book club friends, either. She'd never really had girlfriends, because she'd been isolated as a kid and then spoiled as a young woman, but she had them now.

It was new, and it was lovely.

Kane hooked a left into the next gas station and drove up to a pump. He turned off the engine, then swiveled to look at her, sliding those mirrored shades down his nose.

"I'm not one-hundred percent sure I believe everything that comes out of your mouth, Sunshine. Seems to me a woman willing to live in her car and scrub toilets, especially one as smart and lovely as you, doesn't want to call attention to herself. But know this—if you're scared somebody's going to find you, if you have any doubts about your safety, you have me at your back. And not just me. Alex, Ethan, Blaze, Chance, and Seth are there too. You need help, you ask. Nobody touches one of our own and gets away with it, you hear me?"

Her heart thumped painfully. Her throat squeezed. "I hear you," she whispered.

He slid the glasses on again. Grinned. All he needed was some chewing gum and he could be 1986 Tom Cruise in *Top Gun*. The arrogance. The bravado. The certainty he was God's gift to women.

"Good girl. Don't forget it, either."

He got out of the Yukon, whistling as he pumped gas.

Cocky, arrogant, beautiful idiot.

Chapter Seven

FIRST THEY WENT TO THE INDIAN RESTAURANT. KANE ordered chicken vindaloo—spicy—and garlic naan. He'd wondered what Daphne would get, thinking she was probably a chicken tikka masala girl. Mild. Plain naan.

Nope, not at all. She ordered chicken saag, asked for spicy, and her own garlic naan. Then she proceeded to eat everything as if she hadn't eaten in two days. Of course he ate all his food, but he was a big guy and he worked out often. She didn't eat all the rice, because there was a lot, but she mopped up sauce with her naan and ate all the chicken. When she noticed him watching, she arched an eyebrow.

"What?"

"I was wondering where you put it all."

She frowned at him. "Seriously, Kane? Are you food shaming me?"

"What? No." He shook his head emphatically. "Of course not. I'm just amazed you've got room."

"I ate yogurt for breakfast and nothing for lunch because I was busy, so I'm hungry now. Also, if you talk to the women you date about how much they're eating, how the hell are you getting so many of them in bed?" She mopped up more sauce with her naan. "Because that shizz would make me ragey."

He held up both hands. Daphne was as prickly as a cactus tonight. "Sorry. Didn't mean to be offensive. Just making small talk."

She finished the bread and smiled at him. "Actually, I know. I'm just razzing you."

"Brat," he said, throwing the balled up wad of paper from his straw at her.

She ducked and stuck out her tongue at him. "You missed, old man."

"Old man? Seriously?" He was only slightly offended. And trying not to think about her tongue and all the places he'd like it.

She leaned back in her chair and crossed her arms over her chest. He found himself wishing she'd move those arms lower so that her breasts would be forced upward. Like a pushup bra, but with her arms.

He gave himself a mental shake to clear the image.

"Hey, you insist on calling me a kid, I'm calling you an old man. Or gramps. I kinda like that one, too. Should we tell the salesperson you're my dad tonight?"

She was roasting his ass over a barrel. He probably deserved it, but shit, he was only trying to protect her. From *him*. Keep her from making a mistake. If he gave in to the tingle of desire he felt every time he looked at her, it wouldn't turn out well. No matter what she'd said earlier about meaningless sex and scratching an itch.

"I think we can skip that scenario. How about I just be your friend?"

She shrugged. "Suit yourself, gramps."

"You're going to keep busting my balls about this, aren't you?"

"What makes you say that?" She batted her eyelashes.

He snorted. "Come on, Sunshine. Let's get moving and find you a car. Before I dump your ass on the side of the road and make Blaze and Emma come get you."

"Like you'd do that," she said, standing.

He gathered up their trash and tossed it as they walked out the door. And then, for reasons he wasn't certain about, he walked her to the passenger side of the Yukon and opened the door for her. It wasn't that he didn't do things like that when he took a woman out, but she was Daphne and he was determined to keep her in the friend camp. Friends opened their own doors.

She gaped at him, and then smiled and slid into her seat. "Thank you."

"You're welcome."

He started the Yukon and headed into traffic. Daphne tapped her fingers on the armrest, gazing out the window with her head turned away from him. He wanted to know what she was thinking about, but he also didn't want to know. Would asking her be the kind of thing he'd do with a friend? Or was it showing too much interest in every little thing she did?

Good lord, he really didn't know how to be friends with a woman who wasn't in a relationship with one of his teammates. If Rory or Emma or Callie were sitting there, what would he say?

"You planning on going to the Independence Day celebrations in town?"

She swiveled around to look at him. "Not sure. You?"

"Hadn't planned on it. I don't care for big crowds and loud booms all in the same space. Pretty sure the other guys are the same way."

She nodded. "The fireworks sound too much like gunfire, right?"

"Yep. I'm not wigged out by it or anything. It's the addition of the crowd. That's when I start thinking too hard about how easy it'd be for some nut to open fire, and how I'm gonna stop it if so."

"I hadn't thought of that."

"Most people don't. But I do. The guys do."

"Which is why y'all are so good at the defensive training. Have you ever thought of hiring more people to work the range and you guys building the self-defense business into something bigger? You could do survival training, complete with camping trips into the wilderness. The Bankhead Forest is only an hour away, or you could just disorient them on Monte Sano. I know there are a lot of people who'd pay good money for that."

He could hear the excitement in her voice as she talked. Daphne was the one who'd structured their schedule to allow for more training, and she booked the groups and individuals into the appropriate classes. It'd started as a logical part of the business, but he could see where it could be bigger.

If they were really in business to be in business. If this was a real gig and not a cover.

"It's a thought, but I don't think any of us are ready for that yet. We like what we do."

She seemed to deflate a fraction. "I know. It's something to think about for the future, maybe. When you want to grow beyond the range and the consulting. Don't get me wrong, the range is a great business. You could do even more with it, really. But it requires help beyond the seven of us and two part-timers."

The seven of us. He always thought of his team as six people, but she was right there were seven. Because she worked at the range every day, too. He liked the way it sounded to include her.

"What kinds of things did you have in mind?"

"You have a beautiful property and two houses on it. Some of the trees are huge and gorgeous. They'd make great backdrops for wedding photography. You could create an event space that people could rent. And not just for weddings, but birthdays and one-day business conferences. Think security presentations with catering and a hundred guests paying a premium to be there." She waved her hands around. "It's a lot, I know, but these things *can* work."

They reached the first car dealer and he found parking before turning to her. "What do you know about event spaces and catering? Is that something you did before?"

Her enthusiasm seemed to fold in on itself. "I, um, it was just an idea. I read a lot, that's all. You have a beautiful property and a lot of potential. It wouldn't have to add work for any of you, not if you hired people to oversee that part of the business, to get bookings and arrange for the seating and food. It's just a thought."

He couldn't help but stare at her. Something was prickling inside his brain, tickling the corners, making him think. Not that he hadn't wondered about Daphne's past before, but this was the first time she'd really talked about something in a way that told him she *knew* what she was talking about. It was more than reading. She'd been involved in this kind of thing. The event space and catering, that is.

Nothing wrong with that, but the fact she didn't want to tell him was concerning.

"It's not a bad thought. Seems like it'd be a lot of work, though."

"Maybe it would," she said, her voice smaller than

before. "Like I said, it was something I read and then I started thinking about how it could apply to the range. I tend to get carried away sometimes."

She sounded more apologetic than he liked, and he couldn't help but touch her arm to reassure her. The contact with her skin was like a lightning rod to his groin. He focused on her pretty face, the way strands of her red hair had fallen out of her ponytail and framed her face. The light smattering of freckles across her nose and under her eyes. Her pretty, pale green eyes that reminded him of a cool, clear stream in summer that reflected the moss in its depths.

Her lips were full, kissable, and they parted as her eyes met his and held. All he needed to do was lean forward…

He shook himself, took his hand away, and the fog in his brain cleared. "It's a good idea. Getting carried away is how all good ideas become reality, don't you think? I mean what about the guy who thought the most efficient way to ship a package across town overnight was to actually send it to a hub in another state and then fly it back to be delivered the next day? Sounds crazy, right? But FedEx works or it wouldn't still be around."

Her smile was soft, and he knew he'd said the right thing. "I hardly think my idea is FedEx, but thanks for not laughing at me."

"I would never laugh at you, Sunshine. Not for being filled with enthusiasm over ideas."

Her smile widened. "But you *would* laugh at me."

He grinned. "Oh yeah, definitely. Like if you squirt mustard on your shirt when you're trying to put it on a hotdog, I'm laughing."

"I don't like mustard, so guess that one's out."

He clutched a hand over his heart. "What? No mustard on your hotdogs? What kind of barbarian are you?"

"I prefer ketchup."

"Damn, honey, that's brutal. Ketchup? Here I thought you were civilized."

"You'd be surprised," she said, opening her door. "You coming with me or what?"

"Coming."

She jumped out and shut the door, then walked around to the front of the vehicle to wait for him. He stared at her back, wondering what kind of secrets she carried.

Because it was becoming clearer to him than ever that she was hiding things about her past.

Chapter Eight

It only took four hours, three dealerships, and a lot of growling on Kane's behalf before he pronounced a vehicle up to his standards. It was a twelve-year-old Hyundai Santa Fe with more than a hundred thousand miles. It was silver, boxy, and nothing like her sleek Porsche.

But it started up, purred, and drove well. It also had the added advantage that she could sleep in it if she had to. Best of all, the total price was only three hundred over her budget. She refused Kane's offer of help, knowing she could scrape that much together before they came back with a cashier's check tomorrow.

She lived frugally and saved religiously, two things she'd never done before leaving New Orleans.

"You know," Kane said as they drove along pitch dark roads on the way back to Sutton's Creek, "you could have probably gotten a loan for part of the price, made payments for six months, and then paid it off entirely. That's a good way to establish credit when you're young and starting out."

"Thanks, Grandpa, but I prefer to pay cash."

"What happens when you want to buy a house some-day?" he asked, ignoring the grandpa crack entirely. "If you don't have credit, you won't be able to get a mortgage."

Daphne blew out a breath. "What if all I want is a tiny home? And I save the money for it?"

"Guess you could do that."

"Do *you* own a home?"

"I see what you're doing. The six of us have the range and the two houses on the property. You know that."

"Yeah, but you don't own a home of your own. Though I guess you probably make payments on this big beast." She slid her hand along the leather armrest. The Yukon was top of the line with leather, wood trim, and big displays with touch screens.

"Nope. Got it used and paid cash."

She folded her arms over her chest and gave him a look. "And you think I need to buy a car on credit?"

"I didn't say I never bought *anything* on credit, or that I don't have a credit score. All I'm saying is you need a credit score."

"Nah, I'm good. If I don't have the cash I don't need the thing, do I?"

He snorted. "You're unlike any woman I've ever met."

She wasn't sure whether to take that as a compliment or if it was the usual thing where he tried to keep her in a box of his own design.

"Why? Because I don't want a Chanel purse or designer jeans?" She'd had both, and she'd left them behind. "I don't think you can really generalize that to all women, by the way. Do you think Rory ever wanted a designer anything in her life? She's beautiful and her clothes suit her, but none of what she wears has a designer label."

"You don't want those things either but you know the labels and you know if Rory's wearing them or not?"

"I watch television," she said with a sniff. "And I read celebrity gossip sometimes. I wouldn't say I know every designer there is, but I know the more popular ones."

She knew designers because she'd had a closet full of clothes, handbags, and shoes. She'd defined herself by those things at one time. Before she'd realized the true cost of that lifestyle.

"Okay, I give up," he said. "But I'm telling you, Sunshine, one of these days you're going to need a credit score for something. You're lucky the Suttons didn't want one before they rented the apartment to you."

"Lucky, or I found the right apartment and the right people? There's always a way, Kane."

She didn't know that for sure, really, but arguing with him was turning into a sport these days. Most of the time she enjoyed it. She didn't want to think about what that meant.

"What did that guy say to you today anyway?"

The question was so unexpected that she couldn't stop herself from stiffening. Worse, he saw it because he chose that moment to glance at her.

"Nothing out of the ordinary. I told you before. I just didn't like the look of him—or the way he looked at me."

"Daphne."

"Kane."

His hands flexed on the wheel. "Don't you trust us by now?"

Her throat tightened. "Of course I do. But you're trying to make a big deal out of nothing. What do you want me to say? That he leered? Looked down my shirt? Hell, you did that this morning and I didn't flip out."

He groaned. "Jeez, told you not to mention that."

"I'm not *mentioning* it. I'm just pointing it out to tell you it happens. The dude didn't say or do anything other than stare creepily. Sometimes a woman doesn't want to be stared at, but when you're serving the public, you have to be nice."

"Don't be nice. Tell guys like that to fucking get lost."

Daphne shook her head. "Not how you run a business, dude. You're nice to the women who ogle you. And don't tell me they don't, because I've seen it happen. Also, don't you dare tell me it's different because you're a man. I'll put my foot up your ass the next time I get a chance if you do."

"You fucking kill me sometimes."

"Yeah, well you annoy the hell out of me. Guess that makes us even."

He was silent for a few minutes. It was too good to last.

"Is that why you liked Trigg? Because he didn't leer at you or make you uncomfortable?"

Daphne sighed. Today was Kane's chatty day, apparently. But if she didn't answer some of his questions, he'd keep bugging her. Better to answer the easy ones. Maybe he'd forget about the difficult ones.

"Warren is a good man. Yes, I liked him because he treated me like I was special. He didn't make me uncomfortable. He's respectful and kind, and though I know I'm not the right woman for what he wants in his life, I'm still sorry we broke up."

"You'd go out with him again if he asked."

It wasn't a question, but she answered anyway. "He won't ask."

"But if he did."

"If he did, I'd say yes."

In truth she didn't know what she'd say, but she was feeling just prickly enough to tell him she would. Just in case he didn't like the answer.

"So long as he's a good guy, I guess I can understand it."

"He is."

Too good, actually. He lived his truth, followed his religion, and deserved somebody who shared his values. Daphne had always known she wasn't that person. Didn't mean she hadn't wanted to try, though.

She craved a normal life, thought she could have it if she tried hard enough to be somebody different.

But she was always going to be an O'Malley, no matter how far she ran. That was the kind of stink you couldn't wash away.

By the time Kane drove up behind the Sutton building, it was almost ten o'clock. Daphne gathered the folder with her car paperwork and started to thank him for going with her again, but he turned off the engine.

"What are you doing?"

He pushed his door open. "I'm going upstairs so I know you get into your apartment safely."

"You don't have to do that, Kane. Just wait for me to unlock the back door and get inside the building."

He put a foot on the pavement. "Going up, Sunshine."

He shut the driver's door before she could respond, then walked around and opened her door before she could hop out. Kane had been opening car doors for her all evening, and it was disconcerting. Not that she minded it, but for a man who'd treated her like his annoying little sister for so long, it was decidedly weird.

She slid to the pavement and he shut the car door. She led the way to the building, turning to face him when she stood on the top step. He was a step below her, which put their eyes on the same level. Her heart thumped at being so close to him. Especially after that morning and the way he'd responded when he looked down her shirt.

She'd spent months wondering why he didn't seem to find her attractive, why he hit on every woman he encountered except her. She still wondered, but at least she knew he'd liked what he'd seen. She wasn't as repulsive to him as he would have had her believe.

"Thanks for your help, Kane. I'm really happy to have my own car again."

"You're welcome."

She waited for him to get the hint. Instead, he gently took the keys from her hand and inserted one into the lock. The correct one, she noted. How did he know?

He twisted it and tugged the door open. "After you."

"You don't have to go upstairs with me. This is good enough."

Because it was already awkward between them. If he went upstairs, it'd be even more so at her door. Did she invite him in? Shut the door in his face? If she invited him in, and he said yes, then what? Offer him a beer? Suck his dick until he saw stars? Shove him onto the couch and ride him like a bucking bronc?

Yes, please.

She wanted to do it even more than she had before. Was it because she knew he had a heart in there? That he wasn't just a charmer who saw women as conquests to be made? He'd had a wife, and he'd lost her—and that made Daphne want to hug him tight and stroke his hair before losing herself in his arms.

"Sorry, Sunshine, but it's my duty to make sure you get inside safely."

She pushed the visual of a gloriously naked Kane from

her brain. She was letting sympathy tell her lies about how it would go, and that was not cool. Kane was still Kane. He was still annoying as shit.

"Okay, fine. But this is overkill. The outer door is locked. Blaze and Emma live on the second floor. Plus there are security cameras in the hallway and Blaze gets alerts. Do you really think it's necessary for you to go up three flights of stairs just to watch me unlock my door?"

"Yup. Now get moving."

"Where are you on other nights when I come home alone?"

His gaze narrowed. "You often go home alone in the dark?"

"I did last night after book club."

"So maybe don't do that again, okay? At least not until Nathan Fader leaves town."

Daphne's insides liquified, and not in a good way. "You know his name?"

"Of course I fucking know his name. The dude made you uncomfortable."

"Kane, so help me God—"

He put a hand over her mouth. Daphne blinked at him in shock. Then she bit his finger. Lightly, not hard. But enough so he'd know she didn't like it. He dropped his hand and growled at her.

"Listen to me, for fuck's sake." He pushed her into the interior of the building and closed the door behind him. "He's not a resident here, he's passing through, and he's been to the range two days in a row. He made you uncom-fortable both days, and while that may not mean anything other than he's a dick, I can't in good conscience let you be alone in dark parking lots and entering buildings. If you don't want me here, fine, but until this douche leaves town, at least call Blaze and Emma to come downstairs and wait for you when you've been out. It's Safety 101, Sunshine. Somebody makes you uncomfortable but it's not enough to call the police, you deploy the buddy system. I'm your buddy and I'd feel better making sure you get into your apartment safely. Can you let me do that? Please?"

Daphne swallowed. Her buddy. Always her buddy. Couldn't he at least appear to be struggling to keep her at arm's length the way she was with him?

"Sure, buddy. Come on up and watch me walk inside. I can think of nothing more delightful than shutting the door in your face anyway. Gramps," she added for good measure.

She whirled and started up the stairs. Kane trailed after her. "Now what's got you pissed off?"

"Nothing at all, *buddy.*"

"For fuck's sake, Daphne," he growled. "You are the prickliest fucking female I've ever met."

"Well at least I'm female now."

"What?"

"The *parts*, idiot. This morning you didn't want to count me in the female column and you definitely didn't like it when I pointed out I had all the parts."

He stomped along behind her until they hit the third-floor landing. Then his fingers were on her arm and he spun her until she collided with his chest. A second after that, her back was against the wall and his hard body pressed into her from breast to belly to hip.

It was a shock, and it was delicious at the same time.

His fingers spanned her jaw, tipped her head back, his hand sliding to her throat. He held her firmly but gently. His thumb glided along the side of her neck until he found her racing pulse.

"The reason I don't want to think about your parts, Daphne," he said, his voice whisper soft and growly at the same time, "is that if I *do* think of them, I'll want to touch them. All of them. I'll want to lick this throbbing pulse until you moan, and then I'll want to suck your nipples into tight little peaks. Worst of all, I'll want to find out how wet you are when I do those things. I'll want to stroke my fingers into your hot, tight little pussy until you're begging for my cock."

"You aren't convincing me this is a bad idea yet," she whispered.

He leaned forward and nipped her earlobe. The hard press of his cock against her told her he was as turned on as she was. How the hell they'd gone from arguing about him walking her upstairs to completely horny in a matter of minutes was a mystery, but here they were.

"But it is, Daph. Really bad. Because I'll fuck you good for a night. We'll feel fantastic, and we'll want more and more. But when the sun comes up and reality sets in, I'll be gone. And it won't happen again because I'll be done. Once I've had you, I'll be finished with you. The mystery is gone, the ache, the need. You won't know why, and you'll look at me with hurt in your eyes. I don't want to hurt you, Daph. I really don't. So let's not go there in the first place."

Hurt and anger spun together inside her. She wanted to shove him away and she wanted to kiss him senseless and prove him wrong. There was really only one option though.

Daphne shoved his chest with all her might. It wasn't a lot compared to the strength of Kane Fox, but he got the hint and stepped back, dropping his hand from her throat, his other hand from her hip.

"You are *such* an asshole, Kane. I realize you're pretty, but you really think you're God's fucking gift to women, don't you? Everything you've said—*everything*—is based on the idea that all the poor, feeble-minded women just can't help themselves. One ride on your magic cock and they're in love, right? They hound you for more, but woe-is-you, you just can't get the peen up again for the same woman or something. Do you even *hear* yourself?"

He was a dark, hulking presence, hands at his sides, face utterly closed off. She wanted to slap him until he cracked, but the urge sickened her. Was that her O'Malley blood heating up, wanting to punish? Did she want to make him pay for what he'd said? Or did she want to prove to him that he wasn't as unfeeling as he pretended?

"You're right," he said, his voice low and deep, "I'm an asshole. But I know that about myself and I'm being honest with you, no matter what you think about me. I want you. You have to know that I do. How could I not? You're so fucking pretty, and you're always right there where I can see you and think about you. I've jerked off to thoughts of you, and I'll likely do it again. But that's all it can be. It's all I've got to give. And no matter how pissed you are at me, you fucking *cried* that night by the fire when you told everybody that Warren Trigg broke up with you because you weren't the kind of woman he wanted. I already know where this would go if we started, and I'm not going to be the man who makes you cry. So be pissed at me, I can handle it. Call me names if it makes you feel better. Still not changing my mind, because I know who I am."

Everything he'd said was a dull roar in her ears. Most of it, anyway. She'd thought the news of him having once been married was a shock. This was more so.

"You jerk off to thoughts of me?"

He snorted. "Of course you'd focus on that. Yeah, Daphne, fuck me to hell and back, but I do. And it doesn't make me feel good to say it. I'm too old and too broke inside, okay? I feel like shit lusting after you."

Daphne closed her eyes. Damn Kenny for talking her into being so much younger than she really was. She couldn't tell Kane the truth. Even if she did, it'd create more problems than it solved. Then again, was that really his problem with wanting her?

"You're just looking for an excuse to torture yourself. But I'm a grown woman, Kane. So stop obsessing over your advanced age compared to me. Either kiss me or find better things to do with your time."

She waited but he didn't move. "Thought so."

She stepped around him and started for the door.

"Where are you going?"

She threw a look over her shoulder. "It's late and I want to go to bed. I'll see you in the morning."

He followed her to her door, though she didn't want him to, and stood just out of her sight while she fitted her key to the lock. She was annoyed with herself and irritated with him and it took her a moment to get the key jammed in.

When she turned it, there was no resistance. She turned the key the other way and the lock engaged.

"Kane," she forced out past the sudden tightness in her chest.

Someone had been inside her space. Might still be.

She didn't have to say another word before he acted. Kane dragged her from in front of the door and pushed her against the wall, anchoring her with an arm. She heard rather than saw him draw a weapon.

"Stay here," he commanded, his voice barely more than a growl. "If you hear sounds after I breach the door, I want you to run down to Blaze and Emma's and hammer on their door until they let you in, you got me?"

"Yes." Her heart was a wild animal in her chest,

beating against the cage of her ribs. "Kane," she whispered as he tensed for action beside her.

"Yes?"

"Please be careful."

He grinned, and for some reason the fear in her chest eased a tiny bit. "I got this, Sunshine. Don't worry."

A moment later, he was in motion.

Chapter Nine

KANE'S EMOTIONS HAD BEEN BOILING OVER WITH DAPHNE, making him say and do things he otherwise wouldn't. But charging into danger was something he understood instinctively. He blasted through the door and ghosted from room to room, looking for an intruder.

Didn't take long to discover that no one was inside. There were some open drawers, a pillow on the floor, but nothing was wrecked. He lowered the weapon and returned to get Daphne, who was still against the wall where he'd left her. He had to admit he'd had his doubts she'd stay.

Her eyes were big, her skin pale, and he couldn't help but draw her into his arms and squeeze her for a moment.

"It's okay," he said, his mouth against the fragrant cloud of her hair. "There's nobody here."

Her body sagged in his arms and he stepped back, took her hand, and led her inside. "Tell me if anything's out of place or missing."

She nodded, her arms wrapped around her body as if she were cold. Only a moment ago, he'd have said she was hot as a firecracker, telling him off the way she had. Calling him an asshole and vain at the same time. He hadn't blamed her, because he'd been a dick, but if the end result made her think twice about getting involved with him, then it didn't matter, did it?

She walked through the apartment, him following, looking at everything as she went. She didn't close the drawers that were opened, didn't pick up the pillow. She stopped in her bedroom door, hesitated, then walked inside and over to the queen-sized bed against one wall. Daphne didn't have a lot of stuff in her apartment. He hadn't expected she would since it wasn't that long ago she'd been living in her car.

There was the bed, an end table, a bench at the foot of the bed, and a dresser with a mirror. Her bedspread was plain, white, and she had one of those granny afghans that'd been crocheted with black octagons and riots of color everywhere. It was old-fashioned and made him think about the afghan his grandmother had made for his mother. He wondered what'd happened to it, if it was in storage, or if it'd gotten tossed when his parents split up after he'd joined the Army and left home.

The afghan was rumpled, and there were drawers open in here as well.

Daphne bent to look under the bed, then ran her hands over her bedspread, straightening it. She checked the closet, feeling around in the bottom of it for a moment, then turned to him, that haunted look still on her face.

"It seems okay. Nothing's missing. But what if there's a camera or a listening device? What if some creepy asshole just wants to watch me get undressed? I don't think I can stay here until I know."

The thought of somebody spying on Daphne made his

gut clench. "The equipment's at the range. We can go get it. Or I can see if Ethan's around. He can bring it."

"Thank you."

Kane sent a text to Ethan, then sent an informational one to Blaze since he was downstairs. Ethan responded with a thumbs up and Blaze sent back an exclamation point. He followed it with a text.

I'll check the hallway cameras.

Thanks.

"You don't have to stay here tonight if you don't want to," Kane told her. "You can have the spare room in mine and Ethan's house, or you can stay with Alex. He's living alone these days since Seth moved out."

Not that Kane fucking wanted her anywhere but near him, but he had to offer.

"Thanks. I might do that. Whoever was in here didn't take anything. I locked the door because I always do, but to hear Colleen talk, Melvin could have unlocked it if he's feeling frisky enough. Maybe somebody walked in because the door was open."

She almost sounded like she was talking herself into believing it.

"Tell me you don't really believe that nonsense Colleen spews."

Melvin was the ghost that supposedly lived in the Sutton building and had done since the eighteen hundreds. Colleen claimed he was a fixture. Kane had never seen him. Neither had Blaze, and he lived here full time.

"I don't."

"Good, because I don't either. Doesn't mean the lock isn't faulty. This is an old building."

"The locks aren't that old, though."

"No, but if the wood swelled, could have popped the lock."

Daphne shook her head. "No, because the lock wasn't engaged when I put my key in. I'm certain of it. If the wood had swelled, the lock would have still been engaged inside the mechanism. Somebody picked the lock. Or I didn't lock it this morning, though I'm sure I did."

"How sure?"

"Very, though I guess anything's possible."

They returned to the kitchen where Daphne took a bottle of Scotch from the cabinet and poured some into a glass. "Want one?"

"No. Thanks."

He watched her toss it back, more than amazed at how she didn't even grimace. "You drink Scotch often?"

"No, not really." She poured another small dram and twisted the cap onto the bottle. Then she lifted the glass and sipped.

He smelled the whisky from where he was standing. It had a strong, smoky smell. Not in the least bit feminine or delicate. Not that he expected Daphne to drink feminine whisky, if there was such a thing. He'd learned better than to assume when it came to her.

Her mouth twisted into a half-smile. "I tended bar for a few months once. I acquired a taste for good Scotch because one of the customers was a Scot, and he walked me through the flavor profiles. Naturally I like the expensive stuff, which means I buy a bottle and milk it."

She turned the bottle toward him. "This bottle of Ardbeg was a hundred and twenty bucks, and I've had it for two months now. I'd drink it more often, but I try to save it for when I really want it. I have another one from Bowmore that's not as smoky, and it's cheaper. But there's no such thing as a twenty dollar bottle of Scotch worth drinking, at least not in the US. I imagine it's different in Scotland, though I wouldn't really know."

"I never had a taste for Scotch. Bourbon's more my speed."

She wrinkled her nose. "Too sweet. I prefer the smoke that comes from peat." She sniffed the glass, her eyes closing. "Mmm, so good. Sure you don't want a sip?"

She held the glass toward him. He didn't miss that she trembled and it drove a wave of sympathy through him.

"Sure, why not."

He took the glass from her cool fingers.

"Smell it first," she said. "Inhale that smoke, and think about it."

He did what she told him. The whisky definitely smelled like smoke. And maybe a little bit like a cough syrup his mother used to give him when he was a kid. It wasn't an unpleasant smell, though.

"Take just a sip and hold it on your tongue. Taste it before you let it slide down."

Fucking hell, did she know her instructions were sexy?

He obeyed, surprised at the bold flavor when he swallowed the whisky. "Hey, that's not bad."

Her smile was worth it even if the whisky had ended up tasting like shit to him. Which it didn't. "See? Told you. Honestly, Kane, you should listen to me more often. I'm wise beyond my years."

"I don't doubt it, Sunshine."

He gave her back the glass, then wrapped an arm around her shoulders and hugged her to his side. Like one friend to another. Which, damn, he needed to remember after that exchange in the hall. Her skin had felt like silk under his fingers. Her hair smelled like lavender. He'd wanted, so desperately, to taste her mouth. He'd wanted to do all those things he'd said, and he was still pissed he'd let his ironclad control off the leash like that. There'd been no reason for it, other than she'd been pissed at him, talking about her parts, and he'd been watching her sexy ass sway as she walked up the stairs in front of him.

He'd wanted to fill his hands with her ass and watch his cock disappear inside her as he fucked her from behind. Those had been the things on his mind when he'd pushed her against the wall and put his hands on her.

The only thing on his mind now was keeping her safe.

She leaned into him, laid her head against his side, and huffed a breath. Then she lifted that shaky glass to her mouth again and took another sip.

Footsteps on the stairs told him someone was coming. Probably Blaze. And Emma since he heard a lighter step along with the heavier one.

Emma burst into the apartment first, Blaze on her heels. "Daphne! Are you okay, honey?"

Daphne left his side and went into Emma's arms. Then she burst into tears, which floored him. What the hell was that about? She hadn't seemed *that* scared. Just shook up.

"Oh, honey, I'm sorry. But don't you worry, Blaze and Kane will take care of you and figure out what kind of asshole dared to break into your home."

Kane exchanged a look with Blaze. "Was it a break in?"

"Yeah. I checked the cameras. A man entered the building a few minutes after twelve and went upstairs. He had on a ball cap and a tool belt, so he looked like one of the workers renovating the back apartment. He went inside the back one, but then he continued here and picked the lock. He was inside for about ten minutes. The workers were returning from lunch then. He didn't join them in the other apartment, so not an opportunist."

Daphne had looked up again. The tear tracks on her face killed him. Just killed him.

"What did he look like?" she asked.

"He kept the ball cap pulled down so you can't get a look at his face. He had to have known the cameras were there."

Not for the first time, Kane wondered what kind of past Daphne was running from. Because he was more convinced than ever that she was, no matter what she'd said about not having an abusive ex chasing after her. The idea someone had hurt her made him want to break things.

Daphne swiped her fingers beneath her eyes. She picked up the Scotch from where she'd set it on the counter and gulped it back. "I don't want to stay here tonight."

"You can stay with us," Emma said, and Kane wanted to elbow her for it.

Blaze took one look at his face and knew that wasn't going to fly. "You can," Blaze said. "But if you want to be away from the building, I think going to the farm is a good idea. There's plenty of room. You won't have to even look at Kane's ugly face if you don't want to."

"That's true," Emma said, catching the drift. "You're welcome to stay in our guest room, but Sassy likes to yowl at the top of her lungs around three in the morning. It might be quieter at the farm."

Daphne sniffed. "I want to be somewhere other than here. If I'm downstairs, I'll lie awake and think about somebody creeping around up here."

"Ethan's on the way with the bug sweeping equipment," Kane said. "We'll make sure it wasn't some perv planting cameras, then we'll head back to the farm for the night."

"Should we call the police? Get this on the record?" Emma asked.

"No," Daphne blurted before Kane or Blaze could chime in.

Kane blinked at the vehemence in her voice. "It's not a bad idea, Daph," he said.

"No." She shook her head back and forth until it was a wonder she didn't make herself dizzy. "I don't want the police. Please."

Blaze shot him a look. Kane lifted his brows in acknowledgment before focusing on Daphne again. He didn't know if the Scotch had gone to her head that fast or what, but he thought she was even more spooked by the idea of the police than the intruder.

"We don't need to get them involved," Kane said. "Yet. Nothing's missing. If we find spy gear, or if they return, might be a good idea. Until then, we can handle it."

Daphne seemed to sag a little. "Thank you."

He really, really wanted to know what she was scared of. Wasn't going to push her right now, but it was coming. Because he wasn't letting her keep all this fear and worry inside. Not when she had six special operators to keep her safe and secure.

Ethan arrived about ten minutes later and they swept the apartment for listening gear and cameras. There was nothing, which was a good thing but also curious, because if the dude hadn't stolen anything and hadn't left any listening gear, what the fuck was he up to?

Emma must have had the same thought because she took Daphne's hand. "Honey, I hate to ask this, but have you checked to make sure you don't have any missing, um, underwear?"

For fuck's sake. Kane's head was going to explode at the thought of some dude stealing into Daphne's place to pilfer panties. Not that there weren't sick fucks like that out there, because there were, but why the fuck was she so spooked?

"I didn't, no," Daphne said. "That's disgusting."

"I know. But trust me, they're out there. Want me to help?" Emma looked sympathetic and concerned, and Kane was happy she was there. He wouldn't have thought of that option, and he damn sure wouldn't have offered to help go through her panty drawer.

"Might as well get it over with," Daphne said. The two of them disappeared into her bedroom, leaving Kane, Ethan, and Blaze in the kitchen.

"I don't like it," Kane said, voice pitched low. "If it was an opportunistic burglar, why didn't he take anything? And why didn't he try the apartments downstairs while he was on his breaking-and-entering spree?"

Blaze looked thoughtful. Ethan seemed troubled, though Kane didn't think it was about Daphne since he kept looking at his phone.

"Good questions," Blaze said. "Emma might be right and he could be a panty thief. He might even be somebody from the range who's fixated on Daphne."

Kane didn't like that idea. It made him think about Hannah, about what had happened to her when a man became too fixated on her. Panty theft wasn't funny when seen in that light. It was downright terrifying.

He was ready to crawl out of his skin at the mere thought of someone taking too much interest in Daphne. He'd much rather it was a crime of opportunity, someone looking for money or valuables. But what if it was something more?

"What do we really know about her?" Kane threw out the thought that'd been bugging him. "She had a clean background, but that doesn't mean she wasn't running from something. Or someone."

"Possible," Ethan said, catching up to the conversation. "Has she told you anything?"

"Are you kidding?" Kane said with a snort. "Daphne is tight-lipped about most things if you hadn't noticed."

"Huh, really? She's always pleasant to me."

"Pleasant and forthcoming are not the same things, brother," Kane said. "And have you ever really asked her a question about her past?"

"That'd be a no."

"Yeah, well I have. And you know what she told me?" He paused. "Absolutely nothing."

Emma and Daphne walked into the open living area again. Emma looked concerned. Daphne had a pink overnight bag slung over her shoulder and looked like she'd already known what she would find when she'd agreed to look through her drawers.

"Well?" Kane asked.

"Nothing missing," Daphne said. "Not a pervert who wanted my panties."

"This time," he replied, because it wasn't entirely out of the realm of possibility that some jerk—Fader?—was obsessed with her. He might break in again, steal panties or bras, plant cameras. Kane didn't know what motivated sick fucks like that and he didn't want to know.

All he wanted was to keep Daphne safe. He hadn't been there for Hannah because he'd had a job to do on the other side of the world, but no way was he letting the same shit happen again. He wasn't married to Daphne, wasn't in love with her, but the idea of some asshole snuffing out her spark made his gut clench into knots.

"Can we go now?" Daphne asked, her gaze on him.

"Yes. You got what you need in that bag?"

"One-hundred percent. I'm ready."

"Then we're going."

Blaze and Emma said they'd lock up, Ethan said his goodbyes, and Kane took Daphne's bag before wrapping her cool hand in his and leading her to the parking lot. She wasn't unaware of her surroundings. He watched her carefully, saw the way she scanned the parking lot, the way she stuck close to him. She wasted no time getting inside the Yukon, slouching down in the seat almost immediately.

Everything about her reactions surprised him and bothered him. As if she knew to look out for trouble, to not make herself a target, to move fast and stealthily. It was more than the safety training from the range. It was the kind of wariness that came from experience. Something bad that stuck with someone, made them wary of everything.

He didn't comment as he got into the driver's seat and started the SUV. But when they'd left the lot and turned onto Main Street, he couldn't keep it to himself any longer.

"Daphne, I say this with all the concern of a friend who cares—what the *fuck* is going on?"

Chapter Ten

Daphne stiffened. Her mind raced. She opted for calm disinterest as she turned her gaze on Kane.

The last thing she'd expected was to be back in a vehicle with him, going to the farmhouse he lived in, and bunking for the night. This entire experience was jarring, and her nerves were on edge.

"I wish I knew. Do you think I wanted somebody to break into my apartment and scare the hell out of me?"

"I didn't say that. But why did it scare you so badly?"

"Oh, you mean I should have just said, oh well, la-di-da, no big deal, I'll sleep in my bed tonight and not think twice about some strange man picking my lock and strolling around in my home? Because I assure you, whatever you think is going on, I don't think there's anything worse than your stuff being *violated* by a stranger and you don't know why. It's creepy, Kane. Creepy enough to make me jumpy as a cat in a roomful of rocking chairs—but who wouldn't be?"

Her voice had steadily risen with her little speech until she finished on a yell. She knew there were worse things than her home being violated, but she couldn't admit that to him. He didn't say anything about her practically screaming at him, though she felt bad almost immediately for doing it. But she was rattled and fearful, and he was the closest target.

"Fair point."

"Gee, ya think?"

In truth, she was entirely wigged out. She didn't know that her brother had found her, or that Nathan Fader was an associate of her family's, or that what'd happened was anything less than some creepy dude with a crush on her. She'd encountered a handful of men at the range who seemed a bit more focused on her than she liked, but none of them made her feel as uncomfortable as Fader had.

Still, it could be a coincidence. Her brother wasn't likely to break into her place and let her know he was in the area. His style was more malicious, less artful. Jackson would have been waiting inside with a gun and a cocktail laced with sedatives that he'd have forced her to drink before he carted her back to New Orleans. And he'd have only done that once she produced the evidence she'd stolen. He wasn't going to break in and search her place looking for it when he could simply threaten her into telling him where it was.

She knew his style like she knew her own soul.

Unless he'd experienced his own crisis of conscience, he would not be lurking in the shadows, thinking how to approach her. And she had to think that if Fader was an associate of her father's, he wouldn't be poking around either. He'd simply call the man himself and tell him where to find her. Or he'd haul her back to NOLA in chains, hoping for a reward.

Because no way did she believe her father had shared with anyone other than Jackson what Daphne had stolen from him. He wouldn't want it to be common knowledge. Allegiance only went so far, and there wasn't enough you could pay criminals to be loyal when they thought they might have the key to bring your empire down.

No, her father wouldn't send anyone but Jackson after her. Too risky, especially if he thought she might make a bargain with whoever he sent.

Daphne was spooked, but she wasn't defeated. She wasn't dumb enough to keep that kind of evidence anywhere on her person, or near where she lived. She'd stashed it in the safest place she could find. A place guarded by six former military men with brawn, brains, and plenty of heart.

They had lockers in the break room for the employees, and Daphne had her own. She'd outfitted it with a combination lock so she didn't have to keep up with a key, and she'd stashed the memory card with all her father's business dealings inside. She kept a sweater in there, a pair of tennis shoes, and a couple of books. She'd tucked the card inside one of the shoes, and she periodically reached inside to make sure it was still there.

Paranoia, because who would take it? Nobody knew it was there except her. And nobody knew what was on it.

"You've been acting different since Nathan Fader showed up yesterday," Kane said. "So don't blame me for asking."

Daphne's eyes pricked with angry tears. "I've told you he's creepy. I don't like him, but if you go banning him from the range, I think he's the kind of guy who won't react well."

"And you have experience with those kinds of guys, huh?"

God, this whole thing was turning into a mess. The edges of her two lives were starting to blur, and she didn't know how to separate them again. She thought about the gun she had buried deep in her duffel bag, the one she'd kept packed in case she ever needed to bolt. She was bolting now, but not far.

But what if Kane or one of the guys found the gun? It wasn't registered to her.

It wasn't registered to anyone, which was definitely a red flag.

If the intruder had taken it, she'd be out a weapon. But it was still there. She'd checked when she'd looked in the closet, reaching inside and feeling around until she found its hard bulk.

Thank God.

"I'm a woman, Kane. Of course I've experienced creepy guys who don't like being told no. Again, he hasn't said or done anything wrong. It's me. He creeps me out because he reminds me of someone I didn't like, okay?"

Kane blew out a breath. "Yeah, fine. I've got Seth running a background on him. We'll see where he's from, and where he was today when the break-in happened."

She wasn't sure how she felt about that, but if she said not to do it, that would make Kane even more suspicious. "I want to know what you find out."

Because if she heard the O'Malley name mentioned at all, she was going to have to make a decision—though the thought of having to leave Sutton's Creek made her heart hurt.

"Planned on telling you, Sunshine."

"Thank you."

They reached the smaller of the two farmhouses on the property where the range was located. She'd heard the story from Emma and Rory about how the Jackson farm had been a cotton farm for years until the last generation passed away. When the only living Jackson son had married in the late eighteen hundreds, his parents had built another house on the property for him to raise a family. He and his wife were prolific, producing eight children, but only two of them survived to adulthood. The family had been in decline since, until the last surviving Jackson died and the farm was sold.

Daphne had been inside both houses, and she knew that Kane and Ethan shared the smaller house and Alex had the bigger since Chance and Seth had moved out. She liked both houses, but the smaller one was cozy, like a cottage. There were four small bedrooms on the second floor and a big parlor, dining room and kitchen on the lower level. There was a basement that had been intended for storing food originally, but was now only used when the tornado sirens were blaring.

Assuming the guys weren't up at the range, which had a tornado shelter on the premises.

Kane grabbed her overnight bag from the backseat before she could, then headed up the steps to the wide porch running along the front of the house. He turned off the alarm on his phone before unlocking the door. Daphne followed him inside, weariness flooding her bones as the adrenaline that'd been carrying her along started to subside.

"You know where the kitchen is if you need anything in the middle of the night." He started upstairs. The staircase was in the middle of the house and there was a landing halfway up before the steps turned and went the rest of the way to the second floor. "It's a shared bath, unfortunately, but there's a half-bath downstairs if somebody's in this one. This is my room and that's Ethan's," he said, pointing at rooms across the hall from each other. "This one's a spare, but it's got a bed and dresser. There's a small TV too, if you want to watch anything. Ethan bought a bigger one and put his old one in here."

The room was small but cozy, just like the house. She had a random thought that her closet in New Orleans was bigger. Kane set her bag on the bench at the end of the bed and looked at her.

"I'm sorry somebody violated your space, Sunshine. And I'm sorry for grilling you. It's what I do, though. I'm a security specialist and I can't help but look for reasons shit's happening. I also want to fix it. Which, I promise you, I will."

Her throat was tight. She knew he meant it, but she was also scared for him if it turned out her family was involved. He couldn't tangle with them because they had no qualms about eliminating people who stood in their way.

And that she couldn't handle. She cared about all of them too much, but maybe she cared for Kane a little more than the rest.

"Thanks. It's probably just random, and I'll feel better about everything tomorrow." She fixed a smile on her face. "I'm getting a car of my own. That's something to look forward to."

"It is." He huffed a breath. "Need to say I'm sorry for some of those things I said to you tonight, too. I don't want you uncomfortable because I crossed a line. I was pissed off, but that's no excuse. I like you, Daph, and if I was the kind of guy who didn't have a shitload of baggage to handle, I'd behave a lot better than I do. I'd ask you on dates and seduce you slowly. I'd promise you the stars just to make you smile. Because you deserve those things from a man. You don't deserve my brand of shit."

Her heart hammered and her eyes stung. She wanted to tell him he was wrong, that *she* was the one with the shitload of baggage, and that hers was much worse than anything he could dream.

She didn't *deserve* anything good, not really. Not like he thought she did. But there was no way to say those things without telling him why.

"You don't need to apologize, Kane. I did some shit-stirring of my own. You didn't cross any lines. I pushed, and I shouldn't have done that."

They stood with their gazes locked, not moving. Daphne fought the tug in her soul that urged her to cross the space and wrap her arms around him. She felt her loneliness more keenly than she'd ever felt it before. She wanted to be held. By him. She wanted to curl up beside him and sleep with his warmth surrounding her, his presence guarding her dreams.

Only Kane could do that for her. She was certain of it, and yet she knew it wasn't going to happen. There was no way to breach the chasm between them.

"Goodnight, Sunshine," he said softly, turning away.

"Goodnight, Kane."

The door closed behind him. Daphne swiped angrily at the hot tear that spilled down her cheek.

"Better off this way," she muttered as she climbed onto the bed and curled onto her side.

She was asleep in seconds.

Chapter Eleven

THE SUN WAS BARELY UP WHEN KANE STRAPPED ON A PACK with fifty pounds inside and went for a run through the fields and forests surrounding the farm and range. The terrain was varied with small hills, a creek that switched back a couple of times, and flatland. It made for a good workout, plus it was similar to being dropped just about anywhere, except a desert, for a mission.

Sometimes he and Ethan went together, but not that morning. Ethan's door was closed and the coffee hadn't been started yet. Kane hadn't heard Ethan come back last night before he fell asleep. He'd thought Ethan had headed home as soon as they were done at Daphne's, but apparently he'd been wrong.

No telling what his teammate was doing, and Kane wasn't asking. They were all private men, and though they were brothers and shared stuff with each other, they didn't share everything. Some shit was too personal.

Kane had told them about Hannah's death a long time ago, because what'd happened to her wasn't a secret even if parts of why it'd happened were. How he dealt with everything, how it had affected his life—that was his alone. His to ponder, his to bear. Nobody else needed to know how losing her—and why—had stunted his emotions.

That was his shit.

Hannah had kept secrets until she couldn't anymore, and he often wondered if he could have done something differently. If he could have saved her if he'd recognized the signs. He would never know.

Daphne was a woman with secrets, too. He recognized the signs this time, and it troubled him. Partly because he hadn't thought too much about it until two days ago. Daphne had always been guarded about her past, and he figured it was her right. But the way she'd reacted to Nathan Fader pinged his radar. Hard.

And last night? Shit, that reaction had been far more than being creeped out. She'd been *scared*.

Like she'd believed that whoever had broken into her place was looking specifically for her. Like she'd expected she was the target. He'd expected her to be scared, because who wouldn't be, but her fear was specific and focused.

That's what wasn't typical.

He ran through the woods, birds chirping and squirrels scratching around in the leaves that littered the underbrush even in summer, until he was spent. He'd never be able to outrun the demons that haunted him, but at least he could wear their asses out for a while.

When he reached the house, Daphne was sitting on the front porch, mug in hand, one leg thrown over the arm of the chair she'd settled in, the other curled beneath her. His heart gave a painful thump at the sight of her before beating normally again.

She managed a smile as he reached the steps and strode up them.

"Lookie what the cat dragged in," she said. "A hot,

sweaty Kane Fox. Did you seriously go running with a backpack?"

He grinned as he sat on the top step and shrugged out of the pack—and his soaked T-shirt—before leaning back against the porch column. "Sure did. You don't think I keep my manly figure by eating barbecue and shooting guns all day, do you?"

"Don't forget working out in the range gym."

"That too. Still not enough to keep the BBQ from going to my mid-section."

She let her gaze slide over him. "It would be a shame if the ladies couldn't ogle your abs anymore."

A tingle of awareness prickled to life in his groin at the look in her eyes. He shut it down as fast as he could, but damn, why did this slip of a girl affect him like that?

Not a girl. A woman.

Well, fuck, she'd successfully guilted him into a new way of thinking. There was no going back to calling her *kid* and *girl* and *child,* like he had over the past few months.

He put a hand over his slick abdomen and patted it. "These abs *are* an asset to One Shot Tactical, aren't they?"

She snorted and sipped her coffee. "Newsflash, Mr. Fox. Your co-owners also have them. I've read more than a few testimonials from women quite impressed with the musculature on display at the range."

He blinked. "Okay, that's BS. None of us teach with shirts off."

"No, but you reach for things above your head. You wipe your faces with the hems of your shirts sometimes. Trust me, I've seen every set of abs in the place. And so have the ladies of Sutton's Creek. Which is part of why they keep coming back. Oh, business idea!"

He looked at her suspiciously.

"We rent the event space, like I said, and add sexy men

clad in costumes. You know, like from romance novels. But you have to show chests and abs, so we'll save on shirts and jackets."

"Uh, how about no?"

Daphne laughed, and the sound went straight to his groin. First, he was happy she was laughing. It sounded free and real. Second, he wanted to bottle it up and listen to it on the darkest days.

"You eat anything yet?" he asked, because he needed to think about something besides her laugh.

She shook her head. "No, just made coffee. I didn't want to go through your cabinets or raid your fridge."

"I have to shower, but I'm thinking scrambled eggs with toast and bacon. What about you?"

"Sounds good to me. Are you cooking or suggesting we go to Miss Mary's?"

"Cooking. Unless you want to go to Miss Mary's?"

Her smile was mischievous. "Are you kidding? And miss the sight of famous ladykiller Kane slaving over a hot stove? Hell, I might even film it for Instagram. Can you do it shirtless?"

He shook his head. "Fuck no. It's bacon. I'm not risking these abs with hot grease sizzling and popping everywhere."

"Oh come on. What's a little grease burn compared to the delight of womankind? Bet business will be up fifty percent if we try it."

He got to his feet and stretched. She amused him. He was glad she was in a good mood. Meant she wasn't focusing on the break-in. "You're diabolical, Miss Bryant. And shockingly mercenary."

"No, I just have a mind for business opportunities. It's not my fault if I can see the dollars rolling in."

He left her on the porch and hurried to take a shower

and dress. By the time he came back down, she was in the kitchen pouring another cup of coffee. Ethan's door had been open, but he wasn't there.

"Did you see Ethan?"

"He said he was going up to the range early because he had some things to do."

"Gotcha." Kane took eggs from the fridge along with bacon and butter.

When he laid strips of bacon in a dish and put them in the microwave, Daphne gasped. "Cheater!"

"It'll be perfect, promise."

"I'll believe it when I see it."

"You put it on for a minute a slice, then you can do thirty seconds at a time if it's not crispy enough. Works every time. An old friend taught me that trick, and I've done it that way since. You should try it next time you cook breakfast."

Daphne arched an eyebrow. "Actually, I don't cook."

"You don't cook? How do you eat?"

"Um, restaurants? Convenience food? Sandwiches?" She shrugged. "I just never learned."

"I'm surprised your parents didn't teach you, being nomads and all. Seems like a survival skill you'd want your kid to have."

"You'd think. But they weren't exactly the best parents." She went about taking bread from the sleeve and putting it into the toaster. "I can handle toast, though."

"I just taught you bacon, so that's two things."

"Toast and bacon. Wow."

"Yeah, but add mayo, lettuce, and tomato and you've got BLTs."

"Ohhhhh, yeah. I didn't think of that."

He scrambled the eggs, explaining the process, and they sat down to eat. Daphne was like a kid tasting new flavors in some ways. He didn't know if she was exaggerating to make him feel good, or if she really was that amazed at the fact he'd fixed breakfast for her.

Didn't matter, really, because he'd liked doing it.

When she finished, she sat back and looked around the kitchen. It was an old farm kitchen with white cabinets, an ancient gas stove that still worked, and formica countertops. Nothing as impressive as the renovations the Suttons had done on the apartments in their building. He figured she was comparing and finding it lacking. Didn't bother him since he had no real attachment to the place.

"This house has a good feel to it," she said, surprising him. "Like people loved it for a long time before it fell into decline."

He looked around. "It's just an old house to me."

"It's more than that. I wish I could buy it and live here, walk to the range for work, plant a garden and grow my own food." Her tone was wistful. "It's a fantasy since I wouldn't know how to cook the food—but maybe I could learn. Anything's possible, right?"

"I think it is," he told her, because he believed it was true. "You just need a goal and a plan, then you work your ass off to get to the goal."

He'd lived his life that way more than not. Being a special operator was all about goals and plans and working so hard you felt it in your bones for long after the mission was complete. There were some things you couldn't achieve no matter how hard you tried, though.

Making another person be who you wanted them to be. That was fairly impossible.

"Exactly." She stood and started to gather the dishes. He reached out to stop her, closing his fingers around her wrist. She stilled, their eyes locking.

Electricity snapped in the air between them. He

wanted to kiss her, but that was the last thing he needed to do.

He let her go, breaking the conduit, and sanity returned. "You don't have to clean up," he said, belatedly remembering why he'd touched her in the first place.

She looked disappointed, or maybe he imagined it.

"It's the least I can do, Kane. You cooked breakfast, not to mention let me stay here in the first place. I'll wash dishes."

He scraped his chair back. "Fine. But I'm drying."

Her smile arrowed into his soul, made him want things that were impossible. "If you insist."

"I do."

He grabbed a dish towel and joined her at the sink, taking the dishes from her and drying them thoroughly before setting them on the counter. He was careful not to touch her again, not to create that electric connection that would have him wanting to strip her jeans from her long legs and lift her on the counter so he could do all the dirty things he wanted to do. The things he'd thought about in the middle of the night when he couldn't sleep.

"How many places have you lived?"

He felt her stiffen beside him as she handed over a pan. "Why do you want to know?"

"You said your parents were nomads. I thought that meant they moved a lot."

She seemed to relax a fraction. "We didn't move as often as you'd think. My dad liked to park somewhere remote and stay until the spirit moved him to go somewhere new."

"Guess you were probably home schooled, huh?"

"Yes."

"What kinds of work did your parents do to afford that lifestyle?"

Daphne stilled for the second time, turning to him. "If I said I wasn't comfortable talking about it, would you stop asking questions?"

He searched her pretty face. "Why does it bother you so much to talk about it, Sunshine? Did they steal things? Con people? What has you so upset?"

Her face paled before red flooded her cheeks. Her eyes flashed as she tossed the sponge into the sink and dried her hands on a paper towel. "My dad had an inheritance, okay? And yes, I'm sure they stole things when that ran out. Shoplifting, check fraud, that kind of thing. I'm not proud of them, Kane. I'm not proud of who they were or who I am when I think about it. Talking about it upsets me, but you don't seem to understand that, so I'm outta here. Thanks for breakfast."

She tossed the paper towel in the trash and stalked from the room.

Secrets. She definitely had them.

And he intended to find out what they were.

Chapter Twelve

"WE'RE SHOOTING TONIGHT, AFTER THE RANGE IS closed."

Daphne jerked her head toward Kane. He'd sat behind one of the counters again, a tray with gun parts arrayed before him. She'd informed him icily that he didn't have to stay near her all day, but he'd clearly ignored every word she said.

She wasn't mad at him anymore for asking her questions. She was mad at herself for overreacting. If she'd kept her cool and made some shit up, he wouldn't have been the wiser. Instead she'd gotten upset (still made shit up, though) and now he had to be wondering why.

Which was the last thing she wanted. But she'd slept like crap because she kept dreaming about Nathan Fader breaking into her apartment, looking for the memory card she'd stolen. Then she'd dreamed of Jackson finding her, his face split into a gleeful grin as he told her in a kid's singsong voice that she was in soooo much trouble with Daddy.

She had not been on her game when Kane started

prying and she'd acted like a lunatic. She didn't kid herself that he'd forgotten either.

"Why are we shooting?" she asked. "Do you need to practice?"

"Always, babe. That's how you keep your skills sharp. Can't ever assume you've reached mastery because as soon as you do, you'll find out you don't have it at all."

"Wow, since when did you branch into Zen lessons? Guns, defense, and Zen. You're a Renaissance Man, Kane."

"Very funny. But you aren't distracting me, Daph. We're picking up your car today, and we're returning here to shoot."

She wanted to tell him no, she'd get an Uber to Huntsville to get her car, but after this morning she wasn't rocking the boat any further. "Do I at least get dinner out of it?"

"Yeah, you get dinner. And you can stay at the house again tonight if you want."

Her heart thumped. She did want to. Because until they found out who'd been in her apartment, she didn't want to go back. At least not without a serious alarm system. She'd let herself grow complacent with the building's security, which consisted of motion-activated cameras with phone alerts (not to her, though), and Blaze. Not that Blaze wasn't a good line of defense, but he wasn't *her* line of defense. He was Emma's.

"I might do that. Thanks."

"You can stay as long as you need. Oh, and I'll be installing a security system for you, courtesy of One Shot Tactical. Take a couple of days between ordering the equipment and install."

Daphne blinked. "You don't have to do that."

It was an automatic response, but the truth was she

wanted it. She should have asked a while ago since it was part of the range's business, but she hadn't quite known how to without giving a reason for wanting security. The *why* was what had stumped her because what if they got suspicious about her excuse or asked questions she couldn't answer?

She'd told herself she was overthinking it, but in the interest of better safe than sorry, she'd kept quiet.

"We're doing it so don't argue."

"I'm not arguing. Just let me know what I owe."

"Nothing. You're an employee. Consider it one of the perks."

She wasn't arguing with that, either. "Thank you."

"You're welcome. We should have done it a while ago. Just never thought of it."

"You mean nobody ever broke into my apartment before, and Blaze lives in the building."

"Yeah, that too."

A man entered the store, a woman behind him. He strode purposely toward the display cabinets with the weapons while she stopped just inside and looked like a deer in the headlights. Daphne gave her a sympathetic smile when she made eye contact. Kane was already talking to the man so she got to her feet and made her way to where the woman had decided to look at purses.

"Those are concealed carry purses," she told the lady. "Were you looking for something to conceal a gun?"

The woman's eyes got big. "Oh. Oh, no. Nothing like that. I should have known." She smiled. "I wondered why you had purses in here. They're pretty, too."

"Mm-hmm. They come in a range of styles and colors. All of them have a hidden pocket, quickly accessed, so you can hide your weapon. What do you shoot?"

"I don't." She jerked her head toward the man. "Andy does. He wants me to learn, but I'm scared of guns."

"You don't need to be scared," Daphne said. "You just need to learn how to handle one safely. We offer beginner classes for ladies. You'll be with other beginners, and our instructors will explain everything. Would you like to sign up?"

The woman shot a look at Andy again and lowered her voice. "I don't think he'd like me to spend money on a class when he says he can teach me."

"Well, if you change your mind—or talk him into it—it's twenty-five dollars for an hour, and that includes gun rental and a box of ammo. Can't beat that."

"Thank you. I appreciate it."

"Josie."

Daphne jerked at the same time the woman turned toward the man. "What, honey?"

"Get over here. Lemme show you this sweet little Sig. It'll fit your hand perfectly."

Josie turned back to her. "Thanks again. Maybe I'll talk him into it."

"You can access the class schedule online." Daphne handed her a business card. "Good luck."

The woman—Josie—smiled and went to join her man. Daphne swallowed the acid boiling up into her throat.

It was a name, just a name. Not a rare name, or an unusual one. Josephine. Josie and the Pussycats.

Josie.

Her name.

The name she'd left behind when she fled.

She returned to her desk and tried to concentrate on the spreadsheet in front of her. But the numbers might as well have been written in hashmarks for all the sense she could make of them. She pushed to her feet because she needed to move. She went to the employee break room and took a Diet Coke from the fridge, opened it, and swigged a big mouthful of fake sugar.

First there'd been Nathan Fader and his belief he'd seen her before. Then the break-in at her apartment. And now that name—*Josie*—being called out across the store like it was nothing. Like it didn't signify a dead past to her. Or freeze the marrow in her bones to hear it said so casually.

The couple was gone when she returned to the front. Kane sat at his work station, the tray with the gun disassembled on it. He was flipping through pages on the computer. Daphne went over and leaned against the desk, needing a distraction. He looked up and her belly tightened. Why did he have to be so damned attractive?

"What's up?" he asked.

"I'm tired of looking at numbers and needed a break. What are you working on?"

"Trying to find information on a modification. So far, no dice."

She picked up the slide. It was a Glock 19 with an extended magazine. This version would hold nineteen rounds. It wasn't a monster, like a thirty-three round mag, and though it didn't fit flush in the handle, it wasn't so massive as to make it hard to conceal. Basically, a classic pistol.

"What kind of modification?"

He handed her the trigger mechanism. "This is a modified trigger. The mechanism has been lightened to allow for faster pull times. The reset is shorter and it takes less pressure to pull, so you get a faster response. Means somebody can get off a lot of shots quickly."

Daphne turned it over in her hands, examining it. She knew all about mods because her dad was an expert gunsmith. Once, that'd been his entire business. Before he'd expanded his operation to cover such delightful subjects as money laundering, gun running, loan sharking, illegal betting, and pimping. He still worked on the guns, because he enjoyed it, and he'd taught her and Jackson as much as they could absorb.

Jackson had absorbed more than she had. Her talents lay in numbers and business, while Jackson was destined to be a craftsman like their dad. When he wasn't being a ragey dick, that is.

She turned the trigger again, ran her fingers over it—and felt something. When she held it up, everything inside her went cold. There was a small diamond etched on the inside of the mechanism.

Her breath shortened, her ears rang. The diamond was her family's secret calling card. Always had been. Her dad had made this mod—or Jackson had.

"Daph? What's wrong?"

"I…" She dropped the mechanism in the tray and pulled in a breath. "I'm just, um, feeling kind of off. Maybe your bacon was rancid."

It was an attempt to lighten the moment that failed. Kane frowned at her. Hard.

"You look like you've seen a ghost."

"Haha, are you side hustling at The Mystic Chick these days? Because Colleen's the only person I know who sees ghosts."

Kane was on his feet, his hands on her arms. He gently guided her to his chair and made her sit. Then he grabbed a bottle of water from the small fridge behind the counter, opened it, and put it in her hand, completely ignoring the Diet Coke she'd set on his desk.

"Drink, babe. Be still for a little while. You need to go home and rest?"

She shook her head and sipped the water. It was cold going down her throat. Felt good. The soda was a guilty pleasure, but the water was what she needed.

"No, I'll be fine, really. Maybe I need to eat. It's been a few hours since breakfast. Low blood sugar and stress combined, probably."

"Then we need to get you some lunch. What do you want?"

"I don't care."

"You have to care. Town like this one with so much good food available? It could be something from the Dawg, or maybe you'd like a sandwich from Miss Mary's? You like Miss Mary's club, right?"

"Yes."

He took out his phone. "I'm ordering it. What else do you want? Fries?"

"Fries are good. Kane, you don't have to do that. I'll get a granola bar from the break room. It'll be fine."

"Nope, ordering myself a club too. Gotta check with the guys and see if they want anything. Don't go anywhere."

"Where am I going?"

"I don't know, but don't."

She rolled her eyes. "Not leaving. Sitting right here until you get back."

He nodded and left to go take orders from the guys.

Daphne breathed slowly, staring at the tray with the disassembled gun, until he returned a few minutes later.

"Order made. It'll be here in about twenty minutes."

"Great. Thank you. Let me know how much I owe you."

"It's a sandwich, Sunshine. You can get it the next time."

"Fair enough." She sipped the water. "Sorry I

distracted you from your work. What are you trying to find out about the mod?"

"Who made it would be a nice start. This was the gun that was used to take Nikki hostage last month."

Daphne's insides twisted. "Really? Wow. I thought the FBI would have it."

She'd learned things about these guys she hadn't known before that night, namely that they were some kind of military team who had combat experience. She knew they had training because they were military, and because she'd seen them in action in the self-defense classes, but lots of military people had the training.

What many didn't have was the actual time in combat.

These guys had it, and she knew that by the way they'd behaved that night. She'd suspected it before, but nothing told the story like that night had. She wouldn't have been there if they hadn't all been sitting around a fire out back of the range, grilling and drinking, when the call from Seth came in. She'd been drunk, but not so drunk she didn't pay attention to what'd been going on.

The drama had been over by the time they'd reached Seth, Callie, and Nikki, but the guys had split up and then come back together after they'd searched the area. When they'd split there'd been no words, only a few hand signals she hadn't understood. When they'd returned, she'd listened to them talk about perimeters and tangos, observed the way they all spoke the same kind of language, how calm and methodical they were in the face of that kind of violence, and she'd come to the conclusion they were no strangers to it.

There was also the fact Agent Corbin kept turning up like a bad penny. That woman made her nervous. Every time she arrived, Daphne thought the FBI was about to take her into custody for questioning about her family. So far, Agent Corbin didn't seem interested in her. Thank God.

"They had it. Now I do. Temporarily."

Her skin was hot. "They couldn't figure out who modified the trigger?"

It took him a few seconds to respond. "That's a good observation. I'd ask you to keep it to yourself."

"Who am I going to tell?" Her heart thrummed. "What have you found? Anything?"

"Not yet. There's a diamond on the inside of the guard. Etched. I don't know who made it."

She liked that he didn't lie to her about it. He had no idea she'd found it because it was well hidden. Not to mention most people wouldn't know to look. He'd seen her hold up the trigger, but the diamond was easily missed. It was safe for him to assume she hadn't found it.

"Why do you need to know who made it?"

He picked up the trigger and turned it over. "Just another piece of information. That's all."

There was so much more that he wasn't telling her. She knew it, because she knew what her family was involved in. The gun was stolen, modified for the client, and untraceable. But how did it end up in Sutton's Creek? The man who'd taken Nikki Crowell hostage had been someone Callie knew. He'd wanted her to steal information from her work and give it to him, but she'd refused.

Daphne had chalked the incident up to industrial espionage at the time. And it still could be, but where had the man gotten the gun? Her father was careful about who he sold his guns to. The diamond pattern was a hidden sign to the gun's quality. It wasn't anything he used in his legal gun work and it wasn't traceable to him.

Kane could turn his computer upside down and he wouldn't find anything linking that weapon to John

O'Malley or Crescent City Armory. On the legal weapons, the customizations, her father's symbol was the fleur-de-lis. He wouldn't put that on stolen guns.

Only those who knew could identify the weapons as coming from the O'Malleys. Didn't mean they could prove it, though. Her father was vain, but he wasn't stupid. Jackson, however…

Seth ducked his head through the hallway entrance. "Got a minute?"

"Yeah," Kane said. "Is it just for me, or can Daphne come too?"

"She can come. It's about Nathan Fader."

Chapter Thirteen

Seth had his laptop open in the office they shared. Kane stood back to let Daphne walk in first. She took a seat in one of the chairs, perching delicately on the edge like she expected she might need to jump to her feet at any moment.

Some of the color had returned to her cheeks, but she still seemed shaky. Needed that food to arrive ASAP.

Seth turned the laptop so the screen faced them. A photo of a man—unsmiling, grim—stared back at them. He had buzz-cut hair and a small scar at the corner of his mouth.

"Nathan Fader, thirty-nine, from Mobile, Alabama. No criminal record though he's had a couple of arrests for assault. The charges were dropped in each case. The interesting thing is that he has a Federal Firearms License. He buys and sells guns privately instead of through a storefront. He's likely in the area to broker a deal of some kind, probably checking out the local ranges and stores while he's at it."

"That's it?" Kane asked. He wanted more. Something

that put Fader near the Sutton building yesterday. Something that said he could be their guy.

"Not quite. He travels around, but one of his favorite places to frequent seems to be New Orleans."

Daphne shifted in her seat. It was subtle, but Kane noticed anyway. He noticed everything about Daphne, whether he wanted to or not.

"What's in New Orleans?" Kane asked. "Anything? Or he just likes the nightlife?"

"Don't know. There are dealers he could be visiting, though I don't have hard evidence. One of the bigger ones in town is Crescent City Armory, but there are others as well. Man named John O'Malley owns it. He's something of an artisan gunsmith, though my sources say he has his fingers in more than guns."

"Like?"

"Illegal stuff. Organized crime. If it's true, he's pretty slick about it. He's never been hauled in over any of it." Seth shrugged. "All this to say that Fader isn't overtly shady, but he may be involved with shady people. Again, no evidence he's involved with Crescent City Armory or John O'Malley in any way. Still doesn't explain why he'd break into Daphne's place. You said he didn't hit on you, right?"

Daphne nodded. There were two spots of color in her cheeks. "That's right. He never said anything inappropriate. I just think he's creepy and intense. He might be socially awkward for all we know."

Kane shoved a hand through his hair. "So Fader is a creep, but not a criminal. And why would he escalate to breaking in when he hasn't tried to ask Daphne out? If she'd said no, then maybe. But it never progressed that far. Then again, he might just be unhinged that way."

The other possibility, and he couldn't say it in front of Daphne, was that the break in had nothing to do with her and everything to do with them and the fact she worked here. What if, instead of Fader being the culprit, it was connected to the Dashevsky Group in some way? A fuck you for being involved in the takedown of Dima Smirnov?

Wasn't likely, but he'd mention it later.

"Maybe, but he'd be risking his license if he were caught. There are plenty of tradesman coming and going in the Sutton building," Seth replied. "Nothing was taken, so maybe whoever broke in did it for the kicks. It's possible we're overthinking it."

"Yeah," Kane said. "Maybe. I still don't like it. We need an answer so we'll know it's safe to return. Daphne doesn't want to hang out with me and Ethan indefinitely." He turned to her. "Though you can. Long as you want. Stay until you're comfortable going back."

She bowed her head to look at her clasped hands. "Thanks. I appreciate it."

"That's all I've got," Seth said. "If something else comes up, I'll let you know."

"Thanks, man. Appreciate it."

Kane stood and waited for Daphne. She seemed a bit shaky on her feet so he stuck close while they returned to the front of the building. The food arrived about five minutes later.

"Stay," Kane said when Daphne started to get up to go to the break room. "Eat at your desk."

He put the container in front of her along with napkins and several packets of ketchup. She arched an eyebrow at him. He knew he was being bossy, but hell, the woman looked faint.

"Did I smell food?" Ghost said, walking in from the back.

"Yep." Kane handed him the bag with the rest of the

food. "Got mine and Daphne's. We're gonna sit here. She's feeling kinda faint."

Ghost took the bag. "You okay, Daph? Need the afternoon off?"

Her mouth was full so she shook her head. "Staying," she finally managed.

"Okay, but if it gets worse, go home. We'll manage."

She swallowed and took a sip of water. "Thank you. I'm fine, though. Just hungry. I'd rather be here."

Ghost nodded. "You got anything on that trigger yet?" he asked Kane.

"Not yet. Whoever made the mod, they don't advertise. I'll keep looking though. Never know what might pop up."

"True."

Ghost left and Kane ate his sandwich while scrolling pages on the computer. So many fucking aftermarket parts for Glocks. But none with a diamond etched in the metal. Agent Corbin thought it unlikely that Smirnov had changed out the trigger himself, but she didn't know everything. He might have done so if he didn't like the feel of the trigger. Some people wanted a shorter pull. Could be as simple as that.

Everything didn't have to be some big conspiracy theory related to Viktor Dashevsky and his shadow army. Though it was disturbing that citizens of this country would flock to a Russian oligarch's banner in the first place, but Kane had decided a long time ago that he was no longer surprised by what people did. Or what they believed was true despite all evidence to the contrary.

"Thank you for including me in the briefing," Daphne said.

Kane turned to her. She'd either finished her food or stopped eating because the container was closed. "You're welcome."

"I appreciate knowing what Seth found about Fader."

"You deserved to know. He made you uncomfortable. And since you wouldn't let me ban him for breathing, it was the least we could do to include you."

"I want to stay at your place for a while. I won't feel safe until the security system is running."

He hated the fear in her eyes. He'd do anything to alleviate it. "You can stay, Sunshine. We've got the room. Ethan won't care."

He hadn't asked, but he knew Ethan well enough to know he'd want Daphne to feel safe, too.

Kane polished off his last french fry and closed the container. "You excited about your car?"

He wanted to get her thinking about something else, see that soft smile tease at the corners of her lips again. Daphne had been happy this morning, before they'd started work. Somewhere between then and now, she'd deflated like a helium balloon with a slow leak. He couldn't quite pinpoint the moment it'd happened, but she'd been sliding downhill all morning.

Maybe it was the lack of food that'd made her that way, but he wasn't so sure. It hadn't been that long since breakfast, and she'd eaten well then. But every time they talked about the break-in and who could have done it, she seemed to shrink in on herself. He wished she'd tell him why she was so spooked, but she wasn't going to. Daphne was close-lipped about herself.

A lot like he was, actually. Hard to blame her when he was the same way.

"Yes, I'm excited," she said.

He could tell her smile was forced rather than natural. Still, he'd take it until a real one showed up.

"I need to go to the bank and get the cashier's check this afternoon. I already called and Miss Lewis said it's not a problem so long as I'm there before the lobby closes at 4:00. I thought I'd go after lunch…" Her expression fell. "Crap. Warren's car's at the Sutton building."

"I'll take you. We can leave here at three, head to the bank, then go get your car."

"That works too. Thanks, Kane. You've been a really big help lately."

"Like I told you, you're one of us. We stick together and we help each other out. You'd do the same for me."

"I would, but I think we'd have to limit it to giving you rides. I'm no good at cars, and no way am I throwing myself into danger for you."

"When did I throw myself into danger?"

She rolled her eyes, and it made warmth bloom in his belly. If she could do that, maybe she was starting to feel like herself again.

"When you entered my apartment last night without knowing whether anybody was inside. What if they'd attacked?"

He wanted to laugh but he didn't. She was serious. "Trust me when I tell you I didn't do anything without experience to back me up and a plan. What I did wasn't dangerous to me. If I'd found somebody in there, different story. *For them.*"

She shook her head. "You can't know that. How can you know that?"

"I know, Sunshine. It's not arrogance or masculine bravado. *I know.* And I'll tell you what else, I'm not the only one. Any of the guys would have done the same, and they'd feel the same way about it. The only danger was to whoever was inside."

"What if it was a hitman?"

He blinked. "Seriously? In Sutton's Creek?"

She frowned at him. He got the hint.

"Okay, sure, a hitman. Because this is an episode of a TV drama, not real life. A hitman wouldn't have made the mistake of leaving the door unlocked. Which means you'd have gone in first. Hard to say what would have happened next, because it depends on what the hitman wants. Even then, I wouldn't have hesitated to act."

"You're crazy, you know that?"

Her eyes were wide and her voice soft so he knew she didn't mean it as an insult. She was genuinely shocked that he would willingly engage on her behalf.

"Not crazy. Just well-trained. Anybody touches you—*hurts you*—they die."

Chapter Fourteen

"Anybody touches you—hurts you—they die."

Those words danced around Daphne's brain for the rest of the day. She'd been looking right at him when he said it. The vehemence in his voice. The conviction.

It still made her shudder. And not in a bad way, which wasn't a good thing. The fiercer Kane Fox got, the more she wanted to throw herself into his arms and beg him not to let go.

Not a very independent thing to do, alas. It was probably that dang Fae romance she'd read for book club. No hero was fiercer than a Fae when it came to protecting the woman he loved.

The woman he was bonded to through blood or destiny or whatever.

It was exhilarating to think there could be a man who loved you so much he'd do anything to protect you. Even sacrifice himself, which of course would never happen in a romance novel because the happy ending was crucial.

Not that Kane was in love with her. He was just a good guy whose profession was protecting people. She thought of her dad's enforcers. They'd protected her family because they were paid to do it. No other reason. If the cash hadn't appeared, or if someone had taken over the O'Malley territory by force, those men wouldn't have done a damned thing to save her if she'd needed it.

Kane would. Payment or not. Because that's the kind of man he was.

She tried to concentrate on work, but she kept thinking of Nathan Fader—and hearing her father's name on Seth's lips. When he'd mentioned Crescent City Armory, she'd thought she might throw up. It only got worse when he talked about her dad and the criminal connections.

Of course people *knew* John O'Malley was a crime boss. But like most crime bosses he was careful, thorough, and he knew who he could pay off. That's why she hadn't dared to go to the authorities. Somebody would have reported back to her dad, and she'd have been silenced.

One way or the other.

By the time Kane came to get her so they could go to the bank and then pick up her car, she'd managed to calm her racing heart enough to believe she wasn't in imminent danger of a heart attack. It helped that Nathan Fader hadn't shown up to shoot. If he had, knowing he was in the gun business and frequently spent time in New Orleans, she'd have probably walked out the back door and kept going until she reached the farmhouse and curled up into a ball on the guest bed.

Not knowing if he knew her father was almost worse than knowing. If she knew, she could make plans. Get out of town. Instead, she was in stasis. Afraid to run, afraid to stay.

She hated the uncertainty. The fear.

But she logged off her computer, grabbed her purse, and followed Kane to his SUV. It took a couple of hours to get the cashier's check, drive to Huntsville and pick up her car, and then return to Sutton's Creek. Kane insisted she lead the way back. She glanced into the rearview from time to time, making sure he was there. He always was, the big black Yukon staying right behind her. Not that anyone from her old life knew she was driving a silver Santa Fe, but it was still comforting to have Kane watching her back.

They'd agreed to meet everyone at the Dawg for dinner, so Daphne drove straight over there and parked. She'd thought about declining, saying she was tired, but the truth was she felt better around the guys and their women. And she needed to eat, so why not?

Warren's old car was still in the parking lot where she'd left it. She'd promised to get it back to him this week and he'd said there was no rush. She was grateful for the use of it, but it felt good to have her own wheels again. To not have to rely on anyone else to give her rides or loan her a car.

If she wanted, she could pack up and leave town. Nothing was stopping her. If she got even a hint that Nathan Fader knew her family, she could hit the road.

Except she didn't want to go anywhere. She wanted to stay in Sutton's Creek with her friends. Not just friends, but a family. One she'd chosen, and who had chosen her. It was comfortable with them, and it was fun. Though she always worried they might make a different choice if they knew who she really was. Or the kinds of things she'd once believed were normal.

"How'd it drive?" Kane asked, walking over as she got out of the vehicle.

She pressed the key fob to lock the doors. "It was good. No rattling or shaking."

"No rattling or shaking is definitely good."

"Hello, lovely people!" It was a feminine voice, raspy,

as if its owner chain-smoked from the moment she woke up until she went to bed again. Which she probably did.

"Hi, Ms. Wright," Kane said.

Colleen appeared from the direction of the Dawg. She almost glowed in the evening sunlight. She was wearing a purple caftan with silver thread woven throughout that sparkled when she moved. Her hair was silvery and thick, falling to her shoulders and curling under. She was holding a stack of paper in her hand.

"It's twenty-percent off energy crystals at The Mystic Chick this week." She thrust a paper at them. Daphne took it. Kane did not. Colleen turned her attention to Daphne. "Reba and I are restarting our cemetery walking tours this weekend. You won't want to miss that."

Daphne was used to this kind of thing in New Orleans. The city was filled with people interested in the paranormal as well as those who profited in some way—ghost walks, voodoo shops, haunted hotels. Colleen Wright was delightfully kooky, which Daphne couldn't say about all the mystical entrepreneurs she'd encountered in the Crescent City.

"Why did you quit the tours before?" Daphne asked, skimming the flyer for the happenings at The Mystic Chick. There was a talk on haunted furniture, a seance circle night, the cemetery tours on weekends, and how to charge your crystals using the light of a full moon.

Colleen waved her hand. "A simple misunderstanding, my dear. Reba tripped and fell into an open grave. Well, I tell you, there was much screaming and wailing because Reba was wearing a new dress designed to please the spirits, specially blessed by yours truly, and she was furious she'd quite possibly ruined it. She was *not* terrified, as some have suggested."

Colleen sniffed as if the idea were ludicrous. Daphne,

meanwhile, thought she'd scream her head off too if she fell into an open grave.

"The customers were fine, of course—and indeed it was one of our customers, a rather large man, who had to help her get out of the grave. Though he kicked up a lot of dirt trying and caused a big mess. Plus there was all the cursing, but that was mostly Reba. But I digress. Anyway, the groundskeeper was furious because the ceremony was scheduled for early the next morning due to a potential rainstorm later that day. And there was a big mess to clean up before the family arrived. Anywho, he banned us permanently, but I've been working on the mayor for months and she finally agreed. The Mystic Grave Walk is back!"

"That's great," Daphne said. "I'd love to come, but I just bought a car so I'm afraid I can't spare fifty dollars right now."

"No no, my dear. For you, only twenty-five. Consider it a little congratulations present on your new purchase."

"I, um, thank you. I'll do my best to come one night soon."

"You do that. Well, must dash over to Kiss My Grits and drop some more of these flyers. The crystals are flying off the shelves—well, not literally. I put a stop to that, I assure you. Come get your protective crystal while they're on sale, Miss Bryant. I have a feeling you need it."

Colleen glided away as Daphne gaped after her.

Kane put a hand on her elbow and pitched his voice lower. "She's not psychic, Sunshine. It's a wild guess, nothing more. She wants to sell crystals. She's not making a prediction."

He prodded her toward the Dawg and she went, glancing down at the flyer again. He was right.

Of course he was right.

"You mean you don't want to attend a seance night and talk to spirits? Or charge your crystal by moonlight?"

"No thanks."

Belatedly, she remembered his wife had died. "Kane, I'm sorry. I shouldn't have said that about the seance. It was insensitive."

He stopped and turned her to face him. "It's okay, Daph. It's been ten years. I don't fall apart over the mention of her. People die, people live. The ones left behind learn to keep living. I'm not upset Colleen holds seances, other than I don't believe it works. Colleen believes what she believes, but she also doesn't give people hope of talking to their loved ones just to rob them blind. Rory said that her granny used to see Colleen so she could talk to her dead kids. They had a monthly appointment, but Colleen only charged her a dozen eggs or a gallon of fresh milk or produce from the garden. Small things. Things a grieving farmer's wife could afford. She's not a bad person, just a quirky one."

Daphne was glad to hear it. If Colleen had been fleecing people, it would have been a major disappointment. "I like her. She was one of the first people to welcome me to town. She even told me to be prepared because my job at the Wheeler Inn wouldn't last very long."

"She's a busybody, but I like her too. She makes me laugh. Most of the time anyway."

She studied him. "You sure you aren't upset about the seance crack?"

His expression was clear. "I'm not upset. Swear it."

"Well, I'm still sorry I said it. I wasn't thinking."

"Do you know everything about everyone you meet? Do you know what kind of innocent remark might be insensitive to someone because it brings up bad memories?"

She shook her head.

"Right. Don't overthink these things, Sunshine. Somebody gets upset, you apologize and move on. Somebody tells you it's no big deal, you move on. Got it?"

"I got it."

"You done apologizing now? Because I need some of Theo Harper's fried chicken or my stomach's gonna eat itself."

"All done."

They went inside the Dawg and found the gang at the usual tables pushed together. Rory smiled and waved from the bar. Of course she was still working, because she was Rory, but she'd slowed down a little bit. She didn't work every night anymore, and she'd agreed to Theo's suggestion they hire a couple more people to tend bar and wait tables.

"Do you have a new set of wheels?" Callie asked.

"Yes I do! Very happy." Daphne reached for a chair, but Kane pulled it out for her.

She sat, conscious of the way his friends exchanged glances. Kane took the chair beside her, because it was the only one left. He didn't usually sit next to her in public, and she found it distracting. His leg touched hers from time to time while they ordered dinner and ate, and his voice was disturbingly close to her ear whenever he spoke.

By the time he got up for a game of pool with Chance, she practically sagged in relief.

Not because she didn't like him close, but because it was like sitting next to a live wire and feeling the energy prickling along her nerve endings. She wanted to fly into the light like a moth.

Emma and Callie moved closer once the guys got up to

watch pool and take their turns too. Nikki was at the stable, preparing for a horse show next weekend, but Rory left the bar to join them when Waitress Nikki kicked her out and took over. All the Bookalicious Besties in one place, except for the teen.

"Did that Neanderthal really find you a car?" Rory asked. "Or did he bail at the last minute when you went to pick it up?"

Emma snorted and Callie tried to hide a smile.

"He did," Daphne said. "I handed over the check and drove it back. It's in the parking lot."

"Oooh, I want to see," Rory said. "But not right now. My feet are killing me."

Emma arched an eyebrow. "I told you, ma'am, more breaks, less stubbornness."

"I know, I know. I'm on a break now, aren't I?" Rory put a hand on her belly. It was just starting to show a little bump. If you didn't know, then you'd think it was normal weight gain. "My doctor said everything is going well. My blood sugar is controlled, and the baby is developing normally for where we're at."

They all expressed happiness at the news. Rory was a type 1 diabetic, and though she was healthy overall and took care of herself, pregnancy was harder and potentially more problematic for someone with her disease. She pretended to be stubborn about breaks and working less, but the truth was she knew her own body and did everything she could to give herself the rest she needed. Daphne hadn't known any of them long, but she knew that the Rory of six months ago and the Rory of right now were not the same person in terms of workaholic tendencies.

"So," Emma said, exchanging a look with Rory and Callie. "Inquiring minds want to know if you kissed that man senseless yet."

Daphne's entire body flamed hot. She glanced quickly around before leaning toward them and pitching her voice low. "I told all you nosy beyotches that was *not* going to happen. Y'all read too many romance novels."

They laughed.

"Right, sure," Rory said. "You read them too, my Bookalicious Bestie. And I've never seen a woman who needs a good orgasm more than you do." She cut a glance at Emma. "Well, I have, but Emma Grace solved the problem by shagging the hell out of Blaze at the time."

Emma bumped shoulders with Rory but Rory only laughed. "Come on, you know it was true."

"It was, but you've got all the subtlety of a red flag waved in front of a bull. Despite pretending to be British or whatever with the shagging talk."

Rory rolled her eyes. "Nobody's listening to us talk, babe. Even if they were, it's obvious you're shagging him on the regular. Same as I'm doing with Chance and Callie's doing with Seth. And I like that word because it sounds sooo polite. Anywho, nobody is surprised about what's going on with us, Emma Grace. But what we *need* to happen is for Daphne to take the bull by the horns because Kane never will. Even though he wants to."

Daphne loved these women. She'd never had friends like this before, mostly because she hadn't known she needed them. And even though she thought she probably shouldn't, she leaned in and told them about finding Kane shirtless at the range and what'd happened next.

Emma's eyes got big. "You did not say that! Oh my God."

Rory smacked the table. "Ha, I knew it! You *did* take action. Maybe not a kiss, but something even better."

Daphne laughed. "I did say it. And I don't know if it was better than kissing him because he didn't take me up on it. Honestly, short of making him strip nekkid at gunpoint, I don't know what else is left. Kane has an iron will, and he's decided I'm not what he wants. Maybe it's best that way."

Kane thought it was. He'd said he had nothing to give her. Right after he'd told her he masturbated to thoughts of her. Not that she planned to mention that exchange. It was too charged and too personal. For both of them.

"Honey," Rory said. "You've got the goods. Parade around naked in his house. That will jumpstart his engine."

"Uh, Ethan lives there too."

Rory waved a hand. "Minor inconvenience. You'll figure it out."

Daphne wasn't sure she would. Or could. Maybe, considering everything else going on in her life right now, it wasn't a good idea anyway. She needed to worry about staying clear of Nathan Fader just in case, watching her back, and praying that he never figured out why he thought she looked familiar.

She didn't know if he'd ever been to The Diamond Queen or not, but if he had she really hoped he never put Daphne and Josie in the same thought. Ever.

The talk moved to Callie and Seth for a while, and their plans to buy the farm they lived on in the absolute middle of nowhere. The owner was talking about selling, and they had big plans for renovating the house and building a bigger barn should he decide to actually pull the trigger and let the place go.

Daphne had been out there a few times now, and she could see the appeal. The house was nothing special, but the land was stunning. Rolling pastures, woods, and not far from the river. You could walk to it if you were so inclined. It was a long way to Research Park where Callie worked, but her plan was to quit her job at some unspecified date in the future and do consulting work from home. Seth seemed to be completely on board with the idea.

Nikki had one more year of high school and then it was college, but she was already talking about going to the University of Alabama in Huntsville and getting a STEM degree. It was a bit of a change from the girl who'd just wanted to be a horse trainer, but that's what teenagers did. They changed their minds.

Daphne had never had the luxury. She'd always been destined to work in the O'Malley empire. Trained for it from birth practically. Her father hadn't trusted just anyone with the books, but he'd trusted her once she'd gotten her accounting degree and proved she could handle it. She'd handled it so well she'd gotten to take on The Diamond Queen when Jackson had shown he didn't have the vision or the ability to run an entertainment venue.

"Hey, you ready to go?"

Kane stood over her and Daphne forced a smile. Thinking about her family always made darkness seep through her veins like spilled ink.

"I'm ready."

It was only eight o'clock, but she had a sudden desire to get out of the public eye. A chill skittered down her spine. She peered into the corners of the Dawg, looking for a threat. All she saw was Bonnie Warren, the intrepid mail carrier, leaning toward her husband of fifty years and giggling like a schoolgirl. Judy Simpson from the Bee was at a table with Celia Lincoln, scribbling on a pad of paper while Celia talked. Probably taking notes for her upcoming issue. The tourism issue, in which the Wheeler Inn was bound to figure predominantly.

There was nothing suspicious happening in any dark corner. Just people eating and drinking and having a good time. Daphne said goodbye to her friends, who made meaningful eyebrow gestures at her now that Kane was there. She shook her head slightly, laughing, before walking to the parking lot with Kane.

"What was that about?" he asked.

She decided to play dumb. "What was what about?"

"The contortions Rory made with her eyebrows. Emma and Callie did it too, but Rory's the obvious one."

Daphne's skin heated. "It's an inside joke. About the book we're reading."

He must have bought it because he didn't press further. When they reached her new ride, he opened her car door, his arm brushing against hers. She shivered anew, but for a different reason this time. A more pleasant reason than thinking someone was lurking in the shadows, watching her.

"I'll follow you," he said. "But remember we're shooting tonight, so stop at the range."

There went the warm feelings. "I'm tired, Kane."

"No excuses, Daphne. We'll spend an hour. Don't tell me you won't feel better having a weapon once you go back to your place."

There was nothing she could say. She'd hoped he'd forget about it, but he clearly hadn't. Which meant she had a choice. Shoot and shut him up, or keep making excuses.

Excuses would only last so long. Eventually, Kane was going to make her step onto the range and hold a pistol in her hands. Might as well be tonight since she couldn't avoid it forever.

"Fine. I'll see you at the range."

Chapter Fifteen

DAPHNE DRAGGED HER FEET LIKE A KID BEING TOLD TO DO chores, but they were finally in a lane and Kane had laid out two guns on the table in front of him. He'd selected a smaller Sig that shot .380 caliber bullets to start her off and a 9 mil in case she started to feel brave.

She'd said she wasn't a beginner, but he didn't know if she'd said it to get out of the class he'd wanted her to take or if she'd been telling the truth. Guess he was about to find out.

Daphne stood behind him, leaning against the back table, arms crossed over her chest. She did not look happy to be there, but damn if he was letting another day go by without knowing if she could defend herself. He'd never taught Hannah to shoot. She'd never wanted to. Would it have saved her? Probably not, but he'd never know.

He'd shared his theory with the guys that maybe the break-in was related to the Dashevsky Group and Dima Smirnov. They all agreed it was worth considering, which made it even more critical that Daphne know how to defend herself. She'd want to go back home eventually, and she'd be alone. Kane would feel a lot better if she was armed and knew what to do with a weapon should somebody try again when she was home.

He set the target at five yards, which was close, and turned to her.

"You coming over here to learn how to load the pistol or what?"

"I know how to load a pistol, Kane."

She had her ear protection around her neck and he did too. He slipped his on and she did the same. "Come show me then."

She stalked over to the bay and he stepped back to watch. Daphne didn't wear perfume, but her hair always smelled good. Like lavender and sunshine. He wanted to touch it, wanted to wrap a few strands around his fingers and see if they were as silky as they looked. Her hair was a deep, gorgeous red. He didn't know if she colored it, but he doubted it. The girl didn't even wear makeup, so he didn't think she'd spend time coloring her hair.

Then again, what did he know? He'd thought he'd known his own wife and he hadn't.

Daphne stared at the guns, her head bowed. She took a breath. Then another.

He was about to tell her to step aside when she picked up the Sig. She chose the correct magazine, slipped it into the grip, flipped the safety off, and pulled the slide to chamber a round. He opened his mouth to tell her what came next, but she hit the magazine release, dropped the mag into her hand and pulled the slide again to eject the bullet. Then she dry-fired the pistol, calmly collected the unspent round, pressed it into the magazine again, and placed everything on the table before turning to him.

Belatedly, he told himself to close his mouth. Something swirled in his belly, something hot and dark and needy.

Whoa and damn.

Kane didn't know if he was turned on by the lavender in her hair or by the way she'd handled the weapon. But he was definitely turned on after that display. He was working overtime to turn everything off again. *Son of a bitch.*

"Okay, so you've got the basics down."

He sounded lame even to him.

Daphne smirked. Damn, she was pretty. Her green eyes flashed fire at him and her chin tipped up.

"More than the basics, Grandpa. I told you I can shoot."

"Who taught you?"

The fire in her eyes banked. "My dad. He believed in defending his family and he thought we needed to know how to handle a weapon. I didn't have a choice, so I learned."

When she'd said her parents were nomads, he'd envisioned some kind of weird hippy thing where they were pacifists and didn't eat animals. He had not envisioned a gun-loving father who made his family learn how to handle a weapon.

A mistake he should have known better than to make. Never make assumptions about people. Assumptions got you killed. Or got others killed. Something he knew all too well.

"Let's start shooting then."

"I can do that. But we'll need to move that target."

He pressed the button to bring it closer.

"No."

He glanced at her. She'd turned those hot eyes on him again. Daphne seemed to be simmering beneath the surface. He didn't know why, but he had to admit it was exhilarating to watch her glowing and sparking as she moved.

Like an explosion waiting to detonate. What would happen then? He'd had a glimpse of it in the gym a couple of days ago. His dick remembered all too well if the way it started to ache was any indication.

"Where d'you want it?" he growled.

"Send it to fifteen yards."

"You sure about that?"

"Yes, I'm sure."

He sent the target. When Daphne stepped up to the board, she didn't pick the Sig this time. She grabbed the Glock and slammed the magazine home, racked the slide like an expert, then placed the gun on the table, barrel facing into the range. If he had a dollar for every time a woman couldn't pull the slide of a pistol because it was tight and she didn't know how...

"You first," she said, taking a step back.

"I shoot every day. I'm not the one who needs practice."

"Humor me. One shot, Kane. Let me see what you can do."

He grumbled as he picked up the gun and sighted it. When he was on the exhale, he squeezed the trigger. The answering boom, the metallic pop of the empty shell being ejected, the weight of the gun in his hand as well as the smell of hot gunpowder, were as familiar and comforting to him as homemade apple pie was to other people. He laid the gun down and brought the target closer.

There was one hole in the target, dead center. Kane turned to her. She looked pensive. She chewed on the end of her thumbnail as their gazes met.

"You win," she said with a fake smile. "Can we go now?"

He grinned at her. "Nope. Your turn. I did what you asked, now you show me what you've got. If it's not a bullseye, that's okay. I've had a helluva lot of practice to be able to shoot like that. I don't expect you to do the same."

"I was afraid you'd say that," Daphne said with a sigh. "Move it, Gramps."

She hip-checked him and he stepped out of the way. She pressed the button on the side of the wall separating shooting bays and sent the target downrange. Twenty yards instead of fifteen. He didn't know what she was playing at but there was no fucking way she was going to land a shot anywhere near his.

She picked up the gun, widened her legs and carefully settled her right hand into her left. Then she lifted the gun and stood for a long moment, staring downrange. She took so long he thought she'd put it down again, tell him she couldn't do it.

A moment later, the quiet shattered.

Boom, boom, boom, boom, boom, boom, boom, boom.

Metal pinged as spent shell casings hit the floor in quick succession. They never allowed students to rapid fire a pistol. Or anyone but the most experienced shooters, and even then only at certain times for safety reasons. Rapid fire was dangerous in the wrong hands.

Daphne placed the gun on the board and hit the button to bring the target back. He expected to see wide shots everywhere, but that's not what was there. Kane blinked, and then blinked again.

Surrounding his bullseye in an almost perfectly spaced circle were eight holes. Eight fucking holes at twenty yards.

He stepped up beside her. She studied the target, a frown on her face, as if she hadn't just done an amazing bit of shooting.

"Sunshine," he managed. Croaked, really. "What the fuck was that?"

"I know, I know. The shots aren't even and these two —" She pointed at two holes in the paper. "—aren't aligned. Can't make them all perfect, I guess."

He took her by the shoulders and turned her. Amazement coursed through every inch of him. And something else as well. Desire. Hot, fierce need. Because of a target and a few holes?

Didn't make sense, and yet it made perfect sense. He'd been boxing Daphne up in his head for so long, keeping her behind a fence labeled *No Trespassing*, telling himself that she was young and sweet and innocent to the ways of the world.

She'd just blown through that fence. Literally in some ways. She was young, sweet, but maybe not innocent to the ways of the world after all. Girl could blow a perfect circle in a target at twenty yards. Twenty fucking yards. It took a shit ton of practice to do that.

"You look surprised," she said, her voice soft.

"Baby, if you revealed you were one of Colleen's aliens wearing a human form, I couldn't be more surprised. Where the fuck did you learn to shoot like that?"

"Girls can shoot, Kane. Maybe not the ones who show up here for a lesson from a gorgeous dude with muscles and then make eyes at you the whole time, but a lot of us are competent."

"That's more than competent, Daph. It's fucking mission-ready. Your dad must have made you shoot for hours every day."

"Something like that," she said, her gaze dropping.

He could see the pulse in her throat, the way it thrummed. "You never told any of us. Why?"

She shrugged out of his grip and walked away, turned to face him when there was distance between them. Then she flung her arms out as if angry or frustrated.

"Because it's not important. Because I was hired to work up front, not to be an RSO or teach classes or anything like that. It doesn't *matter* that I can shoot. I don't need it for my job."

He understood and yet he didn't. Why keep something that big a secret? She was working in a gun range and she was an expert marksman. Unless she hated shooting because she'd been forced to do it. Kind of like a kid forced to play piano for hours a day.

Something his mother had tried to get him to do when he was eight. He'd hated every minute of it. To this day he could do scales like frigging Mozart, but he'd forgotten everything else. He'd quit piano at thirteen, but he had a lot of years of sitting at the instrument when all he'd wanted to do was go outside and play with his friends.

Kane shoved a hand through his hair. "You don't want to do this anymore, I take it? Prefer I put everything away and we go to the house?"

She closed her eyes for a moment. "No, it's fine. We can finish. I don't *hate* shooting, Kane. But I don't love it either."

"Do you have a gun?"

"No. And I don't want to buy one."

He didn't ask why, but he thought he knew. She ran many of the background checks on people who bought at the range, and she knew the process required. Filling out the ATF form, submitting it to the NICS. All the system did was look for criminal convictions, mental health issues, drug use, domestic violence orders, etcetera.

But the woman didn't want to apply for credit, insisted

on paying cash for her car. She'd filled out the required employment paperwork when they'd hired her, but maybe that was her one exception. It would be hard for anyone looking for her to access that kind of information anyway.

Hell, it'd be hard to access any of the information—but only having one point of entry wasn't a bad strategy. The more places your data went, the more opportunities to be found.

"You could buy one of mine. Private sales don't have to go through the system."

It was a loophole that some states were still trying to close, but the gun lobby had so far kept it from happening.

She arched an eyebrow. "You aren't worried I'll rob a bank with your gun and then you'll have to answer questions? What if I have a record, Kane? You might be selling a gun to a criminal."

"If you think Seth didn't check you out before we hired you, you're not as smart as I thought you were."

"I'm sure he did. But the NICS.... Well, there could be things in there you boys don't have access to."

He cocked his head. "Are you trying to make me suspicious, Sunshine? Do you want me to tell him to dig deeper?"

She shoved her hands into her jeans pockets and shrugged. "You can do what you want. I'm not worried. I was merely pointing out you have to be careful about selling weapons privately. You never know where they'll end up."

"Yeah, I'm aware. Still think you need one, though. I'll take my chances and loan you one. If you decide to head over to the Perrys' cattle farm and rustle up some cows, I'll say you stole it from me."

She rolled her eyes. "I don't need any cows, Gramps. Got plenty of bull around this place."

"But you'll accept the pistol?"

She hesitated. "If it makes you feel better, yes."

"Honey, knowing you could shoot the balls off that bull at twenty yards makes me feel a whole lot better than I did."

She tilted her head to the side and looked at him like he was a puzzle to be solved. "Were you worried about me, Kane?"

Why lie?

"Somebody broke into your apartment and spooked you. And since we don't know who or why, yeah, I worried about you. Still do, but now I know you've got terrific aim, I'm not worried about you being alone in your apartment when you're ready to go back."

"I'd really rather not have to shoot anyone. I'm a target shooter."

"Understood." He clipped on a new target and sent it to twenty-five yards. "So let's shoot some targets. Best shot wins."

She arched an eyebrow. "Wins what?"

He gazed at her, suddenly overwhelmed by an urge to tug her into his arms and hold her close. What would it be like if this woman was his? If he let himself try again?

He shook his head and gave her a smile he didn't quite feel. "Dunno. How about the winner gets to decide what they want and the loser has to do it or buy it or whatever?"

"Okay, but I'm not buying anything over fifty-dollars. Just so you know."

He laughed. "Got it, babe." He clipped another target to the bay next door and sent it out. "Which weapon you want?"

"I'll take the Glock."

"Figured you'd say that. What's the objective?"

"Three rounds. One in the center, one in the forehead, one in the throat. Bonus points if you can hit the eyes too."

"Lock n'load, baby. Prepare to get smoked."

She grinned at him, and he felt an ache in his chest. "Game on, Gramps."

Chapter Sixteen

KANE WON, BUT ONLY BECAUSE SHE WAS A LITTLE RUSTY.
Her three shots had been perfect. The eyes got her though.
One was higher than the other while Kane's were perfectly
spaced.

He was, naturally, gloating about it. Such a peacock of
a man.

But he cared about her, and he made her heart skitter
whenever he called her Sunshine. He'd only started that
recently. Maybe because she'd laid down the law about
calling her kid. Whatever the reason, she liked it.

She left her Santa Fe at the range and he drove them
the short distance to the house. She would have walked,
but it was dark and he'd mentioned coyotes and bobcats
when she'd stated her intention. She was out after that.
Guess the country wasn't so different from the big city
when it came to times to avoid the streets. Or the driveway,
as it were.

"Maybe a lobster dinner," Kane said as he parked the
truck. "Haven't had one of those in a while."

"Not sure fifty would cover it. Maybe dial down the expectations there, Candy Kane."

He snorted. "Candy Kane? Really?"

"It just occurred to me."

"Gotta tell ya, babe, you're years late on that one. It occurred to Jillie Robbins in the second grade."

"There you go then. I'm not a second grader. Takes longer to think up cheesy jokes."

They got out of the truck and went into the house. Ethan's door was closed, the television droning quietly in the background. Daphne told herself to say goodnight and go to her room, but she lingered.

So did Kane.

"Hey, you wanna sit on the back porch with a beer for a few minutes?" he asked. "I'm keyed up after that. Need to come down first. Afraid I don't have any Scotch though."

"Beer is fine."

She took her purse and the paperwork for the Santa Fe to her room. It was quiet in there and the bed was inviting. But Kane was waiting, and she couldn't say no. She liked being near him, liked the way he both settled her and made her feel like a live wire at the same time.

Not only that, but she was also aware her time with him was probably limited. The diamond-stamped trigger and Nathan Fader were two things connected to her past. Well, potentially in the case of Fader. But if a third showed up, time to boogie.

No matter that she didn't want to. No matter that her life wouldn't be the same if she did. She'd stolen records when she'd left New Orleans when she should have also stolen money. Enough to leave the country and hide out somewhere far away.

Hindsight was a bitch. She'd be cleaning motel rooms

for the rest of her life if she didn't *do* something with the information she had.

And if she did do something, if she trusted the wrong person—or if her father's connections went deeper than she knew—she'd be painting a giant target on her back. She wanted to tell Kane, wanted to ask him for advice, but years of conditioning held her back.

He was waiting for her in the kitchen. He handed her a beer and they stepped onto the back porch. It was screened and there was outdoor furniture with thick cushions. She could envision plants, an outdoor rug, a lamp. Some wall hangings and maybe wind chimes. She imagined it raining softly while she sat with a book in the afternoons and read. The air would be crisp with rain, soft with flowers, and she'd never want to leave.

She didn't know why she was so drawn to the old farmhouse, but she loved the beautiful craftsmanship of the wood floors and tall windows. The house had been built with love, and though it needed some updating, she could imagine it with new bathrooms and a new kitchen, the wood floors waxed to a shine, the wood around the windows and doors stripped of paint and taken back to the original color.

It could be a home worthy of HGTV. Something you'd see in a magazine.

She shook off thoughts of a future that wasn't in the cards and looked doubtfully at the settee.

"Is this clean? Spider free?"

Kane had already flopped onto a chair. "Ethan's a neat freak. And he's scared of spiders but don't tell him I told you that. Yes, it's clean. I doubt there are any spiders. Ethan sealed the gap beneath the screen door once he evicted the previous eight-legged tenants."

Daphne shuddered. Then she took out her phone and

shined the light around the chair, bending down to look underneath too. When she decided it was safe from spiders, she sat, sighing at the comfort of the cushion.

"This furniture did not come with the house, did it?"

"Nah, Ethan found it and I split the cost with him. Don't know where he got it, but he didn't pay too much for it. Why?"

"It's comfortable. Guess I'm surprised."

He sipped his beer. "Don't know why. Nobody likes a hard chair under their ass. Me and Ethan included."

"Well, no, but I guess I'm surprised that you'd want to sit outside like this. Enough so to buy furniture."

"It's nice in the mornings and evenings. Spring was good too, except when all the pollen started. Couldn't keep anything clean."

"I guess not."

Warren's car had been yellow for two months. Everyone's had. If you ran it through the car wash, it was yellow again the next morning. But once spring had sprung, the pollen died down and everything was green and gorgeous. Or colorful and gorgeous.

"What would you have wanted?" Kane asked. "If you'd won the bet."

Daphne twisted the bottle in her hand. "I don't know. Cash probably."

He snorted. "Should have known."

"What's that mean?"

"Means I've observed you're careful with money. You don't seem frivolous at all. Hell, you saved six grand in a matter of months so you could buy a car with cash. Who does that?"

She was proud of herself, really. She'd never had to think about saving or living off what she had in her previous life. "People without credit cards. People who don't believe in buying things they don't have with money that isn't theirs. People who don't want debt to hold them back."

She'd been frivolous at one point, and she'd spent big, but she'd always had cash in the bank to pay her credit cards each month. The only thing that'd changed now was she paid with cash these days. And had a lot less of it.

He studied her quietly. "You aren't typical, are you?"

"Typical how? A lot of people my age aren't buying into the overconsumption culture anymore. Debt keeps you tied down, keeps you working a shitty job and never owning anything. I like my freedom. If I decide I want to move along to a new place, I could. Pack up the car, give notice at the range and my apartment, and go somewhere new."

"Is that what your parents did?"

She hated the lie she'd told, but there wasn't a better one. "Whenever the mood hit, yes, that's what happened."

"Where are they now?"

Fuck.

"Kane, honestly." She sighed. "My mom died when I was eighteen. My dad's still around. We don't speak anymore. Happy?"

All true statements.

"It pains you, and no, that doesn't make me happy. You don't know where your dad is?"

"Nope. Don't care either."

He was quiet for a while. Daphne took a sip of her beer, let it slide down her throat and burn into her stomach. She'd never been much of a beer drinker. Still, the burn felt good because it forced her to center herself.

"I don't talk to my dad either," he said. "He and my

mom divorced after I joined the Army. He was abusive. Not physically. Mentally. To her, to me. She died three years ago. After living her entire youth with that asshole, she ended up dying before he did. Lung cancer, and she never smoked a day in her life. He did, though. He's still breathing and taking up space while she's gone."

Her throat was tight. He'd lost his mother and his wife, and he had a father he didn't speak to. It was hard to imagine someone as charming and vibrant as Kane having such heartbreak in his life. It sucked.

"I'm sorry, Kane. Life's not fair, is it? The biggest assholes never get what they deserve."

She thought of Jackson and her father. Of the kind of shit they were doing now, and she despised them for it. Wanted to bring them down. But she was afraid.

Afraid she'd go down while they kept doing what they always did. Nothing would change and people would still suffer. Her included.

"Sometimes they do," he said softly. "I've been a part of it. But it's definitely not often enough."

She blew out a frustrated breath. "I wish somebody would make me queen of the world for a week. I'd make some adjustments."

He laughed softly. "Not a bad idea. But people would go back to doing the shit they always did once you were done. The greedy and lazy ones, that is. Gotta say though, as much shit as I've seen in my life, I know the world is more good than bad."

"I'm not so sure."

"I've been in places where people barely had anything to eat, or a roof over their heads, much less a wad of cash to buy a car. But if one of their neighbors needed help, they were there, giving what they had. I've seen people run into burning buildings, toward burning vehicles, into churning oceans, to save a person they didn't even know. Because they couldn't stand by and do nothing. That's what gives me hope—that the default setting of humankind is essentially good."

Daphne gaped. "Wow, and you call *me* Sunshine? I think you're the Suzy Sunshine around here, Kane. I'm firmly convinced people are greedy, grasping, and out for what they can get."

"Not gonna argue with you. Many of them are. But it's easier getting up in the morning with hope in your heart. At least for me."

Hope in your heart. She liked the sound of that. And she'd felt it more often than not since she'd settled into life and work in Sutton's Creek. Not when she was at the inn, because Celia Lincoln was overbearing and irritating, but once she'd started at the range. The people were good. They helped each other, looked out for each other. She was part of that tribe, but a dark part of her insisted she wouldn't be if they knew who she really was. What kind of family she grew up in.

The panic that always simmered beneath the surface started to bubble.

"You know, I think I need to go to bed," she said, getting to her feet.

He uncurled from his slouch and sat up straighter. "You okay?"

She managed a smile. "I am. But I'm tired. Buying a car and shooting guns all in the same day is way more exhausting than I expected it to be."

"A good kind of exhausted, I hope."

"Definitely. Good night, Kane. And thanks for the help."

"Night, Sunshine. Hey," he said when she'd taken two steps toward the door.

"Yes?"

"That was some amazing shooting. Best I've ever seen anyone besides my guys do. If you want it kept secret from them, I'll do that. Think you should crow about it, but your opinion's the one that matters."

His words made the knot in her throat tighter. Not the ones about shooting, but about it being her choice whether or not others knew.

"It's okay," she said. "I don't mind if they know. But I don't want it to change anything. I don't want to teach classes or do RSO duty."

"Understood. One more thing—you want eggs and bacon again? Or waffles?"

"You don't have to cook for me, Kane."

He got to his feet, towering over her as he motioned her toward the door and followed her inside. He dropped his empty bottle into the recycle bin. Why did he have to be so flipping sexy doing something that simple?

"You can't cook. I can. And before you get excited, the waffles are frozen. I stick 'em in the toaster oven, slather 'em with butter and drizzle on the maple syrup—real, of course."

"How do you have abs? Seriously, how?"

He dragged his shirt up and patted his very flat belly. "These abs? My award-winning, panty-melting abs?"

Her mouth went dry. "Those abs, Candy Kane. Do you have others tucked away somewhere?"

He grinned at her. "Nope. I workout, babe. You've seen me do it. It's the only way to maintain my manly figure to the peak of perfection."

Daphne rolled her eyes, but she was charmed. Because that's what Kane did. He charmed people.

"I am seriously going to bed now. I'll let you know in the morning what I want to eat."

"Whatever you want," he called after her.

Daphne trudged upstairs, then closed her door and leaned against it. Whatever she wanted?

Because she wanted a *lot*. None of it involved bacon.

Chapter Seventeen

KANE WAS TAKING HIS TURN IN THE FRONT OF THE RANGE, technically the store area, when the man Daphne had said was creepy walked in with a range bag slung over his shoulder.

Nathan Fader, private gun dealer, man who creeped women out.

Still, the man had done nothing to him, so Kane slapped on a smile and swaggered to the counter. "How ya doin?"

Fader looked shifty. Or maybe Kane just thought he looked shifty because he automatically didn't like the man on Daphne's account.

"Fine." He looked around. "Where's the pretty girl who's usually here?"

Kane's gut tightened. He told himself not to lead with pummeling the man's face. Instead, he scratched the back of his neck and tried to look nonchalant. "I'm guessing you mean Daphne. She's got business elsewhere at the moment. Why?"

Fader shrugged. "No reason. She was nice. I guess I thought she'd be here every time."

"Nope, not today." He picked up a clipboard and set it on the counter. "You want to shoot?"

Fader's eyes narrowed for a moment. He reached for the clipboard and turned it. "Yeah."

He filled out the paperwork, produced his license and cash. Kane assigned a shooting bay and handed over a target. "Happy shooting, mister." He waited a beat, until the man turned toward the doors to the bays. "Been thinking you should know something before you go."

"Yeah? What's that?"

"Daphne's a beautiful woman and I get why you'd be interested. But she's my fiancée, so I'll have to ask you to move along when it comes to her. We clear?"

Fader's expression seemed to harden. "Yeah, we're clear. No offense meant, man. Maybe put a ring on that finger, save yourself the trouble of having to issue threats, though."

Kane really didn't like this dude. But there was no reason to throw him out. Yet.

"Not a threat, my man. Just the truth. That's my woman, and I'm mighty crazy about her."

Fader nodded and disappeared through the range door. Kane's temper simmered beneath the surface. Maybe Fader hadn't broken into Daphne's place, but he bore watching. He'd mentioned her with a gleam in his eye that Kane didn't like. It was the same look he'd seen on the faces of hunters when they sighted the prey they planned to shoot. There was no other description for that look. It was predatory, plain and simple.

When Daphne returned from picking up lunch, Kane went to the break room to meet her. She looked up, smiling, and his heart stuttered in his chest. *What the fuck?*

He'd told Fader she was his fiancée so the man would know she wasn't alone, that she had someone looking out for her. That she was off limits. But for the barest of moments he almost wished it was true. Not the fiancée part, because he was never doing that again, but the part where she was his woman.

But then he came to his senses when she arched an eyebrow at him. "What's wrong, Gramps? Acid indigestion from too much bacon and eggs?"

He shook himself. "Huh?"

"You look constipated. Like something's off."

Daphne opened the bag from the Gas n'Go. The odor of BBQ was already assailing his nostrils, but it got even better when she started pulling containers from the bag. She'd offered to do the lunch run today, and he'd reluctantly agreed since the Gas n'Go was nearby and not smack dab in the middle of town.

"Sorry, babe. The smells distracted me. I'm hungry."

"Seriously? You had a big breakfast four hours ago."

"I'm a big guy, what can I say? Plus I ran five miles in full pack this morning before you even dragged your pretty little ass from bed."

"Well, when you put it that way…" She kept pulling out containers, not looking at him any longer.

"Fader's inside the range. You should stay here until he's gone."

Her body went rigid for about half a second before she visibly relaxed. "Oh yeah?" she asked, eating a fry from the box she'd opened. Pretending she didn't care when in fact she cared a lot.

Dude had to have said something to her, but she wasn't telling Kane what that was. Made him want to go wrap his fingers around Fader's throat and squeeze until he got an answer.

Ghost wouldn't approve, so he wasn't doing it. But damn, he wanted to.

"Showed up about thirty minutes ago." He was *not* telling her that Fader had asked about her. He didn't think she'd appreciate that. "And, uh, I may have told him a little lie. Just because."

"A lie? About what?"

"I said we were engaged."

Daphne's eyes bugged out. Then she started laughing. And didn't stop as she sank onto a chair and grabbed a paper plate from the stack in the center.

"You know I regret telling you that, right?" he grumbled as he sat across from her and picked up a pulled pork sandwich. "And why is it funny anyway?"

"Sorry," she said, swiping beneath her eyes with a napkin. "I appreciate it, really, but I was just imagining the collective wails of the local women when they discovered their favorite instructor was off the market and about to get hitched. Lainey Bowen in particular will lose her shit when she hears."

"I went out with Lainey twice, and that was earlier this year. She'll be fine."

"Sure she will."

He ignored her. "A, I'm not currently dating anyone. B, I did it so *if* that douchebag has intentions toward you, he'll have to reconsider. You should be thanking me, not laughing."

Daphne took the top off her sandwich and poured on some barbecue sauce, giggling from time to time. He liked his with coleslaw on top, which was how they served it in the south, but Daphne got her coleslaw separate and ate it from the container with a fork. She put the top of the bun back on and gave him a look. Then she snorted.

"I'm sorry. It's not funny. It's sweet. Thank you."

He ate a forkful of green beans, still feeling slightly put out about the whole thing. "You're welcome."

Ethan and Blaze came striding in. Seth was RSO since they only had one shooter at the moment, and Ghost was in Research Park. Chance had taken Rory to an appointment with her endocrinologist.

"Thanks for going to pick up lunch, Daph," Blaze said as he sat and plucked a pulled pork sandwich off the pile.

The sides were family style, and they all had paper plates to scoop their choices onto. Except for Daphne's coleslaw, which was a single serving.

"You're welcome."

"How'd the new car drive?" Ethan asked.

"Great! The AC works, which is fantastic, and you don't have to jiggle the door handle a certain way to get it to open. Though I'm grateful to Warren for the use of his vehicle," she added. "But this one is definitely a step up."

"Guess it was worth the wait," Kane said, shooting *told you so* looks at his teammates. They'd ridden his ass for the past couple of months about finding a car, but it was good he'd waited. The Santa Fe had been a better deal than she'd have picked up in the spring.

"I'd say so," Daphne said, happily stabbing some mac and cheese onto her fork.

Kane made a face at Ethan and Blaze. They rolled their eyes.

Seth wandered in a few minutes later and grabbed a sandwich. "Fader just left," he said as he took a seat. "He's pretty tight-lipped about his reasons for being in town."

Kane gaped. So did Ethan and Blaze. "Wait—you tried to make small talk with him?"

Seth gave them a look. "Uh, yeah? Need to know more about him. Where was he when Daphne's apartment was broken into, that kind of thing. He said he was in Huntsville on the day in question. Had a meeting. That's all I got out of him. Except I've got the plate number for his rental now so I'll see what I can find out about the GPS coordinates that day."

Daphne was blinking, hard. She put her fork down and picked up the napkin again.

"You okay, Daph?" Seth asked.

"Fine," she said with a sniff. "Think I've got an eyelash in my eye."

"Hey," Kane said, wanting to move the conversation to something that wouldn't make Daphne cry while also giving her a chance to recover. "Daphne failed to mention it, but she's something of an expert marksman."

Three heads turned to look at her. Which was *not* what Kane had intended. She dabbed her eyes again and then rolled them. Well, at least she'd recovered enough not to get mushy because they cared about her.

"Candy Kane exaggerates. I can hit a target."

"Exaggerates, my ass. She put a perfect round circle around my bullseye. Rapid fire. At twenty yards."

"Wait," Blaze said, his head turning from Daphne to Kane to Daphne and back again. Seth looked like he'd encountered a puzzle he couldn't solve. Ethan was looking at Kane like he was waiting for the joke. "You're saying that Daphne put a circle around your center shot? At twenty yards?"

"Yeah, dumbass, that's what I'm saying. She's been holding out on us. She's a crack shot."

"Kane," she grumbled. "Swear to God." Then she took a breath and smiled. "Yes, I can shoot. I'm not a beginner. I never mentioned it because nobody ever asked, plus I wasn't in the mood to step onto a range and see if I could still shoot as well as I used to. Kane, in his overbearing way, decided I needed to learn so I could defend myself. But he didn't bother to find out if I already knew how to handle a weapon. So I showed him."

"I have so many questions," Seth said.

"Me too," Blaze added. Ethan nodded.

"It's no big deal," Daphne told them. "Eat your lunches. I'll fucking demonstrate if you need me to, but not until after I've eaten this sandwich and had some more mac and cheese. And I want my banana pudding, too. Hell, come to think of it, I'm going to be too full after all that, so maybe after the range closes."

"No offense, Daphne, but I really need this demonstration," Blaze said. "Not because I don't believe you can do it. I just really want to see it."

Daphne gave a long suffering sigh as she waved her fork around. "Fine, fine. But I already told Kane I don't want to teach any classes or do RSO duty unless I absolutely have to, okay? I don't want to be involved with the retail side. I'd really prefer nobody wants me to do that."

"Think you've got enough to do," Seth said. "If you don't want to do retail, you don't have to."

"I hope you don't mind me asking, but how did you learn to shoot so well?" Ethan asked.

She shot Kane a look. He had the feeling that if she could get him alone right now, she'd knee him in the balls. But hey, she wasn't fucking crying anymore.

"You know how some kids have to join a sport or play an instrument and practice it all the time, even when they don't want to?"

The guys all nodded.

"That was my dad, except his instrument was a gun. And he insisted I practice. I had no choice."

"Sorry to hear that," Blaze said. "Nothing you're forced to do is fun. Badly as I want to see you shoot, if you don't want to, none of us are gonna make you."

She smiled at him. Kane felt a pinch of jealousy in his soul that she never smiled at him like that.

"Thank you, but I offered. Kane may be overbearing and a dick sometimes, but he's right that I need to stay in practice. It was probably one of the workmen who broke in and it'll probably never happen again. But I should be able to defend myself if it does."

"Wasn't trying to be a dick, babe," Kane said, feeling unfairly picked on.

"I know, Gramps. It just comes naturally."

The guys snorted.

"Shut up and eat," Kane grumbled at the three of them. "And mind your own business."

Ethan grabbed a fry and pointed it at him. "But yours is so much more fun."

Chapter Eighteen

"Hey," Kane said, poking his head into the store area. "Got the security system in. I can install it for you after work."

Daphne's heart skipped. She wanted the security, but she also didn't want to go back to her place just yet. The farmhouse felt safe, despite Kane's presence next door to the guest room. The only thing dangerous there was her attraction to him.

"Great. Thanks."

Kane stepped through the door and walked over to hitch a leg up, half-sit on her desk. "I'm just installing it, Sunshine. You don't have to go back yet. There's no rush."

She leaned back in her chair to look up at him. A curl of dark hair fell over his brow and he shoved it back, then reached for one of the peppermints she kept in a jar on her desk and popped it into his mouth. She imagined him sucking her nipples the way he sucked that lucky peppermint and her mind turned to jelly. Not only that, but the floodgates of bodily responses opened and her panties grew damp.

"I don't want to impose," she said, her voice sounding a bit warbly to her own ears.

"You aren't imposing. It's a guest room. The bed and TV are there, the bathroom situation works because Ethan and I are men and don't need six kinds of body lotion to moisturize with—"

"What? I do *not* have six kinds of body lotion, Kane. You're making that up."

He grinned. "Yep, totally. But I like it when your eyes flash and you look indignant."

She frowned. "Why would you like that? Means I'm annoyed."

"Dunno. Just think you're beautiful when you're annoyed."

She tilted her head to one side. "Are you okay? Because I'm beginning to think that bacon really did a number on you. Or maybe it's the pulled pork because you are *not* acting like yourself at the moment."

He shook his head. "You know, most women say thank you when I tell them they're beautiful. You wonder if I'm okay."

She fished out a peppermint of her own, because she needed something to do, and slipped it into her mouth. "Because you don't talk to me that way. This is a new development."

He picked up another peppermint and tossed it in the air, caught it. "Yeah, well you kind of forced that shift in perspective when you accosted me in the gym a few mornings ago."

"I did not accost you. You were being a dick."

"I seem to remember there was a discussion about dicks." He tossed the peppermint again. "Sorry if I pissed you off at lunch, by the way."

"You didn't. I was surprised at the way you did it, that's all."

"You were about to cry. I couldn't let that happen."

He'd noticed? "I was not about to cry. It was a hair in my eye."

"Yeah, you were. You were as surprised as the rest of us that Seth attempted small talk with a customer, which we all know he hates. And he did it because of you. Because you're one of us and he wanted to help you. That got you in the feels."

Daphne folded her arms over her chest. "Okay, fine, yes. I was feeling teary. But I'm not a little girl and I can regulate my emotions. I just needed a second."

"Which I gave you by introducing the topic of you being a badass."

"Wait, I thought you were apologizing. Now you sound like you want a pat on the back."

"I'm complicated."

Daphne snorted. "You are not."

He grinned and her heart thumped. "You're right, I'm not. Mostly not. Just give me good food, hot sex, and plenty of sleep. I'm a happy man."

"Noted," she said while things south of the border did a spicy dance. "Though I'm going to assume you didn't mean me for the hot sex portion."

He managed to look horrified for half a second. Which was *sooo* not good for her ego.

"No, of course not. We're friends. You don't fuck around with friends if you want to stay friends."

Disappointment flared inside her. "Probably a good policy. Though sometimes being friends first makes things better."

His gaze sharpened. "You speaking from experience?"

"I'm speaking from romance novels."

He seemed to relax a fraction. "Got it." He tossed the peppermint up again, caught it with his mouth. "So you still planning to stay with me and Ethan or what?"

She thought about going home. It'd be easier to mope around her apartment with a hankering for Kane than it would be to stay in the same house, wanting what he clearly did not. It'd also be slightly wicked to take care of herself with him next door. Fun, even.

Which had nothing to do with her answer.

"Staying tonight, but I should probably go home soon. Y'all don't need me taking up your space any longer than necessary. Plus you'll want to free up your schedule."

"My schedule?"

"For all that hot sex you need. Probably be awkward making somebody scream with me next door."

His jaw worked. The buoyant mood of a moment ago was gone, replaced by something a shade more irritated. "I'm fine. There is no schedule."

"Maybe there should be, because you look awfully tense right about now. How long's it been since you got laid?"

His eyes widened. "I'm not discussing that with you. What the fuck, Daphne?"

"Hey, friends talk about things. I'm being friendly here. Concerned. You seem tense and I'm thinking maybe you need a good orgasm or two. I could be wrong. Maybe it's just constipation. Might want to lay off the fatty foods and get some fiber in that case."

He opened his mouth. Closed it. Then he stood. "You know what? I better get back to work. Things to do. We'll touch base on the installation later."

"Sure thing."

"Thanks for the peppermint."

"You bet. I'm putting fiber pills on the shopping list for

the break room, by the way. Anything else you can think of?"

She was having too much fun, but the look on his face just made her want to keep going. She blinked at him innocently, pen poised over the notepad beside her keyboard.

"No. And I don't need fiber pills."

"Hey, no shame. Old men like you need to regulate their gut health. I read about it somewhere. When I wasn't reading about how to get a man to marry me or make my youthful skin glow, I mean."

"I'm outta here."

"Kane?" she said before he could reach the exit.

He stopped and turned, hands shoved in his jean pockets. Made his arms look bigger and unbearably sexy.

Focus, Daphne.

"Yeah?" he grumbled.

"As your friend, I need to tell you something. Are you listening?"

"Unfortunately, yes."

"Good. On behalf of womankind everywhere, you really need to know that not every woman you meet needs or wants a commitment from you. Women are capable of hot, dirty sex for the sake of sex just as much as you are. Sometimes all we want is a really good orgasm. Remember that the next time you're worried about some pretty little filly getting too attached, okay?"

He swore, probably more to himself than her, and disappeared down the hallway.

Daphne snickered.

Chapter Nineteen

Daphne was driving him crazy.

And she wasn't supposed to. He was supposed to have a handle on this attraction. Yet every time he went to talk to her lately, every time he tried to steer their relationship—well, *not* a relationship, but a friendship—back to the boundaries he understood, she hit him right between the eyes with a metaphorical sling shot.

Like rock, meet forehead; down he went. Then he floundered and tried to figure out what the fuck he needed to do to steer them off the rocky shore of sexy town. Before they crashed and burned on the boulders of *this is a bad idea* beneath the surface.

Before he found himself willing to do or say anything to get her beneath him.

Because if he did that, he wouldn't stop until he'd lost interest. Because he always lost interest, even when he wanted there to be more than just sex. Then what? It'd be awkward as hell around here, especially if they didn't agree on calling it quits. And if they didn't agree, and he hurt her because he was done, the guys would be pissed at him, and he'd be an asshole in the eyes of everyone he cared about.

He dragged his attention back to researching the modified Glock and found nothing. Once the fucker had 'disappeared' at sea, there was no trail. Which there wouldn't be with professional traffickers involved. But whoever'd put that trigger in—and he was still working on the assumption Dima Smirnov had not made the mod himself—had to know the gun was hot. Maybe that's why the diamond was impossible to track down. It could be a trafficker marking meant for the illegal trade.

Kane reassembled the Glock and put it in the safe. He hated to tell Ghost he couldn't find anything, but it was the truth. They needed more information from Diana Corbin about other guns in the missing shipment. That might help, or it might not. Why the fuck they were being asked to do it in the first place irritated him like a splinter in a finger. Painful, annoying, but not life-threatening.

At two, he headed into the meeting room at the front of the building to brief a group of ladies who'd signed up to learn about self-defense. The class would meet four times over the course of two weeks and they'd learn a variety of techniques to keep themselves safe from predators.

It was a mixed group, from women in their twenties to their seventies. They smiled and nodded at him, some of them batting their eyelashes. He winked and smiled and made jokes, but his heart wasn't in it today.

All he could think about was what Daphne had said. *Sometimes all we want is a really good orgasm.*

Of course he knew good orgasms were key, and he prided himself on providing them. But she'd also said not every woman wanted or needed a commitment, and he'd spent his adult life operating on the assumption they did.

Which, quite frankly, was a little embarrassing in retrospect.

How many of the women he'd dated had been secretly laughing at him when he'd given them his spiel about having a good time and not wanting a relationship?

Probably more than he realized. Women tended to be more subtle than men, and now he imagined them gazing at him indulgently, wishing he'd get on with it so they could have sex and go to sleep. Instead, he'd been giving the speech about having fun and not getting serious.

By the time six o'clock came and the range closed for the day, Kane was doubting everything he'd ever said to every woman he'd ever slept with. Which was a lot, though nowhere near as many as his teammates thought. Sometimes when they thought he was going out with a woman, he wasn't. Sometimes he went by himself to the river and sat on the dock, watching the water and the birds flying along the shore.

He'd done that a lot since moving to Sutton's Creek. He wasn't sure why. Dissatisfaction with the direction of his life? Unhappiness? A vague emptiness that no amount of meaningless sex could fill?

Fuck all, he was *not* cut out for this soul-searching bullshit.

"Hey, you coming to watch?" Blaze said, interrupting Kane's personal pity party.

"Watch what?"

Blaze shook his head. "Your fiancée. Targets. Remember?"

He really wished he'd thought of something to say to Fader besides telling the man he and Daphne were getting married. Because he'd had to tell his guys, just in case the asshole came back, and now they wouldn't let up. Daphne mostly rolled her eyes at them, but it bugged the shit out of him that they found it so amusing.

"Coming."

When he stepped onto the range, everyone was there. Ghost, Blaze, Chance, Seth, and Ethan. Daphne leaned against the table of the shooting bay, arms crossed, legs crossed, red hair wound onto her head in a big, fluffy bun. She shot him a glance and looked away. He felt the absence of her gaze like a physical ache.

Daphne put her ear protection on, then turned and picked up a Glock 19 she must have chosen from the rental weapons. Her fingers were long and elegant as she slammed the magazine home in the grip.

"Everybody ready?"

The guys all glanced at each other. Everyone had their hearing protection on. "Ready," Ghost said.

"Double tap."

The target was set at twenty yards, like last night, and Daphne squeezed off two shots. Then she stabbed the button to bring the target sailing back to her. As it got closer, the guys started to murmur. Daphne had hit the bullseye dead center and then put another into the target's forehead. They were both kill shots.

Kane felt something like excitement and pride start to fizz in his veins. Not that he had anything to be proud about. He hadn't taught her. But damn, she was amazing.

"Now I'll put a ring around the center. Eight shots."

She sent the target back, lined up her shots, and rapid fired eight of them into the target. When she brought it back, the holes ringed the one in the center. It wasn't a perfect circle, which he knew would bug her, but it was damned impressive.

"Holy shit," Blaze said. "That's really fucking good."

"Good?" Kane replied. "It's more than good. It's fantastic shooting."

"Yeah, yeah. Hold onto your shorts there," Blaze said, patting the air with his hand. "I wasn't insulting your woman. I'm complimenting her."

Daphne ejected the magazine, cleared the weapon, and lay it on the table. Then she slipped off her hearing protection and sized them up. "First of all, I am not Kane's woman. I know y'all find it amusing that he told the creep we're engaged, but *I'm* not amused."

"Sorry," Blaze muttered. "He's just so fun to annoy."

"Agreed," Daphne said. "But I think he had good intentions so I'd appreciate it if you'd stop giving him shit about it."

"Yes, ma'am."

Daphne pulled in a breath. "Second, I'm sorry I didn't mention the shooting thing when you hired me. I didn't think it was important because you weren't hiring me to work the range or teach."

"It's great shooting," Ghost said. "Really great. But you're right. It's not what we hired you to do. You ever want to work the range side, you can. But if you prefer to stick with booking classes and appointments, and doing the office accounting, I got no problem with it."

Daphne dropped her chin a fraction, as if she'd been worried and now she was relieved. "Thank you."

"You're welcome. The only thing I'm going to say about it is with shooting like that, you should be proud. And if you ever wanted to teach a women's class, I think they'd find you inspiring. But that's up to you and nobody's going to force you into it. Okay, moving along—it's Friday. Who's joining me at the Dawg for prime rib?"

Everybody was. Kane had forgotten it was Friday but when Daphne said she was going, he jumped into the fray and said he'd be there too. They locked up and walked outside to get into cars. The sky was black to the west. They weren't expecting a tornado, but severe thunderstorms were possible. Looked like one was on the way if the sky was any indication.

"You want to ride with me?" Kane asked Daphne as he caught up to her in the parking lot.

She stopped and turned, hands on hips. She'd put on big sunglasses that ought to make her look like a bug but were actually pretty on her face. He itched to take that mass of red hair down and spear his hands into it, see if it was as soft as it looked.

These fucking thoughts about her were getting more frequent and he didn't like it. But how to make it stop?

"I'm going to the house to change first. It's hot and I want to wear something cooler. I'll catch up to you."

"I'll come with you."

"You don't have to do that, Kane."

He'd given her the spare key and the alarm codes, with Ethan's approval, so he didn't technically need to go with her. "Do you want to go alone? Fader was here today. If he knows what you drive, he could see it parked at the house, come knock on the door. You want that?"

He hated the fear that crossed her face but he needed her to think. "No, of course I don't. Come on then. It'll only take me a few minutes."

He followed her the short distance to the house and parked his Yukon beside her Santa Fe. The sky was darker now, and the wind picked up as he opened his door and stepped out onto the gravel.

"Better hurry," he said as they went to the front door. "That storm's moving fast. If we don't get on the road soon, we'll have to wait for it to blow over."

He opened the door and Daphne ran upstairs to

change. Kane waited, looking out the window as the darkness spread across the sky. Lightning cracked in the distance and a boom of thunder sounded a few seconds later. Upstairs he could hear Daphne bumping and thumping around the bedroom.

She came hurrying downstairs in a pair of denim shorts and a white button up shirt tied at her waist just as the first drop of rain hit the roof.

"Well, hell," she said as the sky opened up a moment later and the downpour began. "I thought I was fast enough."

"You were fast. The storm was faster."

She dropped her purse onto a chair and blew out a breath. Her hair was still piled on top of her head, her shirt was open in a deep vee to her lacy bra, and her shorts showed a mile of creamy leg that ended in a gold sandal with a tiny heel.

"You going on a date?" he asked.

Her gaze fell over her body, back up to him. "No, why?"

She was going to make him say it. "You look pretty."

Her teeth gleamed white. "Thank you. But why do you sound so angry saying it?"

He shoved his hands in his pockets and glowered. He knew he was doing it, but he couldn't suppress it. "Because I don't want to find you attractive. Because it's inconvenient and dangerous."

She tilted her head. "Dangerous to whom?"

"You. Me. Hell, I don't know. But if I do what I want to do, it has the potential to change everything. I don't want things to be awkward at work."

She laughed softly. "I think it's already awkward, Kane. You just told a man we were engaged today. Then you told your friends, and now they won't stop teasing you about it

—though maybe they will since I told them to. The point is, you want to fuck me but you don't want things to change. You don't want a commitment or a relationship and you're afraid that I'll take things too seriously and get hurt when you have to tell me, again, that you don't do happily ever afters."

Fucking hell, how did she nail it so succinctly? And make him sound like a petulant toddler at the same time?

"My wife was shot and killed by a man she'd been having an affair with."

God, that hurt. He hated fucking saying it, and yet he had to say something. Had to try and explain in his own fucked up way. Everybody knew his wife had been killed. Nobody in his life knew about the affair but him. And now Daphne.

"Kane," she said, her voice soft and sympathetic. "I'm sorry."

"I loved her. And I don't blame her for the affair, not anymore. I was gone a lot. Deployed." And working in a job where he might not come back. He couldn't imagine how frightening that'd been for her. Back then, he hadn't thought much about it. He did now that he knew what it was like to get that call. "She was lonely, and this fucker was there. He was somebody she worked with. They only got together a few times before he got weirdly obsessive. She got scared and confessed everything to me. Yeah, I was fucking flattened by it. We'd been talking about having kids, about me leaving the military, and she hit me with something I hadn't seen coming." He huffed a breath that hurt all the way down to his core. "But we were working on it. I was trying to forgive her, to move on. Then I deployed again, and this fucker—"

"Kane, you don't have to say it."

"Yeah, I do. He'd been watching her, following her. He

broke into our house, tied her up, and raped her repeatedly before he shot her. Then he turned the gun on himself."

Daphne was at his side, wrapping her arms around him. "Oh, Kane. I'm so sorry. There are no words, but I'm so, so sorry."

He slipped his arms around her body and held her against him. It was the first time he'd ever let himself hold her, and it felt so fucking good. She slid against him like she fit there. Like she belonged. Instinct told him to tip her head back and kiss her. Logic convinced him not to.

"Love is hard and messy and complicated. I don't think I'm cut out for it," he said, his throat tight as a drum. "That's why I say the shit I say about meaningless sex. I mean, yeah, maybe it's arrogant and presumptive and doesn't fully give a woman her agency, but it's also honest. I'm not trying to be an asshole. I'm just stating my truth up front."

Daphne tilted her head back to look up at him. Her pretty eyes glistened with tears. "Okay, Kane. I understand. I'm sorry for giving you a hard time about that. It wasn't fair."

His gaze focused on her mouth. Pretty, pink, kissable. His dick was stirring, swelling, aching for release.

"No, you were right about some of it. Why should I assume every woman I meet wants a relationship instead of the same thing I want? It's a sexist view. That's what you were trying to tell me."

"Yes, but I shouldn't have assumed."

He sighed, slid a thumb across her lower lip because he could. "People are complicated. You think you know somebody, but can we ever really know anyone? I thought Hannah was mine no matter what, that we were pledged to each other and that meant nobody could come between us. I was all in, and I thought she was too. But I was wrong."

He wasn't sure, but he thought a shadow slid across her eyes. "No, we never know anyone as well as we think we do."

He was conscious of the fact he didn't know much of anything about her, and he wanted to. But Daphne held her secrets close. She didn't trust him enough to tell him yet. He hoped she would one day.

Lightning lit up the growing darkness and thunder cracked almost immediately after. They both jumped at the power and noise as it shook the house. Daphne's eyes grew big. Kane took her hand and pulled her toward the kitchen. He opened the basement door, flicked on the lights.

"Hold the rail going down. We'll wait it out in the shelter."

"I…"

"You have to go first," he said gently. "I have to pull the door shut behind us. It sticks."

"But there aren't any sirens," she protested.

The wind howled and the house creaked ominously. Kane looked overhead. "I know, but that doesn't mean we shouldn't get in the shelter. Could be an EF-1."

Tornadoes were rated on an EF scale, with 1 being a very small one with some minor damage to 5 being major, the big kahuna of them all. That one destroyed whole towns, turned buildings into rubble, and changed lives forever. Usually, big tornadoes showed up on the radar beforehand. But sometimes small ones could spin up during thunderstorms. They happened fast and quick, and were often identified later, after the damage was assessed.

But it could still take down trees or damage the house, and Kane wasn't taking that chance. Daphne gave him another look, then picked her way down into the basement on her little heels. Kane pulled the door shut, tugging hard where it scraped the floor. Then he went to the bottom and found the battery-operated lantern. Just in time too because the lights flickered in the basement and then blinked out.

"Hang on," he said at Daphne's gasp. A moment later, the basement flooded with light and Daphne let out a shaky breath.

"Not a fan of utter darkness," she said. "I'm not afraid of the dark, but make it pitch black where I can't see my hand in front of my face and I'm freaking."

"No need, Sunshine. I've got you covered. Seat?"

He pointed at the folding chairs he and Ethan had brought down. They also had thin floor mattresses in case they had to shelter overnight—they'd both done enough sleeping on hard surfaces as special operators that they weren't doing it if they didn't have to—and a stash of water. There was a mouse-proof tote with snacks inside, too. Basically, they were prepared for severe weather alerts, which tended to happen often in the spring and fall. Not so much in summer, but there were exceptions.

Daphne took in her surroundings and folded herself into one of the chairs. The basement was clean, with a concrete floor and cinder block walls. It hadn't been that way originally, but someone had worked to update the basement and make it a viable living space at one point. They hadn't finished it out, though. He thought about it sometimes but there wasn't much point since the property wasn't really theirs. In the end, after the Athena Project successfully launched and their mission was done, there would be no need to stay.

Except he liked his life here. His friends were settling down, finding happiness, and though he didn't see that for himself, he liked the town and the pace.

Above them, the house creaked and moaned. Daphne looked up at the ceiling. He looked at her.

"Well, this is fun," she said. "And to think we could be eating prime rib. I should have gone straight to the Dawg instead of changing first."

"The storm is headed their way."

"But the Dawg is solid brick. Old-style brick, not the brick facing they put on houses these days. The people inside probably won't know anything's going on."

"True." He grinned to try and lighten the mood. "But look on the bright side—you get to spend quality time with me."

"Yay," she deadpanned.

He laughed. "That's my girl. Puncturing egos with sarcasm as usual."

She looked suddenly sad. "That's the thing though, isn't it? I'm not your girl. And you've got really solid reasons for not going there, I get it. But what if we both miss out on something really great, huh? Even if it's just a hot, sexy, summer fling?"

"You would want that?"

She nodded, and his dick throbbed.

"Why not? I'm not getting any satisfaction at the moment, and it might be fun to get some of that panty-melting lovin' my book club besties are having, you know?"

Jesus did he know.

"And it's not about me being too young for you. You can just can that line of bullshit right now. I'm fairly certain you've never asked to see a driver's license before you got naked with anyone. I mean it's not like you're hanging out at the high school, right?"

"Fuck no. Don't even say that."

She snorted. "Make you uncomfortable, Gramps?"

He reached for her chair, tugged it closer until he could lean into her space. He didn't know why he did it.

"Yeah, it makes me uncomfortable. But you like throwing me off balance, don't you?"

She grinned. "Oh, I really do. You're so cute when you look perplexed or exasperated by something I've said. It makes me happy. It might even make me a little bit hot, if I'm honest."

He did not need to know that. Especially when she was close enough to smell her lavender shampoo, plus whatever other scent she had going that made her smell sweet and clean. He suddenly wanted to throw caution to the wind, put his mouth on hers and see if she tasted half as lovely as she looked.

Then again, if he did that, would she think he was trying to soothe his old hurts? That it wasn't about her so much as it was just getting laid?

Fuck. Too many options and not enough information.

"Kane," she said with that soft, throaty voice. "You're overthinking this. I can see the wheels turning in your brain."

She stood, unfolding her long beautiful legs before straddling him. Then she sat on his lap, facing him, her face only inches from his, her beautiful eyes gazing at him with desire and determination.

He was too stunned to stop her. Hell, he didn't want to. That was the God's honest truth right there.

He. Did. Not. Want. To.

"What are you doing, Sunshine?" he murmured, his gaze fixed on her mouth.

"Taking charge, Candy Kane."

Then she kissed him.

Chapter Twenty

Daphne's heart hammered a mile a minute as she pressed her mouth to Kane's.

She wasn't fully in possession of her wits, clearly, or she wouldn't have taken such a big chance. Straddling his lap? Kissing him? What if he pushed her away? It was possible, and if he did she'd go, but she'd be humiliated to her core.

So deeply embarrassed she might not be able to look at him for a solid month.

His mouth opened beneath hers, his hands went to her hips, yanking her forward until their crotches met, and his tongue plunged into her mouth.

Okay, good sign. Very good sign.

Daphne cupped his face between her hands, pressed herself harder against him, and met his tongue like a woman starved for sex. Which she was. Not in general, but with him.

She'd wanted to get naked with Kane for ages now, quite possibly since that first night when he'd been part of the trio who'd found her in the empty apartment in the Sutton building. He'd taken charge, spreading a protective wing over her, getting her warm and safe, feeding her, and hovering like a mother hen with a baby chick.

She'd been drawn to him from the first few moments, though she'd been in no place to do anything about it at the time. But when she got on her feet again, thanks to him and his friends—her friends now—she'd tried to let him know in every way she could short of actually saying the words that she was available.

He'd ignored her, and she'd eventually realized he always would. That's when she'd accepted Warren's invitation to dinner the first time.

Kane's hands left her hips and went to her shirt. He unbuttoned it swiftly, untied it, and spread the tails open so he could cup her breasts in two big hands. Daphne slid her arms around his neck and arched into him. She was in danger of soaking through the denim of her shorts, but if Kane kept touching her then it was worth a little embarrassment when he discovered it.

If he discovered it. She reminded herself they were a long way from delicious sexy times even if it seemed imminent.

If Kane got some noble thought into his brain, some idea that he had to sacrifice his massive erection on the altar of self-denial, then it was over before it started.

And it *was* a massive erection, she noted. Because she was rubbing herself shamelessly against it as his tongue delved into her mouth and his big hands dragged her bra down to free her breasts.

"Jesus, Daphne," he groaned as she kept moving her hips, seeking more of the electricity that sizzled and popped in her veins. "You feel so fucking good. But if you don't stop moving like that, I'm gonna embarrass myself here with a premature explosion."

She wanted to laugh and she wanted to free him and feel him inside her before that explosion happened.

"Think that's an old man problem," she said, unable to stop herself from goading him. "There might be a pill for it. I'll pencil it in along with that fiber."

His too handsome face went still for a moment. Then he laughed. It was a rusty sound, but it was a laugh all the same. "I ought to spank you."

"Oh, would you?" she whispered, a new flood of moisture adding to the tsunami between her legs. Not that she'd ever been turned on by spanking before, but the idea of Kane's big hand on her bottom was almost too much to think about. If she didn't like it, she could always tell him to stop.

Beneath her, his body was rigid. And not just the part of him she wanted rigid. A torrent of swear words issued from his lips. She silenced them with a kiss. He groaned as their mouths met, then his hands were on her shoulders, pushing her shirt open farther.

When his mouth closed over a nipple, Daphne stiffened, her insides melting at the feel of his hot tongue on her flesh. "Kane," she sighed, winding her fingers in his hair and holding him to her.

He sucked her nipple a little deeper, a little harder, and she felt the answering pull in her center. Her clit throbbed as if each tug of her nipple was a flick along those nerve endings. She couldn't imagine what would happen if he put his mouth there. She wouldn't last two seconds.

Overhead the storm cracked and shook, but Daphne no longer cared. She cared about this. Two bodies melding, fusing, becoming one. They weren't there yet, but she prayed they would be. Soon.

Kane's fingers skimmed the leg of her shorts, but her legs were spread too wide and they were too tight to get a finger in. When he unbuttoned her shorts and tugged the zipper down, her heart ricocheted around her chest. She eased the pressure against his dick, moving enough to give him a way in. His hand slid down the inside of her shorts until his fingers dipped into her seam.

Daphne gasped at the same time he groaned.

"So fucking wet," he said, leaning back to look at her. Her breasts sat up high and proud from the bra cups sitting beneath and her nipples were tight, wet points where his tongue had been.

Kane's fingers slid over her clit, and she moaned.

"I shouldn't be doing this," he said. "But I really fucking want to."

"You aren't the only one involved, Kane. I'm here too, and I really fucking want you to keep doing what you're doing. I want more than that. I want you inside me."

He managed to work two fingers into her and Daphne's walls gripped him tight. "Like this?" he said, his voice a rough purr.

"Yes, but with cock," she gasped.

"No condom. Believe me, Sunshine, I'm not happy about it."

So close and yet so far.

"And we're in a basement," he added. "You're worth more than a basement fuck."

"I don't mind a basement fuck. To start. But then I want it in a few other places. Shower, couch, kitchen counter. Maybe even your Yukon, assuming you haven't fucked half of Sutton's Creek in there."

He dragged her mouth down to his and kissed her hard. "I don't fuck in my Yukon," he growled. "But I'd make an exception for you."

Daphne shivered with longing. "I haven't had sex in

over a year, Kane. And I have an IUD, so no surprise little Kanes if that's what worries you."

He looked at her with hooded eyes, his fingers still inside her body. Still creating havoc with every tiny, shivery movement.

"You aren't worried about me?"

"Nope. You're smart and careful. You wouldn't take a chance. You'd wear a condom every time. And if you want to with me, I don't blame you. But it's been so long and I really, really want to come."

He looked turned on and puzzled all at once. "What about Trigg? He didn't make you come?"

"Warren and I never, not once, did anything remotely resembling sex. He doesn't believe in sex before marriage."

Kane suddenly looked predatory, like a decision had been made. "Out of those shorts, beautiful. Now."

Daphne climbed from his lap and shimmied out of her shorts, letting them drop to the ground. Kane was on his feet, tugging his shirt off. Daphne went for his jeans before he could, unbuttoning and dragging the zipper down until she could free his cock.

His big, beautiful, hard cock.

Thunder boomed, but it was farther away than before. The storm was moving fast, and so were they. She wanted to move fast. She didn't want to give him any time to think, to change his mind.

He shoved the shirt from her shoulders, unhooked her bra, and then she was gloriously naked with all her clothes in a pile on the floor. Her hand closed around his cock.

"Daphne." His voice sounded strangled.

"Mmm, Kane, this is impressive. No wonder they love you," she said, sliding her hand over him.

He caught her wrist. His grip was firm, but not hard. "Look at me."

She did.

"No more, babe. No more talk of anyone outside this room but you and me. It's us in here, not anyone else. And I don't want that in my head when it's you I'm focused on, okay?"

It was a surprisingly sweet thing to say and her heart skipped a beat. "No more," she agreed. It wasn't that she'd wanted to say those things, it was more that she needed him to realize she wasn't falling in love with him over a big dick and a magic tongue. She put her hands on his chest and pushed him back until he was on the chair again.

His cock stood at attention and she thought about dropping to her knees and sucking it, but the floor was hard and she was in too much of a hurry to get him inside her this first time.

Kane put his hands on her hips, rounded them to cup her ass, and pulled her toward him so he could place a kiss beneath her belly button. She threaded her fingers in his hair and let her head fall back, thanking God for thunderstorms.

"This ass is perfect," he said, his mouth against her skin, his hands sliding down, under her cheeks, back up again. He gave her a light swat and Daphne felt the sting in her nipples and her clitoris. It was… way more exciting than she'd expected it to be.

"That's for calling me an old man." He swatted her ass again, the other cheek this time. "And that's for the fiber crack."

"I'm going to call you old every day, just so you know. So long as we're fuck buddies."

He snorted. "Is that what we are? Fuck buddies?"

She straddled him and he gripped his cock, holding it so she could sink down on him. They both groaned as she surrounded him. "Oh my God," she said as her body stretched to accommodate him, as she took him inch by inch until he was home.

His eyes glittered hot as he reached up and took the elastic from her hair. It tumbled over her shoulders like a fall of red silk.

"Fucking beautiful," he said. "This hair. You. This moment."

Daphne fisted her hand in his hair and pulled his head back so she could kiss him. Her tongue speared into his mouth, taking what she wanted. "Just so you know," she whispered against his lips. "I know this is nothing but sex. Your dick is feeling very magical at the moment, but I promise not to fall in love with you."

His muscles tightened as he stood up without breaking the connection between their bodies. It was a move that would've made even the most immune of women swoon. Daphne was not immune. Her legs wrapped around his hips as he held her up, the muscles in his arms corded and beautiful.

He took her to one of the mattresses and laid her down on it, never losing the contact between them. His gaze dropped over her body before locking with hers again. "Need you to hang on, Sunshine."

Then he thrust home—and Daphne shattered.

Chapter Twenty-One

Ten minutes ago, he'd have said his determination not to ever cross the line into sex with Daphne was iron-clad.

Yet here they were, naked as the day they were born.

Kane was buried to the hilt inside her and Daphne was convulsing around his cock after a single thrust. Her back arched, her perfect breasts thrusting in the air as her eyes shuttered and her mouth dropped open.

He wanted to kiss her, and he wanted to watch what happened when he moved inside her. He chose option two. Plenty of time for kissing later. He pulled out slowly, dragging against her walls, then slammed into her again, right up to the point stars danced behind his eyelids.

"Fuck," he swore as sensation traveled down into his balls and up his spine. It wouldn't take much at this rate until he lost it too.

"Yes," she gasped, her body shaking around him.

"Look at me, Sunshine."

Her eyes snapped open, tangling with his. It'd been an alpha male thing to say, a command he'd needed to give like he'd needed his next breath, but he hadn't been prepared for what it did to him.

His heart stuttered and tripped before righting itself and racing to catch up to where his brain was. All he could do until that happened was stare, feeling Daphne's pussy grip him tight as she kept coming.

Move, his brain finally said.

Kane dropped to his elbows so he could bracket her face between his hands and watch her reaction. Then he started moving, thrusting deep and hard, dragging his cock along her walls, pushing inside again, prolonging her pleasure, propelling her toward even greater heights.

"Oh my God," she moaned. "Like that. Fuck yes."

He loved the mouth on her, the way she didn't hold back. The way she named what this was and made sure he knew she didn't expect anything from him.

And yet something about that also disappointed him. Which made no sense. This was pretty much his wet dream come true. Daphne Bryant's luscious body beneath his, taking every inch of him, wanting him to fuck her into a screaming orgasm without expecting a commitment from him.

He'd dreamed about this, jerked off to thoughts of the two of them tangled together, and told himself repeatedly it could never happen.

But it was happening, and while he'd probably beat himself up over it later, he wasn't wasting time regretting it in the moment.

Her eyes closed again, her bottom lip catching between her teeth, and he had a need to make her pay attention to him instead of whatever was happening inside her head. Kane dropped his mouth to hers, speared his tongue into her mouth, and groaned when she kissed him back like she was dying of thirst and he was water.

Their mouths fused, their bodies moved together, and a fire lit inside Kane's soul, burning along the pathways in his brain, along his nerve endings, until he felt like he was about to ignite. He anchored himself more firmly onto his elbows and pistoned into her willing body with a need bordering on primal.

She stiffened beneath him—and then shouted his name as the wave broke over her. Her legs wrapped tighter around his hips, anchoring him inside her. Any thoughts he'd had about withdrawing before he came fled as he erupted, jet after jet of semen coating her walls, draining him of the will to move.

Time ceased to have meaning as waves of ecstasy rolled and rolled before finally fading to something more manageable. Until he came back to himself, still buried inside her, tangled in a sweaty heap of arms, legs, and body parts.

He hadn't felt this good in a long, long time.

"Everything good?" Daphne asked, cracking an eye to look at him.

Her pussy still gloved him, warm and tight and welcoming, and she could ask that?

"Yeah," he said roughly. "You?"

Her smile was the very definition of satisfied even if her next words made him choke. "It wasn't bad."

"Wasn't bad?" he growled, flexing his hips just to hear her gasp.

"Okay, it was fucking fantastic and you know it. Happy now?"

He dropped his mouth to lazily circle her nipple. "Yes. Mostly. Gonna need to do it again, slower this time, and that might help me be even happier."

"I'm there for it. Except, and it pains me to say this, I

think we need to head to the Dawg before our friends send a search party."

"Aw, shit. You're right." He withdrew from her body reluctantly and reached for his jeans, found his phone. Daphne turned on her side as he propped himself on an elbow beside her. "Three messages," he told her while she trailed a hand over his abs. It was this close to tickling, but he liked her hand on him so he didn't stop her.

Ethan: *You coming?*

He turned the phone to Daphne. She snickered. "Coming is why we're late."

"I'm not writing that."

Had to wait for the storm to pass.

Next message was Seth. *Y'all get caught in the storm?*

Yes, be there soon.

Rory: *I hear you and Daphne went to the house so she could change clothes. Did you finally pull your head out of your ass and kiss her? Is that why you're late?*

He turned the phone again. Daphne's eyes widened and then she laughed. "Dammit, she's good. Though I'm the one who kissed you."

"I'll tell her that."

"The hell you will."

"You're right, I won't."

She leaned over to kiss his chest. "I don't want them to know. I think you're with me on that."

He was, but why did it bother him when she said it?

"Agreed."

Her hair was a mess, her eyes were gorgeous, and her body was mouth-watering. She sat up and started to reach for her clothing. "I'm starving. Think it's safe to head over there now?"

"Yeah, I think so. Why don't you want anyone to

know?" he asked, because he couldn't stop thinking about it now that she'd said it so matter-of-factly.

She stopped what she was doing to look at him. "Because it's personal? Because I don't want to endure questions and comments and nosy friends—book club friends, I might add—asking how things are going, if we're moving in together, it we're committed, etcetera. They're all in happy relationships that are headed toward marriage and babies and all that. This is an agreement to scratch each other's itch for as long as we want to, right?"

It sounded empty when she put it that way, but that's what he wanted. "Yes."

"Exactly. I want to have hot sex with you without questions or comments about said sex."

He dragged on his briefs. "You don't think they're going to notice if I stay overnight at your place?"

She shook her head. "No, because you aren't staying. You can leave when we're done."

He didn't like the way that made him feel, but he could hardly blame her for it. He'd been the one who'd set those expectations in the first place.

"You're forgetting something, honey. The cameras in the stairwell show arrivals and departures. Blaze will know I'm there even if nobody else does."

"Well, hell. Swear him to secrecy?"

"From Emma?"

She pursed her lips. "Guess that won't work. Emma won't want to keep it from Rory." She waved a hand. "We'll figure it out. Or maybe we'll be done by then anyway. Meaningless sex doesn't last long, right? Problem solved."

Damn, she was brutal. "And if we aren't done?"

"There's always your Yukon," she said with a grin.

The overhead bulb snapped to life, flooding the basement with more light than the lantern gave off. Daphne had put on her bra and shirt, leaving the tails hanging, but she hadn't put on underwear or shorts as she headed for the stairs with those garments in her hands.

"Where are you going half-dressed?"

She turned back to him. "Really, Kane?"

Her gaze dropped and his followed. A glistening trail of his semen ran down the inside of her thighs.

Fuck, that was hot. Made his dick swell again. Not that it'd ever stopped, but it'd been on the way down until that moment.

"Think we could convince them we had car trouble?" he asked. "Because I want you in my bed so I can take my time for round two."

"Sorry, hot stuff. You know as well as I do that's a suspicious excuse."

He sighed as he zipped his jeans and tugged his shirt over his head. She wasn't wrong.

"Okay, fine. Let's go to the Dawg and eat before we end up with a search party of nosy fuckers at the door."

Chapter Twenty-Two

Daphne was reeling inside. Outside, she was the picture of calm. Or so she hoped.

She'd finally gotten through Kane's barriers. And she wasn't exaggerating when she told herself it was the best sex of her life. Of course Kane knew his way around the lady bits. Not that he'd done much more than fuck her with his massive dick, but he'd known *how* to do it. Not every guy could say that.

She was wrecked from that encounter, and not only because of the physicality. She'd been too wet to be really hurt by anything they'd done, but her body knew it had just weathered a cyclone. Happily weathered, she might add.

Willing to do it again. She'd decided not to let him know that, however. Something told her to play it cool, maybe even hard to get, and Kane would keep coming back for more. Or so she hoped.

She was also reeling from what he'd told her about his marriage. She'd hurt for him when he'd said his wife had an affair, and she'd been angry too. Angry at a dead woman for making choices Daphne couldn't fathom. Kane was, at his core, protective and loyal. At least he was with his friends. And he was honest with the women he dated when he really didn't have to be. A lot of men wouldn't be so honest, but not Kane. He set expectations, even if she gave him hell about it being sexist thinking that women couldn't want the same thing he did from the encounter.

She thought of him returning from a deployment and being confronted by his wife's infidelity. By her lies.

When Daphne thought of her own lies, her chest squeezed tight. It wasn't the same thing, and she had no choice, but she didn't think Kane would appreciate knowing she wasn't who she said she was. That everything about her was a lie.

He was waiting for her in the living room when she reemerged from the bathroom, having cleaned herself up and put on her shorts again. He looked broody as he stared out at the remnants of the storm, the leaves and twigs that'd been blown everywhere, and she wondered if he was about to give her the *I'm-sorry-but-we-can't-do-this-again* speech.

Instead, his gaze slid over her with raw appreciation. Thank God.

"Best not look at me that way at the Dawg," she said, sashaying over to where he stood, telling herself to be bold and confident.

He hooked an arm around her waist and tugged her against him. Then he dropped his mouth to hers and kissed her until her body started to melt. So far, so good.

He steadied her when he let her go. If he hadn't, her knees might have collapsed.

"What was that for?" she asked.

"Does it have to be for anything?"

"No. But you spent so long pretending not to be interested in me. Guess I expect that Kane to reappear."

"Genie's out of the bottle, babe. At least with us."

She caressed his cheek because she could. "I know this is temporary. I can't imagine what you went through, and I understand why you don't want to fall in love again."

He pressed his hand to hers, holding it against his face. "I don't want you to get hurt, Sunshine."

Her heart squeezed. "I know that, and I appreciate it. I'm fine."

She wasn't fine, not really, because everything about Kane Fox only made her want him more. She wanted to be the one who soothed him, held him, spent time tangled in the sheets with him. She wanted to talk to him endlessly, and she wanted to be the one he turned to when he needed someone to listen to him or just be there for him.

"You ready?" he asked. When she nodded, he held the front door for her and then ushered her to the passenger side of his SUV. "No sense taking two vehicles when you're coming back here tonight. And I've got the cameras for the security system in the back. I can install it after dinner."

"Or tomorrow," she said, sliding a hand to his crotch and caressing him. Why not be bold? Why not take everything she could get? "In case you'd like to screw me on a bed instead of putting screws into the wall."

She loved the look on his face, the need reflected there. And his growl as he said, "I can do both, Sunshine."

They didn't talk about much on the way to the Dawg, mostly the weather and the way the storm had blown through and left downed branches and bits of debris. The decorations for the Independence Day celebration were a little tattered as they headed into town, but the committee would no doubt be out in force tomorrow, fixing and replacing as needed.

The parking lot was full when he turned in and found a spot on the outer edge. It was still daylight, but that didn't stop Kane from leaning over, hooking a hand behind her neck, and fusing his mouth to hers for a kiss that had her worried about her panties again.

"What was that for?" she asked when he let her go.

He gave her a cocky grin that hitched her heart. "Because I could. Because I don't have to pretend I don't want to anymore. At least with you."

She couldn't stop the goofy smile that creased her face. "I'm glad you aren't pretending anymore either."

They didn't hold hands as they crossed the parking lot, but she was very aware of him beside her, of the way his fingers skimmed over hers as they walked, the way they went to the small of her back as she went up the stairs in front of him.

When they walked into the Dawg, a cheer went up from their table. "Finally," Rory said. "I'm starving."

She was sitting beside Chance, clearly taking time off her feet and letting others handle the bar. Extraordinary for a Friday.

"I'm sorry," Daphne said, guilt flaring that they'd kept a pregnant woman waiting. "You should have ordered."

"Don't listen to this woman." Chance looped an arm around Rory and pulled her closer. "She just polished off half a basket of cheese sticks. She is *not* starving."

Rory stuck out her tongue at him. "You do not know that, Studly McStudmuffin. Because you didn't get knocked up, I did. I could eat a big slab of beef with some au jus sauce and a basket of yeast rolls."

"Lucky for you it's Friday," Chance said before kissing her forehead.

A bolt of envy took a path through Daphne's heart. Getting laid was one thing. Having someone love you and protect you and want nothing but the best for you was something even better. She would never get that with Kane. He wasn't capable of it, thanks to his wife.

Anger flared deep inside but she smashed it down. What good did it do? The woman was dead and gone, and Daphne had no right to judge her for her decisions when Daphne had never spent a moment in her shoes.

But she wanted to judge her. Wanted to hate her for causing a good man so much pain.

Hard to hate someone who'd been murdered for her mistake, though.

Kane pulled out a chair and waited. It took Daphne a second to realize it was for her. "Thank you," she murmured.

Rory and Emma exchanged a look as she sat. Callie joined a moment later. Daphne's face grew hot as she glared at her three friends. They arched eyebrows. She arched hers back.

Rory waggled hers and bumped Emma. Daphne rolled her eyes, but the heat in her cheeks didn't diminish.

"Oh for fuck's sake," Alex groaned, his gaze on something at the back of the building. Daphne turned her head, along with everyone else who wasn't facing that direction, in time to see Diana Corbin and another man walk in. This man wasn't one she'd seen with the FBI agent before.

He was good-looking, lean, with a look that said he was in law enforcement too. Daphne recognized those types because she'd been trained from an early age to notice the tells. The way someone's eyes methodically catalogued a room, looking for entrances, exits, and vulnerable positions. Looking for trouble. Enforcers had their own way of behaving. Military and law enforcement another. It was in how they observed the room, how they carried themselves.

Enforcers had firepower, legal or not. Law enforcement

and military usually had ingrained skills and a sense of duty.

Her gaze slipped to the pretty FBI agent. There was something about Diana Corbin that made Daphne's insides tighten. She always felt as if the woman could see right through her. As if she knew something wasn't right but didn't really care because it didn't affect her current case. But if Diana had any idea who Daphne really was, her priority list might change.

Something Daphne wanted to prevent at all costs. The FBI had sniffed around Crescent City Armory and The Diamond Queen before, but they'd never found anything to bring her father down.

The memory card in her bag at the range had the potential to be explosive. She wondered what someone like Diana could do with that information. It was enough to bury her father and Jackson, but only if nobody in the FBI was on the take and willing to turn a blind eye to the O'Malleys.

But how to know who was good and who wasn't? Even if Diana Corbin was a good agent, once the New Orleans branch got involved, things could change. Probably would change. And Daphne would have gambled and lost.

"Looks like she's not coming over," Callie said. "Maybe she's on a date."

If Daphne hadn't been looking at Alex at that very moment, she might not have seen it. That subtle tic of his jaw, the hardening of his eyes. He always looked exasperated by Agent Corbin, but was he attracted to her too?

Daphne glanced at Diana and her companion. The woman was beautiful in a classic way. She wasn't gorgeous in the way that made you do a double take, but she had that tall, elegant manner that drew eyes. Her hair was always smooth, always pulled back in a ponytail or a low bun. Tonight it was loose, hanging about halfway down her back, a pale glossy blond that she'd parted in the middle and tucked behind her ears. She also had a red lip going, which wasn't typical.

"Definitely a date," Daphne said, turning to watch Alex again.

"How do you know?" Kane asked.

"Loose hair, red lips, and she's wearing jeans. Fitted and dark, like a casual version of her pants suits, but still jeans."

"Huh," Kane said. "Guess you're right."

Alex picked up his beer and took a drink. "Good. Means she won't be strutting over here to annoy us."

Daphne bit the inside of her lip to keep from laughing. She was fairly certain Diana Corbin didn't strut anywhere.

Amber arrived to take orders. Everyone ordered prime rib. Daphne got a glass of white wine since she wasn't driving. For the first time in weeks, she felt as if the tension she'd been carrying like a weighted blanket had melted away, at least for a little while. A good orgasm—two, in fact —could do that for a person.

Beneath the table, Kane's leg brushed against hers. The first time it happened, she thought it was an accident. The third time, she turned her head casually to look at him. He did not stop talking to Ethan across the table, but he brushed her leg again and she knew he'd done it on purpose.

Which wasn't a problem except that every time he did it, a bolt of electricity zapped along her nerve endings and into her core, leaving her aching and wanting.

Two could play that game.

She kicked out of her sandal and put the bottom of her foot on his leg, rubbed it casually. She felt his body tighten and she refrained from laughing.

"Oh look, there's Paisley," Callie said. "Paisley!"

The librarian turned. Her gaze skimmed over them and it seemed as if she looked pained for a moment, but she waved. Daphne joined the other women in waving her over to join them, but Paisley shook her head apologetically and pointed at her wrist as if to lament the time. Then she was gone, grabbing a To Go bag from the bar and heading for the door like there was a lion nipping at her heels.

Daphne frowned. Paisley had been so friendly and sweet when they'd had book club at the library a few nights ago. She was new in town, learning her way around, and they'd asked her to join them permanently. She'd explained she had a four-year-old daughter at home so she might have trouble with meetings sometimes, but they'd all agreed the book club was meant to be fun and they'd make it work. Paisley had said yes.

Could be a child care issue that had her running out without coming over to say hello but it seemed more abrupt than Daphne would have expected from someone as chatty as Paisley.

By the time they got their food, ate, and spent time talking, it was almost eight o'clock. A country band was coming on at nine and Rory tried to get everyone to stay for it, but Kane shook his head.

"Can't. Gotta install Daphne's security system."

"Is that what they're calling it now?" Rory said with a lift of her eyebrows.

"Cute. Daph, you coming to help?" he asked, giving her a significant look.

"I guess I have to since you're doing me a favor."

With many apologies to Rory for missing the band and lingering goodbyes because nobody in the south ever left the first time they said they were going, they finally walked out of the Dawg and over to Kane's Yukon to get the equipment.

"Oh, I'm so glad I ran into you again," Colleen Wright said as they walked past the back patio of her shop.

They stopped and she glided over in a cloud of incense and cigarette smoke. Reba was sitting at the small patio table, a mug in her hand. She waved and Daphne waved back.

"I wanted to give you this, my dear," Colleen said, taking Daphne's hand and pressing something hard into it.

Daphne looked at the object on her palm. It was a shiny black crystal with a silver chain.

Colleen explained. "I didn't think you were going to come in for one of my protective crystals but I knew you needed one, so please accept this as a gift. Black tourmaline will help to keep you safe from negative energy."

Daphne's heart jumped into a higher gear. "Thank you. But why do you think I need it?"

"I don't know, but my spirit guide tells me you do. And it's my duty to provide that which I can."

Kane slid an arm around her and anchored her to his side. Her body had become strangely cold but his warmth helped. "Daphne's safe with me," he said. "I won't let her come to harm."

Colleen smiled indulgently. "I know. But think of this as an extra layer. Nothing more. I'll let you kids get on with whatever you were doing. Don't forget the cemetery tour tomorrow night. We start at nine p.m. sharp. Reba's testing the kombucha now. Free samples before the tour for all guests!"

Kane guided her toward the Yukon while Colleen returned to her patio and Reba. Daphne clutched the black tourmaline in her hand, her mind throwing increasingly worrisome scenarios her way. When they reached the

Yukon and Kane unlocked it to retrieve the gear, Daphne slipped the necklace over her head. The chain was longer than she'd thought and the crystal dangled almost between her breasts.

"Why do you think she's so convinced I need a crystal?"

Kane sighed as he hefted the bag and shut the door. "Honestly? She probably knows something happened because she watches everything that goes on in this parking lot. She might have seen Ethan arriving the other night, seen us leave soon after. The woman isn't stupid and she can put two and two together. As for why she gave you the crystal?" He shrugged. "Maybe she wants you to pay for the cemetery tour, or tell people about it, or tell them about the crystal. I don't know. Or it could just be that she's trying to be helpful and thinks this is the way."

Daphne took the crystal between her fingers and rubbed it. "Probably right. It's pretty though. Could have been something huge and ugly, I guess."

"Looks nice on you."

"You're just saying that because of where it lays."

He put a hand to his chest and feigned shock. "Are you suggesting I like it because it's nearly between those perfect breasts of yours?"

"Pretty much."

He grinned. "Doesn't hurt, I'll admit."

He lifted his head to look around the parking lot, and then bent and kissed her, his hand sliding around to cup her ass and give it a squeeze before he pulled away.

"C'mon, let's get upstairs," he said. "I need to get this system set up so I can get you naked again."

Chapter Twenty-Three

For a man who'd been telling himself for months that Daphne was off limits, touching her for the first time had opened a floodgate of need inside.

Kane didn't know where this aching desire was coming from, but suppressing it wasn't an option. Not anymore.

He'd wanted so badly to put his arm across the back of her chair at dinner, the way Blaze, Seth, and Chance had with their women. He'd wanted to lean into her, whisper something in her ear, and have her laugh at a joke only they shared.

And he *shouldn't* want that. It was self-destructive and unfair, because he was never going to be the kind of man who could relax into a relationship and think he'd found happiness forever and ever, amen. Daphne and her friends were into reading romance novels where true love reigned. Once the Fae prince—or whatever—chose you, you were together for life.

Yeah, it didn't work that way. He knew from experience. He'd thought he had that with Hannah, but human beings were fallible and unbreakable bonds were fiction.

Didn't mean he wasn't going to enjoy himself when they were alone, though.

He unlocked her apartment door—it was definitely locked—and stepped inside first. He didn't expect there to be anyone waiting, and there wasn't. Daphne followed him in and closed the door.

He meant to be good and install the cameras, set up the system on her phone, show her how it worked, then strip those shorts off and bury himself inside her again.

Not what happened, though. The instant the door was closed, Kane dropped the duffel he'd been carrying and dragged her into his arms. Sitting beside her, touching her, smelling her, wanting her, had driven him crazy for the past couple of hours.

He wasn't waiting a moment longer. Didn't want to. Didn't *have* to.

His mouth dropped to hers, his tongue spearing into her mouth, and all the tightness inside him eased. She wrapped her arms around his neck as he skimmed her body with his palms. He had her shorts off in moments. He thought about freeing himself and taking her right there, against the door, but instead he picked her up and carried her to the kitchen island.

When he set her naked ass down on it, she swore at him. "Fuck, Kane, this granite is *cold*."

"Gonna fix that, babe," he said, pushing her knees apart and dropping to slide his tongue into that heavenly space between her legs.

"Oh my God," she gasped, fisting her fingers in his hair and holding him against her.

He put her legs over his shoulders and then tasted her thoroughly, stroking his tongue into sensitive places, toying with pressure and technique. Daphne squirmed beneath him, having given up holding his head and fallen backward onto the island, her entire body laid out before him like a gorgeous feast.

He took full advantage, tasting her, driving her wild as her body trembled and soft moans issued from her throat. Then he added two fingers to the mix, sliding them into her slick, smooth channel, pressing deep and crooking them to apply pressure inside.

If her sharp cry hadn't alerted him to the orgasm slamming into her, the way her pussy clamped down on his fingers would have. Her walls rippled around him, her body trembling harder than before.

"Kane," she moaned, her body still coming apart.

His dick was hard, throbbing, aching to be inside her, but he made himself wait. He needed her to come again, to listen to the beautiful sound of his name on her lips when she did. He wanted to take his time with her, stoke her passion, make her so hot she pleaded with him to let her come.

He did none of those things. He didn't do them because he had a sudden realization there was no patience, no waiting. Not with her.

He freed his cock, positioned himself, and slammed home. A groan escaped him when he was seated to the hilt inside her. Her legs wrapped around him, anchoring him. His heart throbbed a million miles an hour as he gazed down at the woman on the island. Her red hair spilled over the granite and her skin was rosy. He unbuttoned her shirt and tugged her bra cups down to reveal her nipples so he could suck them while he pumped into her.

It didn't take long before she was moaning again, before her walls clamped down on him. He sucked a nipple into his mouth, tugging firmly, and Daphne imploded with another sharp cry, her legs tightening around him. Not enough to stop him from moving, though.

He loved the way she felt surrounding him, the silky softness of her walls. It'd been years since he'd gone bare inside a woman. Maybe he shouldn't have done it with her, but when she'd said she had an IUD, he'd wanted nothing more than to be inside her with nothing between them.

Maybe that's what made the sex with her feel so fucking fantastic. It wasn't the same with her as it'd been with others. It was something more.

He shook his head to clear it. It couldn't be *more*. Sex was sex.

Still, his brain insisted this was different. Better. More intense.

He bent to kiss her, to quiet the chaos in his head. Her tongue speared into his mouth, her fingers raking his shoulders, and his balls tightened. He could hold off, quiet the churning, build up again slowly. But he didn't want to. He wanted to feel everything now.

He cupped her ass with one hand, angled his hips, and drove himself home. Electricity sizzled through him, his release exploding as he pumped into her twice more, draining his balls and his strength as he came hard inside her.

He lay with his torso on hers, his cheek against her neck, breathing hard and feeling like he'd just done twenty miles in full pack. He was drained and energized at the same time. He wanted to scoop her into his arms and take her to her room, lay her on the bed, and cuddle up beside her for hours.

He didn't do it, though. Instead, he kissed her again, then stood and pulled her upright on the island. She wrapped her arms and legs around him, and he dropped his mouth to her collar bone, tasted the salt of her skin.

"Much as I'd like to stay right here, there's work to do."

"Mmm," she said, stretching against him like a cat. "I suppose you have some screwing to do that doesn't involve me."

"True. But once it's done, it's done. Then I'll focus on you again."

"Sounds like a plan."

He stepped back and tucked himself away, zipped his jeans. Daphne hopped down and strolled toward her bedroom, her ass bare. He couldn't tear his gaze away until she was out of sight. Then he sighed, shook his head as if to ask what he'd gotten himself into, and went to retrieve the duffel he'd dropped. Something slid across the floor when he picked the bag up.

He frowned as he bent to pick it up. It was a playing card, ornate, with a two-headed queen and a diamond. It wasn't the typical playing card from a box store pack, but a version he'd never seen before. He turned it over. The back design was black with a fleur-de-lis in gold.

Daphne strolled back into the open living area wearing jeans this time, her shirt buttoned and tied in a knot at her waist. Her red hair was loose and flowing and she had a smile on her face that made his heart squeeze.

"You lose a playing card, babe?" he asked her as she approached.

The smile faded, replaced by a wary look. "What? No. Why?"

He held up the card. "This was on the floor near the door."

All the color drained from her face. He moved to steady her before she fainted. Not that he knew she would, but with the way the blood left her face, he had no doubt it'd made her light-headed. He steered her to the nearest chair and sat her down on it.

He placed the card on the table beside her. She stared at it but didn't touch it. A tear slid down her cheek before she raised her head to gaze at him.

"I'm sorry, Kane. So sorry. B-but I need your help one more time." She swallowed, clasped her shaking hands in her lap. "I need to leave town. Now."

Chapter Twenty-Four

They'd found her. Her father. Jackson. They knew where she was and they were coming for her. They wanted her to know she couldn't run far enough, couldn't hide forever. The card was a warning, and a promise. It was also a giant fuck you because they didn't believe she could escape them again.

But she wasn't going to stay in Sutton's Creek like a lamb to the slaughter and let them take her easily. No fucking way. She had to *go*. She'd figure it out as she went, but staying was not an option.

She started to surge to her feet, intent on grabbing a few things and getting the hell out. Going back to the farm, getting her bag, talking Kane into taking her to the range so she could retrieve the memory card, and then disappearing into the night.

But Kane stopped her with a hand on her shoulder. Held her firm so she couldn't stand. She thought about fighting him, but what good would it do? He knew all the moves because he taught them. She might have the element of surprise on her side, but mostly all she'd do is piss him off.

"You need to tell me what this is," he said, nodding at the card on the table. "And you need to tell me why you're terrified. Who left this for you? What does it mean?"

She dragged in a breath, her mind racing with plans—and terror. "I can't. Not here. We need to go, Kane. Before they find me."

"Who?"

She surged to her feet. He didn't stop her this time. "Are you listening to me? We need to go before they get here. I'll tell you on the way back to the farm."

His expression was a mix of anger, frustration, and resignation. "Okay, fine. At least tell me what I might be facing from here to the parking lot."

Her heart skipped. "Oh, God. I didn't think of that."

And she should have. Jackson might be waiting, intending to trap her. He'd have his enforcers, and they'd be armed to the teeth.

"It's my job to think of those things." He took out his phone and turned away from her. A moment later, he was talking to somebody. "Hey. Got a situation here at Daphne's place. Gonna need backup to get her to the vehicle and back to the farm… No, nobody here, but I don't know if they're watching the place… Okay, great. Thanks."

When he turned back to her, gone were all traces of the man who'd been playful and fun earlier. "The guys are going to check out the parking lot, see if anybody's out there. Ethan and Alex will follow us back to the farm, make sure nobody else does."

She could breathe again, but barely. She nodded, unable to find her voice at the moment.

Kane made her wait while he checked the hallway,

then he returned for her and they left the apartment, locking it behind them and heading down three flights of stairs. When they got to the bottom, he made her wait until his phone pinged with a text. Then they went outside to find Ethan's truck sitting at the bottom of the steps. Kane hustled her into the passenger seat, tossed his bag in the backseat, and went around to change places with Ethan. He handed Ethan his keys to the Yukon and then they were heading out of the parking lot and back to the range.

"Start talking, Sunshine," Kane growled.

She thought about lying, making something up he'd believe, but she was tired. So tired of lying and running and looking over her shoulder. Tired of hoping for more and believing she didn't deserve it. She'd finally gotten something good—him—and now it was over before it'd really started.

"Before I do, I need you to know it's dangerous. These are dangerous people, Kane, and I don't want anything to happen to you or the guys. I don't want Emma or Rory or Callie or Nikki to be in their crosshairs. I don't want *any* of you hurt, so you really just need to let me grab my things and disappear."

His hands flexed on the wheel. "You seem to think you have a choice. You don't. If I know what's going on, there's every chance I can help you. And if I can't, if leaving is the best thing for you, then I'll help you do that."

Daphne bowed her head and covered her face with her hands. Tears pressed hard behind her eyes, clogged her throat, but she refused to cry. If anything happened to him, if Jackson hurt him…

Stop.

Kane wasn't helpless or clueless. He was a man who'd served his country, who'd seen combat, and who could defend himself if he knew what he was facing.

She lifted her head, swallowed down her tears, and turned to look at him. She wanted to watch him when she told him who she was. Wanted to see the disgust and anger she knew she'd find there. She needed to see it to stop her heart from bleeding. Her stupid, stupid heart that'd loved this man from almost the first moment she'd seen him. He was going to hate her, and she wasn't about to shield herself from it. It was the only way to get over the heartbreak.

"You'll be glad to hear this part. I'm not twenty-three. I'm twenty-eight. No cradle robbing for you. How awesome is that?"

He didn't look at her but his body tightened.

"My name is Josephine O'Malley. Josie." Her throat ached. It felt so strange to say it. To say the name she no longer associated herself with. "I'm a woman whose father runs a criminal empire, whose brother is a psychopath, and I was part of that empire until recently. I've laundered money, accepted protection payments, and benefited from money earned off the blood, sweat, and freedom of others. I guess you could say I'm a mafia princess. Mafia in this case being Irish and Southern rather than Italian."

If he was shocked, he didn't let it show. "Who left the playing card?"

"I don't know. Maybe Jackson—that's my brother. It's not quite his style to warn me first, but he's also a psycho who likes to terrorize people."

He shook his head. "The fucking fleur-de-lis. Crescent City Armory, right? John O'Malley is your father?"

"Bingo," she said, folding her arms over her body as a chill swept through her.

"Fader?"

"I don't know him. But he thought I looked familiar, and then Seth said he might be a customer of my father's.

I guess he is since they found me. He must have called Jackson or my father and told them he'd spotted me." She sucked in a breath. "It was stupid to work in a range. I should have left months ago. I never intended to stay anywhere very long because I know they're looking for me. I've endangered all of you by being here."

"Not worried about your brother or your dad. But you know what? You should have fucking told me—told all of us—a long time ago. Knowing what we're facing is critical to mission planning. We never, ever got on a plane without knowing what we were up against. Even when we didn't know everything, we knew *something.* Because our commanders weren't going to let us go blindly into a fight we couldn't understand. Surest way to get killed. But you know what? They respected us—our training, our talent, our worth to the fucking United States Army. They briefed us and we got the job done."

She'd never seen Kane angry. She'd seen him annoyed, amused, intense, focused, and determined. She'd probably seen a hundred shades of those emotions and the little ones in between. But real anger? No, never.

Until now.

"If you'd told us weeks ago, we'd have been prepared for this kind of shit. We could have done something to keep you safe. Now we have to defend you from a threat we didn't see coming."

Her heart squeezed—both at his anger and at the idea he still intended to protect her. "I couldn't tell you. Maybe I should have, but you have to understand how I was raised. What I've done—Jesus, I've betrayed them all. The family. Everything they stand for. And yet the training is ingrained in me. O'Malleys don't talk. Because we know what happens when people talk. They die. *I* would die because my father is that ruthless." She dragged in a breath. "He's killed people, Kane. When he suspected one of his men was skimming profits, dear old Dad ordered his death—and the deaths of his family. Jackson personally took care of it. He won't hesitate to eliminate all of you because you helped me." She shook her head. "I wasn't ever going to tell any of you the truth because I didn't want you to know. I planned to leave before they found me."

"Yeah, but you didn't, did you? And now you've got a fucking playing card under your door and you're terrified." He swore softly. She didn't say anything because what was there to say?

They rode in silence for a few minutes. But he wasn't done. She'd known he wasn't. He'd been cooling off before he continued.

"What's the meaning of the queen of diamonds? Or does it mean anything?"

"It's me. I ran a nightclub in New Orleans called The Diamond Queen. I *was* its queen. Everybody who was anybody frequented my club. My dad did business there when he wasn't doing it at the armory, making deals, meeting clients. Jackson…" She shuddered. It was Jackson who'd started her down this path. "He was doing things I didn't know about, things I didn't approve of. When I found out… Well, too little too late, I guess. But I decided I had to get out."

"Anything else you need to tell me?"

Her heart was in her throat, her stomach in her shoes, and everything felt surreal. But she'd come this far. In for a penny, in for a pound, as John O'Malley always said.

"I was my father's accountant. I kept the books—both sets—while also running the nightclub. And I copied every-thing before I left. I have a memory card with all the infor-mation from my father's businesses." She pulled in a breath, her body shivering. "It would be enough to bury anybody else, but he has contacts in the police department. Probably has them in a few other agencies as well. I could never be certain so I never did anything with it. If I were to trust the wrong person…"

She didn't have to tell him what would happen. By now, he understood.

"Your father wants the card back."

"Yes. And me too, I expect. I'm too dangerous to let walk free. I know things—and I will always know them."

That was the truth of it. She had the information on a memory card that she could share with law enforcement, if she ever trusted them enough, but she also had it in her head. She knew the books because she'd kept the books. She was a loose cannon so far as her father was concerned.

He would want her back so he could punish her. Then he would silence her permanently.

They reached the farm and Kane drove up to the house and parked. Ethan and Alex parked beside them.

"Wait," Kane commanded when she unclipped her seat belt. Ethan and Alex exited their vehicles. She couldn't see where they went but they reappeared a few minutes later, tucking weapons into holsters and nodding at Kane.

"Let's go," he said.

They went inside the house with its beautiful original features she found so charming, but this time it didn't seem welcoming the way it had before. She stood with her arms folded over her body, watching the three men warily. Kane was angry with her. Ethan and Alex would be too once the truth spilled. They would despise her, and it surprised her to realize how much that was going to hurt.

"Beers?" Ethan asked.

"Hell, yeah," Kane replied. "Daphne?"

"Um, yes. Please."

Alex took a seat, kicking one leg over the other at his ankles and slouching into the chair like somebody who didn't give a fuck about anything. "If somebody would like to tell me what's going on, I'm all ears."

Ethan returned with the beers, passed them around. Daphne sank onto the edge of the couch, but she couldn't relax. Kane didn't sit. He hovered. Ethan stood nearby, waiting.

"You want to tell him or do I?" Kane said.

The easy way out was to let him do it. But it was also the coward's way, and these guys had done too much for her. The least she could do was tell them something they wanted to know before she damned herself in their eyes.

"I know where the diamond on your Glock trigger comes from."

She heard Kane's intake of breath and knew he'd put two and two together. One more thing to be pissed at her about since she could have saved him from spending so much time searching for an answer.

"Go on," Alex said.

"John O'Malley of Crescent City Armory traffics in illegal weapons. He's known for the quality of his goods, and his mods are top notch. The legal weapons are stamped with the fleur-de-lis, his official mark. But his other work gets a diamond pattern. It's basic, untraceable, and denotes a certain quality of the goods. Not everything gets that diamond. Only weapons to very select clients. It's somewhat of a status symbol in the criminal underworld. Can others fake the diamond? Sure. And it's possible that one isn't his mark, that somebody else is faking it for reasons of their own. But a diamond stamped in a hidden location is an O'Malley mark. I can't prove it, but I know it."

Many things were on the memory card, but proof of

the diamond wasn't one of them. It wasn't like her father had a playbook on how to be a crime king. He just had records of the financial aspect of his businesses.

Alex exchanged a look with Kane. "And you know this how?"

"Because I'm Josie O'Malley. John's daughter."

Ethan's eyes widened a fraction. Alex only arched an eyebrow.

"You're his daughter," he repeated. "Did he send you here?"

That question took her aback. "Why would he do that? I never heard of your range until I got to Sutton's Creek. And no, he didn't send me. I left because—"

Her throat tightened and she took a big swallow of her beer, let it scald its way down her throat. Dammit, she should have grabbed the Scotch before they left the apartment.

"I left because my brother, quite possibly with my father's approval, started trafficking vulnerable people into prostitution—mostly women, though some young men too. Undocumented immigrants, people with forged papers, women in bad situations. Teenage girls and boys as well, lured by a promise of a better life with people who care. But they don't care. They only care about money, and by then it's too late to escape. They're trapped. Drugged, trapped, forced into submission. Some are sold, others put into the trade."

She pressed a hand to her mouth to stop the sudden sob that clogged her throat. She'd held onto this knowledge for months, hating herself for not doing anything but also not knowing who to trust with the information. Who to tell so they could put an end to it. One wrong move and she'd be dead. Then those people would never be free.

Kane's hand closed over her shoulder, squeezing. She'd

thought she was out in the cold, forever cut off from any kindness he had to offer, but he was giving it to her anyway.

"We're going to help you, Daphne. We won't let them take you."

Those few words gave her hope. And yet she despaired, too. Her father was powerful. Maybe not here, but his power wasn't solely concentrated in New Orleans. His influence could reach this far, do things to these men she cared about.

Bad things.

No way could she sit by and watch it happen.

"I'm not going back," she said, straightening her spine. "But I can't stay here either. I can't endanger all of you any more than I already have. I can be on my way tonight. All I ask is you keep it a secret as long as possible."

Alex and Ethan gave her the same look that Kane had. A look that said *honey, please.* As if they weren't afraid of anyone or anything. As if they were positive they could control the situation and she was the one overreacting.

"I'm not going to pretend this isn't inconvenient," Alex said, his voice a low, lazy drawl. "It would have been nice to know the details much, much earlier. But we can and we will protect you. It's what we do. Kane, text the others. Tell them we need a strategy meeting first thing in the morning. Oh-six-hundred."

Daphne gaped. They weren't listening to her. They were treating this like a consultation in Research Park when the men coming for her were cold-blooded enforcers for the O'Malley empire. It wasn't the same thing at all. She shot to her feet and stared the three of them down.

"I can't let you risk your lives for me. You don't understand what's going on here. My father is ruthless. My brother is a psychotic asshole who delights in tormenting people. If he isn't here yet, he's coming. And he won't care who he harms—or kills—to get his way. You can't install a security system and take turns patrolling in the dark, or whatever it is you do, and keep me safe. You just can't. Because Jackson and his enforcers do not play fair or show mercy. They will kill all of you, and anyone you care about."

Kane took her by the shoulders and turned her to face him. He didn't look in the least bit alarmed by what she'd said. He looked… indulgent?

"Listen to me. Your fear for us is beyond adorable. I'm touched. The guys are touched. But unless your brother and his enforcers have HALOed into enemy territory with nothing but a few light weapons and packs, with the objective to extract hostages or kill terrorists or kidnap enemy commanders—and have done it repeatedly, over a period of years, and lived to tell about it—then no, we aren't worried about a group of highly armed assholes—and no doubt deadly accurate ones, if your shooting is anything to go by. But they can't have suffered the deprivation, the battles, the training, the endless working to be the best of the best that the six of us have endured. Your shooting is fucking amazing, and I'm sure your brother is the same. Maybe even the men with him. But how many pitched battles have they engaged in, huh? Or is it all superior numbers and firepower intimidating and killing people who can't fight back?"

Daphne stared at him as hope tried to flare again. She forced her brain back to the questions. "Battles? With enemy fighters equally equipped?"

"Yes. How many?"

"I… Well, it has to be zero. Battles are not how it works. A crime boss sends in his enforcers to intimidate or kill. There might occasionally be a battle for territory, but it's not a battle in the sense you're talking about with two sides meeting to fight it out. So, zero battles with enemy fighters. An encounter with return fire a couple of times a year, maybe."

Kane grinned. "I didn't really expect a detailed answer, but that's fucking brilliant. Zero battles with enemy fighters. Do you see why we aren't scared of these dicks now?"

The hope inside her kindled into a small flame. She tried to temper it with reality. "Yes, I think so. But it doesn't solve the problem, not really. Once they know I'm here, they won't stop trying to get to me. You won't ever be safe."

"Not true, honey. Tell them the rest of it. The accounting, the memory card. What you know."

"Memory card?" Alex said, perking up. "That sounds promising. Tell me more."

Chapter Twenty-Five

KANE DIDN'T SLEEP WELL, BUT HE DIDN'T EXPECT THAT Daphne had either. They met in the kitchen a few minutes after five in the morning. He was pouring coffee when she walked in and then halted like a deer in headlights. She took a step back as if she intended to sneak out.

"It's too late. I see you."

She didn't move for a second but then she sighed and walked in. She was wearing a T-shirt and shorts and he resolutely did not look at her legs. Looking at her legs would make him think of how they'd felt wrapped around him, and he definitely didn't want to do that. Shit was too complicated for those thoughts right now.

"I just wanted to grab some coffee. I smelled it, but I thought you'd gone for your run."

"Today's not a run day."

Not to mention he needed to stick close to her now that she was a target. Last night, after she'd told Ghost about the memory card and he'd asked a bunch of questions, they'd determined that Daphne needed to stay at the farm for the time being. Both houses were secure, and there were three special operators on the premises. Blaze, Chance, and Seth could be brought back if needed, but Kane, Ethan, and Ghost were enough for the moment.

Last night had been quiet, but he'd expected nothing less. Whoever had slipped the card under her door wasn't currently planning a full frontal assault on a farm. Not yet anyway.

Kane poured coffee into a mug, added cream, and slid it toward her on the counter. She picked it up, cupping both hands around it as if she needed the warmth, and took a sip.

"Thank you."

"You're welcome."

Silence descended between them.

"I'm sorry, Kane. For everything."

He turned to face her, his heart and head warring. She looked vulnerable and wary. And young, though she was twenty-eight. Five years older than he'd thought she was, but she easily looked younger.

He wanted to wrap her in his arms and keep her close. He was also angry, and he was definitely feeling betrayed that she hadn't trusted him enough to tell him the truth. It wasn't the same as Hannah, he knew that. Hannah had been his wife, committed to him, and he to her. He had no such relationship with Daphne.

Yet it still hurt that she'd kept such a monumental truth from him. And it was worse than Hannah's deception in at least one way. Daphne *knew* she was being hunted by ruthless men, and she'd kept it from everyone. Endangering them, yes. But endangering herself far more.

"You said that before," he clipped out.

"I know, but I'm not sure I can say it enough." She twisted the mug in her hands. "I'm still not sure this is a good idea, but I appreciate that you want to protect me. I'm not sure I deserve it though."

His gut clenched that she could think that way. "You deserve it. Why wouldn't you?"

"Because I'm one of them. I'm an O'Malley." Her voice was barely more than a whisper.

The urge to pull her to him was strong. He resisted. "But are you really?"

She looked shocked. She'd told them last night that she wanted to be called Daphne, which was her middle name. He was glad because he couldn't see her as a Josie no matter how he tried. She still did, though, down deep where it counted. This conversation was proof of it.

"Are you suggesting I'm lying?"

"Fuck no, I'm not. But if you were truly one of them, if you believed what they believe, you'd still be there. You left, Daphne. You stole important information and you left. Did you think they'd ever welcome you home with open arms if you wanted to go back? Or did you know you could never return because they'd kill you if you did? And not only that, they would presumably never stop hunting for you. You knew, and you left."

She shook her head. "I appreciate what you're trying to do, but I've been my father's accountant for the past six years. I've known what kind of shit he was involved in for a long time. Maybe I finally left, but that doesn't make me a decent person. Just means I found a line I couldn't cross."

He wanted to shake her. "Lines you can't cross are important distinctions. I've spent years serving my country, killing for my country when necessary, and I've had to make my peace with it. But there are always lines, and if I'd ever been asked to cross one, I was prepared to face the consequences of refusing. That's how you live with yourself."

Her lip trembled. "You make me sound heroic. But I'm not. I haven't managed to put a stop to anything Jackson and my father are doing. I ran, but I didn't use what I took because I'm a coward."

"You haven't used it *yet*. But you want to, right?"

"Yes."

"Then we'll make it happen. Alex told you last night that we would, and today we'll make a plan."

Her shoulders curved over, making her smaller. "I'm scared. You don't know what they're capable of. This whole thing could explode like a nuclear bomb, wrecking more than just my life. I don't want anyone else to suffer for my mistakes."

He sighed. He couldn't tell her what she wanted to hear. "Sure, there's a chance it'll go wrong. Every single time I went into enemy territory, I had to be prepared not to come back. Because it was always possible that our intel would be bad, or the enemy would know we were coming, or a million little hiccups that could've made the difference in living or dying. And I'm not saying it never went wrong. It did. Plenty. But I'm still here. My guys are still here." He tipped her chin up with a finger, forced her to meet his gaze. "Your choice is to fight or to run. If you run, you'll have to keep running for as long as you live. If you fight? You might just win."

She smiled tentatively, and his heart squeezed. "You're really good at pep talks, you know that?"

He dropped his finger from her soft skin. Touching her ignited the need inside him. He didn't want to need her.

"Part of the service. You want something to eat?" he asked, retreating to the familiar before she wrung an emotion out of him.

"Ethan said he was going for breakfast sandwiches from Clarence this morning. Before the meeting."

Kane scratched the back of his neck. "Yeah, forgot."

"Kane."

"Hmm?"

"You don't have to push me away. I already know that what we did yesterday will never happen again. You don't have to be awkward. I told you I could handle meaningless sex, and I can. Would it have been nice to keep exploring each other a bit more? Absolutely. But I lied to you about who I was, and it wasn't just a tiny lie but a big one. So you aren't interested anymore and I completely understand. Your history has to make lying abhorrent to you, and I get that."

He was rooted in place. She said the words so plainly, so certainly. He'd been feeling like he needed to keep his distance because he didn't know what the hell he was doing anymore. Every idea he'd ever had about not being the kind of man who had relationships started to blur at the edges when he was deep inside her, feeling more alive than he'd felt in ages.

And now that she was in danger? He would move mountains to protect her. Nobody was taking the light from those beautiful green eyes while he was still breathing. He'd take on the O'Malleys and all their enforcers. He'd never allow them to harm a hair on her pretty head.

When he was with her, he became a man who wanted the kind of love and acceptance he saw his teammates getting with their women. For months, he'd remained cynical deep inside while watching them together, thinking it could all fall apart if the team had to deploy elsewhere, if their lives weren't somewhat settled in Sutton's Creek. It could fall apart if the mission fell apart, if they failed in the goal to protect the top secret Athena Project, or if something went wrong and they became the fall guys for mission failure.

Ghost had told them in the beginning they wouldn't get support if they were caught. The president needed deniability and if Ghost Ops went down, they went down alone. Would Emma, Rory, or Callie stick around then? Would they stand by their men, be faithful and strong, and wait?

He didn't know the answer, but he'd started to think maybe it didn't matter. Maybe what mattered was the sense of belonging and love and togetherness you got when you gave yourself completely over to the relationship. Had he really done that with Hannah? Or had her loneliness stemmed from more than his missions?

He tried to think of the young man he'd been back then, full of bravado and testosterone and a sense of purpose that came from his job. His calling. Hannah had been second to the job for the five years they were married. They'd talked about him leaving the military, but he'd never really wanted to. She'd known it, too.

Guilt speared into him. It was the same old guilt as always, but tinged with a new color. The color of his own lack of faith. He'd felt guilty for not being there when she'd needed him most, for not knowing she'd been in a relationship with someone else, but he was also guilty for not *wanting* to change his life to make hers better. To make their lives together better. He'd said the right words, but he hadn't done the right thing.

Neither had she. But she wasn't alone in bearing responsibility for what'd happened between them.

"It's a big lie," he agreed, dragging himself back to the present. "Not saying I don't understand why you felt you had to keep something that big to yourself. And not saying I'm not mad about it either. Whether we're done or not? I don't know that yet."

"I… That's not what I thought you would say. Especially after, um, what you told me about your… uh…."

"Wife?" he finished because she was clearly uncomfortable saying it.

She nodded. "I realize we aren't in a relationship or anything, and there's no deep feeling involved, but a lie as big as mine… Well, I thought it was a dealbreaker."

No deep feeling? Maybe not, but there *was* feeling. That's what was killing him. He cared for her, and that was something he hadn't allowed himself to do in years.

"Trust me, I've been thinking about it. But you're right. We aren't in a relationship and you didn't promise to love me and then break that promise. That's next level shit, and that's not our level."

He could see the hurt in her eyes, but what else could he say? Until he figured it out for himself, he wasn't admitting to feeling anything for her other than the physical attraction he already felt.

She lifted her chin. "Understood."

"Need a refill?"

She glanced down at the mug in her hands. "Nope, I'm good. Need to get dressed anyway." Her smile was lopsided when she looked at him. "For the record, up until the moment you showed me the playing card, yesterday was the best day I've spent in Sutton's Creek. And they've all been pretty good, because I love my life here. Just so you know."

She turned on her heel and left him in the kitchen. He poured another cup of coffee and stared out the window at the dewy fields.

Yesterday was his best day in Sutton's Creek, too.

Chapter Twenty-Six

"You're up, Daphne."

It was a few minutes after six and Daphne was sitting at the table in the break room with all six of the One Shot Tactical men. Alex had suggested they convene in this room where there had hot coffee available and a fridge with drinks.

The range was closed until ten, so there wasn't any chance they'd be interrupted. Unless Jackson and his men decided to attack. But based on what Kane had said last night about battles, she was certain that wasn't going to happen. Jackson was a tough guy in the sense he had weapons and attitude, and he always went in with superior forces, but when she'd considered her brother's activities in terms of what Kane had told her these six men had done, it didn't compare.

Jackson wouldn't storm a gun range in full daylight to get to her. He wasn't that brave, or that stupid.

Good to his word, Ethan had hopped into his truck and gone to the Gas-n-Go for breakfast. The guys were busy chowing down. She'd only taken a bite out of hers because her stomach was tied in knots.

All six of them watched her patiently. Even Kane.

She took a deep breath and placed the memory card on the table in front of her, her heart pounding at seeing it there. Such a tiny thing. Explosive. And vulnerable too. She hadn't checked the information since right after she'd downloaded it. When she'd left New Orleans, she hadn't taken a computer because she didn't want to be traced.

And she hadn't bought one since arriving because she hadn't had the money at first. When she finally did, she no longer cared about having a laptop. She had the computer at work and that was enough. Her smart phone was a burner.

She simply trusted that the information was still there, still secure, because she hadn't done anything to compromise it.

She'd also brought her Glock in its soft-sided case, and she laid that on the table as well.

"You'll find the diamond stamped on the trigger guard. This gun has the same mod as the one you were researching. I have legal weapons, but I didn't want them traced if I got picked up for some reason. It's just another way for my father to find me. This one I took from my brother's office."

It'd been a source of contention that her father had made her give her brother office space in her building, but she knew why now. Trafficking women into sexual slavery was better done in the Quarter, in a night club setting, than a gun range. Easier to move them through. Easier to make them think they were being hired to work at the club.

"It probably went missing at some point before delivery to the dealer," she said. "My father has a network of spies, and he has paid agents on shipping vessels, in ports, and probably even in the factories of some of the manufacturers. The guns go missing, he eventually takes delivery at one warehouse or another, and if the client wants mods, they get done offsite from the armory. Everything that goes through the armory is legal—weapons, I mean. He's very careful about that."

"Jesus," Blaze said. "I thought we were meeting to discuss another incursion at your place—and now your father's an arms dealer?"

"We are," Alex replied. "This is the background story. There wasn't any reason to go into detail last night, so you get the story now."

"Sorry," Daphne said. "Yes, he is. Among other things. My real name is Josephine O'Malley. Daphne's my middle name. Bryant is an alias."

She proceeded to give them a quick summary of the story she'd already repeated twice before. Blaze, Chance, and Seth took it all in. Then Seth got up in the middle of his sandwich and left the room. He was back a few moments later with his laptop.

"Need to research. Carry on."

"That's pretty much it," she said. "My father is a crime boss, my brother is a psychotic nut he unleashes from time to time, and I stole evidence about all the O'Malley businesses. I worked for my father because that's what I was raised to do, but it doesn't excuse the fact I knew what he did wasn't entirely legal."

Seth was typing away on his keyboard, his sandwich forgotten for the moment. Daphne took a tiny bite of hers. It smelled good, and her stomach growled as the knots started to ease now that the truth was out there.

"Do we have any clue who left the playing card?" Chance asked.

Blaze dragged his phone out. "I can look over the past

few days of footage in the hallway. I'm guessing whoever it was timed it for when the workmen were there. Too many people coming and going to keep up with at that point. I've checked the door every night after work and it's been locked. But that wouldn't stop anybody from sliding a card beneath it."

"My initial thought was that it was my brother. Jackson. He's usually not so subtle though—unless he's toying with me. He might want to provoke me into running so he can get me away from all of you." She frowned, thinking. "I suppose Nathan Fader could have done it. I don't know why. If he's the one who told them where to find me, he wouldn't want to give me a heads up. At least I don't think so. Unless Jackson told him to do it so I'd try to leave town."

"I have the info on Fader's rental," Seth said. "The car's GPS places him in Huntsville on the day of the break-in. Redstone Gateway, to be precise. I'd like to get into those parking lot camera feeds," he growled half to himself. "But they changed the system after I broke in the last time. It'll take time to break in again."

Daphne glanced at the men surrounding the table. Not one of them seemed surprised that Seth was breaking into random camera feeds. Then again, it probably had something to do with Callie since she worked in one of the buildings in the complex.

Not that Fader had anything to do with the crap that'd happened to Callie, or the man who'd held a gun to Nikki's head and tried to steal classified information from Callie, but it had to bring up bad memories for him.

"So he didn't break into the apartment," Kane said. "Unless he left the car in Huntsville and found another way into town."

"Possible," Blaze said, "but he can't know what we're capable of. So why go to the trouble?"

"Because he's a conspiracy theorist," Seth said. "That's my guess anyway. Those type of people are paranoid about everything."

"True," Blaze acknowledged. "It could be a fun game in a way. Cloak and dagger shit for the sake of his own self-importance. Though in this case, he'd be right that he was being watched."

Kane sighed and shook his head. "Look, none of that matters. Doesn't matter if he did it, if the tooth fairy did it, or if Daphne's pyscho brother did it. Somebody knows who she is and they wanted her to know they're watching her."

Daphne had finished half her sandwich by now. "Look, this is a lot to deal with. A lot to ask of you all. I know you want to protect me, but I can still leave. If you help me get out of town, I won't be running scared. I can do it smart and disappear where they won't find me, and you can get back to your lives."

They looked at her with blank expressions. Kane reached over and squeezed her hand, let it go again.

"Told you before, that's not how we operate. You're one of us, Daph. No man or woman left behind." He glanced at his friends. "We spent years in the military with that creed burned into our brains, not because they made us do it, but because that's who we are at the core. We won't leave you behind."

She stared at six handsome, stern faces. Kind faces as well, but determined. She'd never had that before. Never had a group of people—or even one person—who would stand between her and the gates of hell. Mrs. Donovan had loved her and tried her best to protect her, but she was one woman and there had only been so far she could go as an employee of John O'Malley. She would have never risked her very existence for Daphne, and Daphne wouldn't have wanted her to.

But these men, no matter how many outs she tried to give them, were willing to risk their lives for hers.

It was sobering. Humbling.

A tear spilled down her cheek and she swiped it away, but she knew they'd seen.

"I don't deserve this," she forced out of her tight throat.

"It's not a matter of deserving," Kane said. "It just is. You're one of us. We fight for you."

Daphne sniffed back the tears, wiped her eyes with her napkin so she wasn't staring at a watery, blurry mass of humanity.

"We need you to fight for us, too," Alex said, his voice soothing and commanding at the same time. "With your permission, I want Seth to download the information from your memory card and analyze it. And then, if it's as explosive as you say, I want to bring Diana Corbin in."

Daphne stiffened as fear rolled like a tsunami inside her. "My father has spies in law enforcement. I don't know if he has FBI agents on his payroll or not, but he has ways of making negative information about him disappear. How do you know you can trust her? And even if you can, how can you be sure she has the clout to make sure this doesn't go away and my father just carries on as usual? Because if he gets away with this, he'll come for all of us. We will never be safe."

Alex leaned back in his chair. "Honestly, I don't like the woman much, but I know she can be trusted. I have my reasons, and I promise you they are airtight. Diana Corbin is no traitor to her profession. She's professional and determined, and she will not take what we give her lightly. She won't fob it off on anyone else either." He frowned as if considering something. "There are things I can't tell you. About all of us. Why we're here. Diana knows the reasons. She was trusted with them by high-ranking people. What we're doing here, what she's involved in—there's every chance your father is connected to it through the weapons trade."

Daphne's gaze shot to Kane. He had the grace to look sheepish at the revelation he too had secrets. She swiveled back to Alex, determined.

"I think if I'm trusting you with this absolutely huge piece of my life—this thing that has the power to end it if not handled right—then I deserve to know what you're involved in. I've spent enough time with my head in the sand."

Alex sighed as if he was the most put upon human on the planet. "Can't do that, Daphne. But I will tell you that we're a military special forces team, and we're here to protect something important. This range, everything we do, is geared toward that goal. We report to the highest levels of government, and that means we have the ears of important people. So does Diana. If anyone can put a stop to the threat your father poses—to you and to others— then it's her. You'll have to trust me on that—and you'll have to keep everything I just told you to yourself, which means I'm trusting you as well."

She stared at him, her heart thudding. She'd played her hand, and though she hadn't gotten precisely what she'd wanted, he'd given her something. What choice did she have, really? It was either run—which they seemed deter- mined not to let happen—or trust them to do what they said they would do.

"When you say special forces team… Is that like Navy SEALs or something?"

"Oh Lord, here it comes," Chance muttered beside her.

Alex let out a breath. Closed his eyes. Opened them again. "Yes, like Navy SEALs. We were in the Army, not the Navy, but we can do exactly what they can do. They get all the glory—SEAL Team Six, Bin Laden, television series, blah blah blah. We are no different. Except maybe we don't brag as much."

Someone coughed. She thought she heard the word "Bullshit" in it. Alex turned to focus on Ethan, who pointed at Kane. The rest of them laughed.

"I do not brag about being a special operator," Kane said. "Never needed to. It's clear I'm exceptionally competent and manly just by looking at me."

"I can smell the shit from here," Seth said, not looking up from his computer.

"Y'all are just jealous. And stop making me look bad in front of Daphne."

"Since when have you needed help for that?" she asked, eyebrow arched.

Kane tilted his head back and sighed loudly. "I'm completely misunderstood around here."

Daphne wanted to laugh, but she didn't. The moment seemed perfectly normal, like something that would have happened just a couple of days ago. She liked it, but she didn't fool herself they were back on solid ground. Especially now that she knew he'd been keeping secrets too. They were going to have words about that.

Eventually.

"Daphne," Alex said, swinging her attention back to him. "Need your permission to move forward."

She fiddled with the card on the table. If she didn't give it to them, then what? Nothing would ever change and she'd always know there were people she might have helped escape her brother's clutches.

"I want to be informed," she said, fingers closing around the card. "I don't want to be patted on the head and told the men are handling it and not to worry. I didn't risk everything to be kept in the dark and told a bunch of shit. I don't expect to be in the loop on your secret stuff, but if it involves the O'Malleys, then I want to know. Deal?"

Alex gave another one of those soul-deep, utterly put upon sighs. One day she wanted to know what that was about. But not today. Today she wanted agreement.

"Unless it involves something we can't talk about, you'll know what we know. Once we know what's on the card, I'll call Agent Corbin to come to the range. You can be at the meeting and tell her anything you want her to know. Will that work?"

Daphne swallowed. She felt like she was standing at the edge of a precipice. When she took the first step, there was no turning back. But what was there to turn back to?

Nothing.

"Guess it has to," she said, sliding the card over to Seth.

He gave her a kind smile as he palmed it. "Thanks, Daph. I'll take good care of it."

"Please do. That's my life you're holding. Literally."

Kane's leg brushed hers beneath the table. Reassuring her. When she lifted her gaze to his, they locked and held until she felt the tension in her body start to ease.

"Seth won't let you down, Sunshine. None of us will. Promise."

There was a quiet murmuring around the table, but she couldn't look away from Kane. He was her strength.

Her will. Her reason for wanting to be better. Not that she could tell him any of that. He'd run screaming if she did.

A throat cleared. "If you two are done with the longing looks," Alex said, "Let's talk about protection."

Daphne must have started because Kane pushed his leg into hers again.

"He means a protective detail. For your safety."

"Fuck me. Yes, that's what I meant. Sorry, Daphne. A protective detail to keep you safe. We need a schedule and a plan. Thoughts?"

Chapter Twenty-Seven

Kane was jumpy as shit. He paced around the small room where Seth was currently working his magic on the computer. The answers weren't as quick as Kane wanted, though.

After the meeting with Daphne, they'd come up with a plan to protect her. Naturally, she was staying at the farmhouse, and though Kane had argued for stashing her there 24/7, Daphne had fought back. She wanted to be working, not sitting around thinking about everything that could potentially happen.

They'd moved her computer to a small storeroom off the hallway so she could work undisturbed and out of site of the public entering and exiting the range. Kane had frowned at the size of it, but Daphne had said she was happy. The room was little more than a closet, but after they'd moved out some of the supplies they kept inside it, there was just enough room for a desk and a chair.

She'd seemed surprised they were going to let her keep working, but Ghost had told her with a smirk that if he'd known they'd had a real accountant on the premises, he'd have given her all the financials in the first place instead of only some of it. She'd managed a smile after that and then immersed herself in the things she did best, like updating the spreadsheet, fielding calls, and booking appointments.

The rest of them were taking turns in the front of the building when it was busy, but otherwise they knew when someone entered and could go up front to greet them. After business hours, someone would be with Daphne at all times.

Him, because he wasn't letting anyone else do it.

Seth had offered to let Luna, the Belgian Malinois he and Callie had rescued, stay with them—if Callie agreed—but Kane thanked him and said he didn't think they'd need her. Still, he was touched that his friend had offered. Daphne had been, too. She sometimes dog-sat for Seth and Callie and she loved Luna.

But Luna, though a Malinois, wasn't a trained guard dog and Kane didn't feel right taking her from her new family. She'd done a good job when Dima Smirnov had grabbed Nikki, but Kane wasn't going to take the chance Luna could get hurt this time around. Fortunately, Daphne had agreed. If anything, she'd been more insistent than he had that she didn't want Luna in the path of danger.

"Josephine Daphne O'Malley," Seth said. "Twenty-eight-years old, five seven, blond hair, green eyes. Wow."

The sound of that *wow* had Kane walking around the desk to look at the screen. The woman staring back at him was stunning—and not his Daphne. This woman had a mane of blond hair, emerald green eyes, and artfully applied makeup. She definitely looked older than the makeup-free redhead he knew.

"You wouldn't know it's the same woman at first look, except you can see it in the face shape."

"I like her better the way she is now," Seth said. "This

woman looks like somebody who could shoot a pea off a fencepost at twenty-five yards."

Which they both knew she could do, looking like that or not.

"She's pretty either way," Kane said, needing to defend her. Didn't matter if a woman wore makeup or not so long as she was happy.

"She is. Just saying I wouldn't make small talk with that one. Our Daphne is friendly and approachable."

Our Daphne. He liked the way that sounded coming from Seth, the man who'd always been lauded for his robotic ability to focus on the facts and not let emotion get in the way.

"She is. How did she get past the security check you did on her originally?"

"Whoever made her fake ID is good. They made an entire background for her that stood up to digital scrutiny. Not that I tried too hard. Have to admit that I accepted what I found and went on with life."

"Why wouldn't you? We were hiring a down-on-her-luck woman we found squatting in an apartment building. It all checked out."

Seth nodded. "It did."

Ghost walked into the room. "What's that memory card looking like?"

"I copied it over and pulled up the files. When Daphne said she took everything, she took everything. There are financial records, documents, and two sets of books for the accounting, one for the legit Crescent City Armory and another for O'Malley's illegal businesses. The second set of books is coded, but Daphne provided the code to read it. Her father's involved in a lot of underworld shit. Drugs, money laundering, protection rackets, prostitution, and gun running. Most of it's funneled through legit businesses like The Diamond Queen, which Daphne ran. The gun business is the biggie. Like she said, they take delivery at various warehouses that O'Malley either rents or owns. He then sells them on, with or without modifications, to the mafia, drug lords, and fringe groups. The Dashevsky Group is on here, and Smirnov's gun came from that lot. The interesting thing is that I found a name from Huntsville, too. Colonel Brent Gannon. Retired U.S. Air Force. He works at the MDA facility on Redstone Arsenal as a contractor. He was asked to retire from active duty two years ago after being accused of harassing a female airman under his command. That's all I know at the moment, but I'm searching for more."

Ghost looked thoughtful. "Diana might know something about Gannon. If he's buying illegal weapons, he might have pinged her radar. We got enough to call her in?"

Seth nodded. "Think so, boss."

"And the human trafficking?"

"It's here. Not part of the financials that Daphne was responsible for, but it's in the documents. Her brother isn't all that subtle, and he's arrogant. He kept records, and he didn't code them. He targets vulnerable women and teens, like she said. He's been at it for a few months, so no telling how many women and kids are affected."

"I fucking hate people sometimes."

"Amen," Kane added.

When you'd seen the worst people could do to each other, it scarred you for life whether you admitted it or not. Didn't mean you couldn't have hope in humankind, but you always expected the worst. That way you weren't surprised.

Ghost rubbed his forehead. "Okay. I'll call Agent Corbin. See what I can get out of her."

Ethan strode in. "Been looking at the camera footage from the hallway of the Sutton building. There was a man who emerged from the open apartment beside Daphne's, went to her door, bent down like he was sliding something under it, and returned to the apartment. Looked to be one of the construction workers. I asked Blaze who was doing the work yesterday but he didn't know. He's calling Emma to find out. Figured we could get a list of who was onsite yesterday."

"Fader could have paid this guy to slip the card under," Kane said. "Or it could be her brother. He might be nearby but lying low."

"Got a photo of Jackson O'Malley?" Ghost said.

"Right here."

Seth turned the screen so they could see. The guy was good-looking, young, with red hair and a red goatee. His eyes were blue. Empty. He looked like the kind of person who tortured small animals for fun. Kane couldn't imagine Daphne and this fucker sharing genes, but the resemblance was too strong to ignore.

"Need to see if anyone's seen him in town," Kane said. Growled, really. "And if anybody's with him."

"Blaze and Chance can go, ask Rory and Theo, then maybe the shop owners on main street," Ghost said. "He might have ordered coffee at Wendy Cochran's, or eaten at Miss Mary's, or even the Dawg. Hell, maybe he bought crystals from Colleen for all we know. But I'd think if someone was asking around for Daphne, we'd know about it."

"We should see if he's at the Wheeler Inn," Kane added. "Might be staying there, waiting for something before he makes a move."

"I'm not talking to Celia Lincoln," Seth said. "She annoys the shit out of me."

"I'll take her," Ethan said. "She's a snooty old bag, but she likes my accent. Thinks it's exotic."

Seth snorted. "Exotic? It's fucking Jersey Shore."

"I'm from Brooklyn, asshole."

"Same difference."

Ethan let out a long-suffering sigh. "Hardly. But then you think pizza's pizza and what's the difference, right?"

"Believe me, I know New York pizza is superior because it's all you talk about. Especially when our asses were stuck somewhere on overwatch duty and I was fucking starving to death. You and the pizza. Always the pizza."

"Fuck yeah," Ethan said. "You want me to talk to that old lady or what?"

"Yes, I do. Thanks."

"Then tell me New York pizza is the best."

Seth groaned. "Dude, it's the best. I'd sell my soul for one slice if it makes you happy."

Ethan nodded. "Happy enough. I'll go see Ms. Lincoln."

The bell for the front door alerted them to a customer.

"I got it," Kane said. Blaze and Chance were inside the range, working on one of the target pulls that'd gotten stuck, and Kane was just restless enough to want to make the trip.

When he reached the front of the building, a man stood at the counter, looking mildly annoyed. Kane's insides tightened at the sight of Nathan Fader. He wanted to throttle the dude, ask if he'd been the one to break into Daphne's apartment. If he'd informed her father she was in Sutton's Creek.

He could do none of it.

"Hey, man. What can I help you with? Want a lane for an hour?"

"No. No lane." Fader studied him, piggy eyes narrowed and cold. "Where's your fiancée?"

He said the word with a sneer. Kane nearly crossed the counter, but told himself it wasn't a good idea. Not yet anyway.

"Not here. What do you want?"

"Just wanted to give her a message."

"Yeah? What message is that? And careful what you say, asshole, or I'll punch your face in."

Fader shook his head. "You even know who she is, or you just a clueless dick she's shacking up with?"

"Man, I'm telling you," Kane said, ice filling his veins. "You do *not* want to fuck with me. You see an Alabama country boy standing here, think he's stupid or something? My man, you have no idea where I come from or what I've done. I can make a body disappear just as well as you and the dick holding your leash can."

"You don't know a damned thing about me either. Just sayin'. You tell Josie to get the fuck out of town. Now. Before reinforcements get here, because they are surely coming for her."

"Who the fuck is Josie?" Kane asked, because he couldn't admit the dude was right. What if that was the objective? But damn, he was shocked at the idea this guy wanted to warn her. Unless he wasn't being truthful. Unless it was all a ploy to positively identify her.

Fader looked disgusted. "I got no beef with her. None. But I'm not the only person on this here earth knows she left town with a boatload of secrets. Her daddy wants them back. Her brother does too. They know she's here. Saw fucking Jackson myself yesterday, right here in this town."

Daphne emerged from the hallway before Kane had any idea she'd do something so fucking harebrained. He wanted to shove her back the way she'd come but it was too late. Fader had already seen her.

"Jackson's in town?"

Fader smirked at Kane, then turned his attention to Daphne. "Yeah, doll, he is. And he's looking for you."

She managed to look queenly and frightened at the same time. He was going to murder her later, but right now he admired her balls. "You told him I was here."

"Not me. This is a fucking gun range. Didn't you think somebody might recognize you? John O'Malley's fucking daughter in the middle of a gun operation?"

She sniffed and frowned. Hard. "I thought about it, yeah. But sometimes hiding in plain sight is the best idea because nobody thinks to look for you there."

"Yeah, well they didn't look for you here, did they? But they damn sure found you. Somebody spotted you and they went running to your daddy about it."

"Why are you telling me this? You're working for my father, aren't you? Why would you warn me?"

Fader's expression grew troubled. "You helped a friend out of a bad situation. This is payback for it."

"Kenny's sister," Daphne said, her eyes widening.

"Yeah. Louanne." His voice cracked on the name. "Good woman. Sweet. Didn't deserve that shit."

Daphne had moved closer. Kane stepped to the side to intercept her. He didn't block her, but he put himself between her and Fader. Just in case.

"You love her."

Kane didn't know how she jumped to that wild ass conclusion based on one moment of Fader saying Louanne's name, but his hard look crumbled. *Direct hit.*

"Nah," he said gruffly. "Kenny's my bud. Louanne is like a sister to me."

Daphne smiled at him, the softest smile Kane had seen.

"Listen to me, Mr. Fader. If you love her, tell her. For all you know, she feels the same. Don't waste time pretending or pushing her away. If the Universe says you're meant to be, you're meant to be."

Fader cleared his throat. "Don't know about that. Anyway, just wanted you to know. Maybe get the fuck out before he catches you."

"Did you slip a queen of diamonds playing card under her door?" Kane asked.

"I paid one of the construction workers to do it. Thought it'd scare her into getting lost again. Looks like I was wrong."

"Fair enough. Did you break into her place a few days ago?"

"No. I came here to warn her, but I didn't do that shit. That's Jackson's doing." He pulled in a breath, his lips flattening. "I've done my part, time for you to do yours, Josie."

Kane didn't like the look in Daphne's eyes. It was a hunted look, scared. He wrapped an arm around her shoulders and pulled her close. "She's safe here."

Fader shook his head. "Up to you, but if you love her, get her out of here. Don't let them find her. That's all I came to say."

Chapter Twenty-Eight

"WHAT THE FUCK POSSESSED YOU TO SHOW YOUR FACE?"
Kane growled, whirling on her when Nathan Fader was
gone again.

Daphne's cheeks flushed, but whether it was with anger
or embarrassment that she'd been so reckless, she couldn't
exactly say. She decided to focus on the anger.

"It was a spontaneous reaction. And it turned out fine,
didn't it? We know Jackson's in town, and we know he's
looking for me." She shuddered. "If you hadn't been with
me that night when we discovered somebody had
broken in…"

She didn't want to think about it. The place had been
turned over fast and not thoroughly, so whoever it was had
gotten interrupted. They'd probably intended to return
later that night when she was alone. But Kane had insisted
on going upstairs with her, then he'd taken her to the farm.
If she'd been on her own, she didn't know what she would
have done. Grabbed her go-bag and fled, probably.

But Jackson, or one of his men, had probably been
watching the place, waiting for her to try and escape. The

fact Kane had been with her had very likely put a crimp in the plan.

"Yeah, we would have found that out anyway. That was a risk you shouldn't have taken, Daphne. No matter what that douche says, he has proof you're still in town. He could run straight to your brother and confirm it now."

She moved closer, until she was toe to toe with him. He had to straighten to keep her head from bumping his chin. "He's not going to do that. If he loves Louanne, and I believe he does, he wouldn't do that. It was my brother who was taking advantage of her, pumping her with drugs so he could use her for himself before he started to pimp her out. I got her out of there. Nathan Fader wouldn't know about it if he wasn't friends with Kenny."

She'd hadn't really known Louanne well, but the night she'd found the woman sobbing in the alley behind The Diamond Queen because Jackson had decided to punish her by not giving her a hit of the drugs she was addicted to, Daphne knew she had to do something.

That's when she made it her mission to discover everything her brother was up to. A search of Jackson's office revealed the sick truth, but it wasn't until she searched her father's files that she confirmed he knew and didn't care.

Her first priority had been to get Louanne out of Jackson's clutches, which she'd done, taking her to her brother. Daphne had known who Kenny was because of his profession, but she'd never had any dealings with him until then.

He'd been grateful, and he'd offered to help her if she wanted out.

Turned out she did. Because she couldn't stomach that life for another moment more than she had to. She also needed time and space to figure out how to bring the O'Malleys down for good.

Jackson had raged when he realized Louanne was

gone, but he couldn't find her. Kenny was too good at his job for that, thank heavens.

Daphne didn't leave right away, because it took a couple of weeks to get her fake ID, but as soon as Kenny provided documents and a background, she grabbed a copy of her father's files and left. She even scheduled a weekend in New York City to give herself a head start. Of course she didn't go to New York. She left the airport in New Orleans and used the car Kenny had arranged for her. It was the old hoopty she'd coasted into town with a few months ago. It had served her well before its noble death.

Kane glared at her. "It's still not a risk you should have taken. I'm trying to protect you, Daphne. We all are, and we need you to fucking cooperate and not do reckless shit!"

Her anger bubbled over. How dare he yell at her when he had his own explaining to do.

"When were you going to tell me you're more than you seem, Kane? Huh? Was that ever going to happen, or did you plan to just let me feel guilty for lying to you when you've been lying too?"

Ethan poked his head through the door. "We can hear you two yelling at each other. FYI. Everything okay?"

Daphne took a step back, feeling like a porcupine whose bristles were standing on end. Kane didn't look any less furious than she felt.

"It's fine," Kane said. "Daphne just showed her face to Nathan Fader, but it's okay because he came to warn her that her brother's in town. Absolutely no ulterior motives or anything. She knows it because he was so honest and truthful about everything else."

"Uhh…" Ethan began.

"Fuck you, Kane," Daphne growled. "You arrogant, lying, *prick!*"

"Oookay then," Ethan said. "I got a lady to see at a motel. Or did Fader tell you for sure that's where to find Jackson?"

"He didn't say where to find him," Kane said. "I guess Daphne didn't ask nicely enough."

Daphne held up her thumb and forefinger. "I'm this close to kicking you in the balls."

"Thanks for the warning. Now go ahead and try it and let Ethan watch me turn you over my knee and spank your ass."

She barely refrained from launching herself at him. "You better not even try."

"You liked it well enough the last time."

"Aaaand that's me out of here," Ethan said before disappearing the way he'd come.

"You arrogant, stupid, bossy bastard," she grated. "I thought you didn't want anyone to know we were fucking, huh?"

"Oh for fuck's sake," someone groaned.

Daphne turned to see Alex standing in the doorway that Ethan had vacated. Her face flushed even redder than it currently was. Not that she could see it, but she damn sure felt it. This had to be what those hot flashes Mrs. Donovan had complained about were like because she couldn't imagine being any hotter in her own skin than she was right now.

"I thought we had an understanding about this, Kane," Alex said. "As in don't fuck with Daphne because we need her too much and don't want her to quit."

He did not sound happy.

"I know. I'm sorry. It just happened."

Daphne closed her eyes as a fresh wave of irritation rolled through. "You had an *agreement* about me? About not asking me out or anything because you didn't want me to get mad and quit?"

Alex managed to look uncomfortable. Which was saying something because the man was always cool, calm, and controlled. Even when he was grumbling about Diana Corbin, which he did every time she showed up.

"It seemed wise at the time. Kane isn't exactly known for his ability to think long term."

Daphne clenched her fists at her sides. That was the reason Kane had treated her like his pesty baby sister for so long? Because they had an agreement? Unbelievable.

"Honest to God, you are the most arrogant bunch of cavemen assholes in some ways, you know that? I'm a grown ass woman. An adult. Responsible, legal, and, whoa—news-flash—capable of thinking for myself. I get to say who I sleep with, not any of you. If I want to throw myself headlong into a hot sexual relationship with a man, it's *my* business. And his, obviously. But the rest of you don't get a say in it!"

She finished that last part on a yell. Alex squinted as if waiting for more words, then opened his eyes when she didn't say another.

"I'm sorry, Daphne. I thought I was protecting you from Kane's charming habit of discarding women after a couple of dates, and us from losing you because he was a dick to you."

She sucked in a breath, trying to cool her anger. "I appreciate the thought. But if everything goes well and I don't die, I'd also appreciate the same respect for my personal autonomy that you probably give to all the men you meet while simultaneously thinking women need protected."

"Ouch," Alex said.

"Direct hit," Kane said. "Think she smoked you."

"I'm feeing the burn, believe me."

Daphne whirled back to Kane. "And you're no better. You entered into this agreement to protect the poor little woman from making a mistake by giving her a choice. For all the two of you knew, I'd have said no to any overtures and that would have been the end up it. I was fucking dating Warren, if you'll remember. Or did you both think Kane is so damned charming he could have stolen me away with a crook of his finger?"

"Uhhh," they both said, shooting looks at each other.

Daphne held up a hand. "Just shut your faces, both of you."

The men exchanged looks again. But they didn't speak, and for that she was glad. It was silent for all of a minute before Kane opened his pie hole.

"None of this changes the fact you took a risk you shouldn't have taken. Showing your face to Nathan Fader was reckless and dangerous. Even if all he wanted was to warn you, you don't know that your brother won't get information out of him one way or another."

Daphne sighed. She had been reckless, but when she'd heard Nathan say Jackson was in town, she'd reacted without thinking. He'd said he wanted to warn her, and she'd believed him because Jackson wouldn't have sent him to smoke her out that way. Then there was Louanne. Kane might not believe it, but knowing how protective Kenny was of his little sis, and how he'd made Daphne's fake documents at a risk to himself if her father found out, she'd known Nathan truly knew him. If he hadn't, he wouldn't have known the first thing about Louanne. He also wouldn't have known her name because it wasn't the name she'd used when Jackson had her in his grip.

She'd been Destiny, not Louanne. Very few people knew her as Louanne.

Still, she'd reacted recklessly and she shouldn't have done that. She lifted her chin.

"You're right, I shouldn't have shown my face. But I did, and I'm not sorry because we learned that Jackson's definitely in town, and that the queen of diamonds came from Nathan. We also know he didn't break into the apartment. I don't think it was Jackson either, but I believe he sent someone to do it. I also think they would have abducted me if you hadn't been there. None of that absolves you from lying to me about your own shit, or from thinking you have a God-given manly right to make decisions for me."

Alex put up a hand to stop Kane from responding. It worked, which surprised her. Then again, in light of the fact they were a military team on special assignment, and Alex seemed to be the one in charge, Kane probably had to.

"It's not his fault for not telling you about us. We aren't authorized to discuss it, but under the circumstances I made the decision to say what I could. If Kane was the sort of man who spilled government secrets, even to people he cares about, then he wouldn't be here. Blame him for whatever you want, but not for that."

She folded her arms in a huff. "Fine. Then he doesn't get to blame me either. I did what I thought was right by keeping my secrets close."

"Not the same thing," Kane growled.

"It is to me."

His mouth opened. Closed. She didn't know if he'd thought better of continuing the argument or if he realized she had a point.

"You two can continue this without me," Alex snapped. "I came out here to say that Agent Corbin will be here at fourteen-hundred. Two o'clock, Daphne. Now if you'll excuse me, I'm going to go stick my head in the microwave and save the government the trouble of shooting me later."

Daphne blinked after him. "What was that about?"

Kane still looked like a thundercloud. "He's the leader. Shit goes sideways, he gets blamed first."

Guilt flared again. "Is it because of me? Will helping me get you in trouble?"

"We won't get in trouble." He rubbed his forehead. "Can you return to your cubbyhole before somebody else comes looking for you? Please?"

"Fine. But you know what? It's pretty shitty that you let me feel guilty for not telling you the truth when you had your own secrets, orders or not."

"I can't help the way it makes me feel."

"Same for me, you know? Even if you couldn't tell me about your secrets, the fact you were mad at me for mine? That you let me think I deserved your anger?" She shook her head. "That's some unbelievable gall right there."

He didn't say anything. Didn't acknowledge she was right or apologize or offer an explanation. Her fury whipped higher.

"You know what? Maybe I don't need you to decide whether we're done or not. Because I'm not so sure I want to be with someone, even a fuck buddy, who can't treat me like an equal. Have a nice life," she said, breezing past him to her tiny office.

He didn't try to stop her, which only made her angrier. She slammed the door and slumped into her chair, the fight draining out of her.

It was over between them as fast as it'd begun.

Chapter Twenty-Nine

"So," Blaze said with a grin when Kane stalked into the break room half an hour later for a bottle of water.

"What?"

"You and Daphne."

Kane twisted the cap viciously. "Me and Daphne what?"

"Ethan said something about spanking. Gonna assume you didn't do that with clothes on."

"None of your fucking business."

Blaze nodded. "Yep, you're right. But you have any idea how happy this is gonna make Emma, Rory, and Callie?"

Kane took a drink. "None of their fucking business either."

"You cut her loose already?" Chance asked, walking into the room. "Man that was fast. I think. When did it start?"

Kane swung his gaze toward his other fucknut teammate. "No. She cut me loose. And recently, though I'll reiterate that it's none of your business."

He also wasn't telling them that recently meant they'd started yesterday. That was a lightning fast fuck up, even for him.

"Whoa, that's not typical. Losing your mojo, old man?"

"Something like that."

He had a fucking headache. And maybe a heartache. He could hear her voice in his head, sneering at him. Telling him she was done because he didn't respect her as an equal. Yeah, maybe it'd been wrong to have an agreement about her, but he also didn't blame Ghost for urging him not to fuck around with Daphne. He didn't have the best track record, and he'd been the object of female tantrums before.

Jeez, those were two words he wasn't about to say in Daphne's hearing. Female tantrums.

She'd eviscerate him.

He didn't miss the look that passed between Chance and Blaze. "How you feeling about it?" Blaze asked.

"Just peachy. We done?"

"Guess so. Just trying to be there for you, man. You don't seem happy."

Kane blew out a breath. "Were you happy when your woman was in danger?"

"Nope."

"Same. Daphne isn't my woman, not that it's anyone's business but mine and hers, but I'm not happy her life's in danger. Not happy she's the key to bringing down an entire fucking criminal organization. We don't know what that's gonna entail, how it'll affect her life. What if they want to put her in witness protection, huh? Or prosecute her for being an accessory? We could lose her forever—"

He couldn't keep going. The reality that he could lose Daphne, that she'd go into protection and he'd never see her again, sat like a stone in his belly. It was the same gut punch feeling he'd gotten when he'd learned that Hannah had been killed. That he would never see her again.

It staggered him, that feeling. Was it because everything was so far out of his control and still spiraling?

Or was he going too soft, wanting what he knew he couldn't have? What didn't really exist, no matter how much his friends might believe in it? Love, as the song said, was a losing game. He knew it better than most.

"We just have to wait and see," Chance said. "Diana's got connections. Maybe she can make the whole thing happen without needing Daphne to testify. And she makes *any* noise about prosecuting Daphne, we'll hide her so deep undercover the FBI won't find her ever again."

"That's right," Blaze added. "We won't let that happen. And we'll argue for protecting her ourselves. She can get another new identity, maybe stop working at the range for a while, go do something else. She can cut her hair, dye it, wear contacts. There are ways to disguise her."

Kane took a deep breath as his heart started to slow again. God he loved these guys. His family. Way more of a family than his dad, the venerable Navy captain, had ever been. Kane hardly ever wondered—or cared—what the old man was up to in Virginia Beach. One thing was for certain, though. He'd have never put himself into any difficulty for Kane.

These guys? They'd plunge head first for him. Same as he would for them, the nosy bastards.

"Thanks."

"For what it's worth," Blaze said. "Took almost losing Emma for me to realize I'd rather take the risk with her than never find out if we could be something. Not sorry I did either."

Kane didn't know what to say to that. Fortunately, the chime sounded for the side door. He glanced at his watch.

"Fourteen hundred. Guess that's our favorite FBI agent," Chance said. "Want me to get Daph for you? Or do you think she's cooled off enough by now?"

"I'll get her," Kane said. He was simmering down now, and he owed her an apology. No, he hadn't been able to tell her about his reasons for being in Alabama and he wouldn't have broken his oaths to his country to do it. But he could understand why she was angry with him for having secrets. In his opinion, hers were more deadly. Didn't change the fact she had her reasons for not telling him, same as he had for not telling her.

It wasn't the same thing as Hannah's lies, and he knew it. Even if he was still pissed about it. But pissed and right weren't always the same thing, and he was man enough to admit it.

Daphne emerged from her tiny office a moment before he got there. She stopped abruptly, her gaze hardening. He held up both hands. "Just coming to tell you Diana's here."

"I know that. I heard the chime, and I can tell time."

Kane sighed. This thing between them wasn't going to get any better unless he took charge and did what he needed to do. "You're right. I was a dick."

"Which time?" she asked, arching an eyebrow.

"Possibly all of them. But I'm specifically talking about keeping secrets."

"Go on."

"Alex told you why I couldn't say anything, and if he hadn't told you what he could, I'd have never said a word. Won't apologize for that. I took an oath to the Constitution and I'm duty bound to uphold it. But you're right that being pissed at you for your secrets is hypocritical. Even if I still think you should have told us so we could help."

She shook her head. "And how was I supposed to know you could help me? What I knew—what everyone knows—is that the six of you retired from the Army and moved here to make your dreams of owning a shooting range and security training facility come true. In what universe does that make you equipped to deal with the mafia, huh?"

She had him there. Much as he hated to admit it.

"Point taken."

"Okay. Anything else you need to apologize for?"

He had to think about it while her eyebrows climbed higher. Any second now and he'd start to sweat. He felt like he was back in fifth grade and Mrs. Chen wanted to know why he hadn't done his homework. He'd had no excuse then and he had none now.

Then it hit him.

"I'm sorry I entered into an understanding not to, uh, flirt with you or ask you out without considering that you can make your own choices."

"I appreciate you saying that. Thank you. Are you just saying it because you want to return to fuck buddy status or do you mean it?"

A hot, sharp feeling bloomed in his belly. "I mean it," he said roughly. There was something about hearing her describe what they'd done as fuck buddies that didn't hit right this time. Which didn't make a damn bit of sense, but there it was.

He didn't have time to work it out, though, because she brushed past him and started toward the break room where Diana Corbin was surely waiting.

FBI agent Diana Corbin. A woman who could take the information Daphne gave her and use it to put the O'Malleys away for good. A woman who wouldn't care that Daphne belonged here in Sutton's Creek with him and the One Shot gang. That she was one of them.

Agent Corbin wouldn't hesitate to use Daphne. To

compel her to testify and then send her into witness protection. Or prosecute her for her part in her family's crimes.

Kane's gut turned to ice. Despair flared hot and deep. He caught Daphne's arm and turned her. There was shock on her face. Fear? God, he hoped not. He couldn't handle making her fearful for even a moment.

He pressed her to the wall, bracketed his palms on either side of her head, crowded her sweet body with his much bigger one. Her eyes weren't fearful as they gazed up at him. They were soft, confused. Maybe a little bit hopeful?

"What's the problem, Candy Kane? Grunt it to me if you can't talk."

He wanted to laugh and he wanted to kiss her. He chose kissing her.

Her mouth softened beneath his, her lips opening. His tongue found hers and he shuddered with the rightness of it. He needed time with her. Time to explore this thing, to find out if his shriveled heart could beat again. If she could heal him.

But time was what they didn't have. Diana Corbin waited. Like her namesake, the ancient goddess of the hunt, she was filled with deadly purpose. She would use any tool at her disposal to achieve justice. Ordinarily, Kane would agree.

But he couldn't agree when the tool was Daphne. When she was a living, breathing, beautiful person he cared about.

Daphne's hands curled into fists in his shirt. She sighed, and he kissed her deeper. He would have forgotten everything but her if not for the clearing of a throat.

"Was just coming to fetch you two," Ethan said apologetically when Kane looked up. "I just got back. Jackson's not staying at the Inn, by the way. Didn't ask around town yet since I had to get back for the meeting, but that's next."

Fuck.

"Okay, thanks. Be there in a sec," Kane said.

"Make it quick. Ghost—shit, Alex—is getting impatient."

Ethan disappeared and Kane's gaze tangled with Daphne's. "Ghost, huh? You got a cool name too?"

"Demon."

"Demon?"

"Yup. Scared an instructor so badly during training that he called me a demon in disguise. It stuck."

"I see."

"Best not acknowledge that you heard that. Or the word Ghost in connection to Alex. Will you do that for me?"

"Yes. Why did you kiss me, Kane?"

He sighed. "Because I'm a fuck up with the words, but I know I've got the kissing down."

She snorted. "So full of yourself."

"A little. Maybe. But Daph—I just. I need you to know I don't want anything to happen to you. I like being with you. I want to keep being with you."

"For somebody who likes his sex meaningless, you're saying a lot of words that aren't."

"It's not meaningless with you. I wish it was, but it's not."

She patted his chest. "Flatterer. Okay, you've made your point. I'm not entirely pissed at you now, and you've made things move down south if you know what I mean, so jumping you later is not entirely out of the question. But maybe we need to get into that room before Alex comes out here looking for us. I have a feeling he won't be so nice if he does."

No, he definitely wouldn't be.

Kane wrapped her hand in his. She looked at him questioningly.

"No point hiding it anymore."

She gazed at their hands, then at him again. "No, I guess not. You okay with that?"

"Absolutely. You?"

She nodded. "One hundred percent."

He lifted her hand to his mouth and kissed it. "I'm on your side, Sunshine. No matter what happens in there, nothing's changing that."

She looked concerned. "Don't get yourself in trouble for me, Kane. I don't want you to do that."

"Nobody left behind, Daph. You're one of us, and I promise you I'm not the only one who'll fight for you."

Her smile was wobbly. "Don't tell anybody, but I think I love you all."

His heart skipped a quick beat. He found himself wanting her to say she loved him specifically, but that was a crazy want.

Because he wasn't somebody who could believe those words even if she did.

Chapter Thirty

DIANA CORBIN COULD HAVE BEEN A PROFESSIONAL POKER player for all the emotion she showed when Alex yielded the floor to Daphne and let her tell her story yet again. After spending so many months saying nothing at all, her soul seemed to grow lighter every time she told the tale.

Didn't make up for what'd been done by her family over the years, but it felt good to stop hiding and start talking. Maybe, despite Diana's poker face, something good would come of the memory card and all the files.

Provided her father didn't manage to pay somebody off first.

Daphne didn't clutch her hands together while she spoke, though she wanted to. She faced Diana squarely across the polished table and explained what she had and why. When she was done, Diana turned to Alex.

"You've looked at this information?"

"Yes."

"And?"

Alex shot Daphne a look, smiled reassuringly. Daphne was still reeling from the existence of the room with the polished table and all the sophisticated electronics that she'd thought was a secure store room until a few minutes ago. She'd thought they were meeting in the break room, but then Alex led the way here and she'd been gawking since.

"It's everything she says it is. Before we hand it over, need to know what you plan to do."

Diana blinked, then sat back in the chair and looked shockingly at ease for once. She picked up the pen on the table in front of her and turned it over a few times. "I can't say too much, but John O'Malley is a person of interest for many reasons. This information could be incredibly helpful to our case."

"So you'll arrest him?" Daphne asked, her heart thrumming.

"Not yet, but yes. I expect the arrests to be wide ranging across the O'Malley enterprise. We won't act until we're certain we can make it stick."

"I want you to arrest me, too."

Kane stirred beside her. "Daphne—"

She turned and put a finger over his mouth, silencing him. He looked angry and frustrated—and scared? Her heart skipped, her stomach clenching tight. "Listen, please. Can you do that?"

He nodded and she knew it cost him to give her that control. But he did it, and she turned back to Diana. "Maybe you plan to arrest me anyway, in which case I'm wasting my breath, but if you aren't, then I need it put out there that you've arrested all of us. Not just my father and Jackson, but me too. I need people to think I'm going down with them. Josie, I mean. If Josie isn't mentioned in connection with any of this, then people will suspect it was me. Some people will know anyway, but if I can throw off suspicion at all…. Well, betraying the family and living to tell about it isn't the way it usually works. I'd like a shot at staying above ground for a few years."

Diana nodded. "I can't say what'll happen when the files reach my superiors, but giving us this information works in your favor, especially if we can take down the O'Malley businesses with it. You may have to testify, but I don't know that yet either. It's too early to say. But assuming you don't, and assuming there's no reason to bring charges against you, it won't be a problem to leak the information that Josephine O'Malley has been taken into custody when the time comes."

Daphne couldn't stop trembling. She'd said her piece, but her body wouldn't give up the flight or fight response. Kane wrapped an arm around her and tugged her against his side. Nobody said anything about it, though Alex heaved one of those sighs of his.

"Thank you," Daphne managed. "I appreciate your help. I really, really hope you can make the charges stick. My father has a way of slipping through even the most tightly woven net."

Diana smiled. It was a cool smile, controlled. As if the woman never let go and allowed herself to be messy and emotional. "Not if I have anything to say about it."

"Now that we've got that out of the way," Alex said, slapping his hands on the table to get everyone's attention, "need you to know that you aren't arresting Daphne in connection with her father's crimes. She's not testifying either, because you've got everything you need in the files she's giving you. I don't care what you have to do to make it happen, but make it happen. Call up those connections and do what you gotta do. Or you won't get another moment of cooperation out of us on any aspect of your investigation into Viktor Dashevsky."

Diana's face was a mask. Daphne had to give it to her,

the woman didn't crack. Her own heart raced a million miles an hour and her eyes pricked with tears. She'd called Alex a caveman asshole, but right now she was glad for his bossiness. Glad for him. For these men who were her friends despite the fact she'd been lying to them for months.

She didn't know who Viktor Dashevsky was, but he was clearly important to Diana if the way she took her time answering was any indication.

"I'll do my best."

"Better than that, ma'am. Because you need us for this rogue investigation of yours and you know it."

Diana's mask slipped. She glared daggers at Alex. "You're an arrogant son of a bitch, Colonel. But I assume you know that."

Daphne glanced at Kane. He squeezed her shoulder but didn't look at her. So Alex was a colonel. That was a bit of information she hadn't known. Explained a lot about how effortlessly he seemed to be in command. And why he had a room like this tucked away behind a steel blast door. Not for the first time since she'd learned they were on a mission, she wondered what they could be doing in Sutton's Creek that was so important.

If she never found out, so be it. The important thing was that they were here and they were on her side.

"Heard it a time or two," Alex said. "I'm sweet as a kitten when you treat me right, though. So be sure you do."

"With incentive like that, how can I say no?"

"My thoughts exactly." He took a memory stick from his pocket and placed it on the table in front of him. "A copy of Daphne's files."

Diana looked expectant but didn't speak. Daphne's gaze darted around the faces gathered and she knew Alex was angling for something else, which was why he didn't slide it over.

"Might as well tell me what you want," Diana said.

"Information. What does John O'Malley have to do with The Dashevsky Group?"

Diana darted a glance at Daphne, but Alex spoke again.

"She's giving you his books, both sets, and she's identified the diamond stamp as originating with her father. Think you can tell her what's going on."

Diana's eyebrows lifted. Daphne hadn't shared the diamond information because Alex had asked her not to. Clearly, he'd had his own plan for doing so.

Diana cleared her throat. "That's helpful. Thank you."

Alex snorted. "You suspected it already. You wanted to see if we could confirm it for you."

"Okay, yes, I had my suspicions, though I certainly didn't anticipate you'd have O'Malley's daughter on your staff." She cleared her throat delicately. "John O'Malley is ruthless and mercenary. He acts in his own self-interest, nobody else's. He would have supplied those weapons to The Dashevsky Group for cold, hard cash and no other reason. But Jackson O'Malley…"

Daphne's heart slammed her ribs.

"He's a hothead, susceptible to influence. Viktor Dashevsky is very good at manipulating people for his own ends. I think he's been grooming Jackson, whispering to him about taking over the O'Malley empire. About joining him in his new world order." She turned to Daphne. "Did your brother ever mention Viktor Dashevsky to you?"

"No, but then we aren't exactly close."

"Hmm." Diana looked disappointed, but nothing Daphne could do about it.

"I'm sure you're right about Jackson, though," she

added. "He would slit my father's throat in a heartbeat if he thought he could get away with it. I would too, if I'm honest. But not so I could take over the business. And I'll tell you this—Jackson taking over would be a disaster. There'd be war in the underworld and it wouldn't be pretty."

As if anything in the criminal underworld ever was.

Diana nodded. "We know Jackson is in communication with Viktor, because Viktor supplies the trafficking victims."

Daphne hated Viktor Dashevsky on principle.

"It's his operation," Diana continued. "It's one small part of how he recruits men for his movement. He plies them with easy targets for their desires, fuels their paranoia and sense of grandeur. It's not the only way, because some people think of themselves as patriots fighting against government corruption, but Viktor's not above using any tool it takes."

"Will bringing down my father and brother stop him from trafficking people?"

"It'll slow him down. My goal is to stop him entirely, but this kind of thing is like a mythological hydra. Cut off one head and several more sprout up."

"Anything else?" Alex asked. "Tell me now because if I find out later that you withheld something, I won't be nice about it."

The corners of Diana's mouth tightened. "I presume you know Jackson's in town?"

"We do. But we don't know where he's staying. Do you?"

"Not yet." She hesitated. "I think he's here to broker a deal for a missing shipment of black market Stinger missiles. Among other things, obviously," she said, glancing at Daphne.

Alex frowned. "How do you know?"

"I have an informant who works with the O'Malleys."

"Wouldn't be Nathan Fader, would it?"

"Not divulging my sources, Colonel."

"He didn't tell you about Daphne though. Maybe he doesn't entirely trust you?"

Diana didn't react. She was back to normal then. "My informant doesn't know where Jackson's staying, and doesn't know the time or location of the meeting yet. I'm waiting to hear. If we can catch Jackson in the middle of a deal, we'll have even more evidence against him than what's in those files."

"You have a team ready for intercepting?"

"Yes."

Alex slid the memory stick toward her. "If you need help, call us."

"I don't think I will, but thanks."

She reached for the stick and their fingers brushed. They both stiffened as if contaminated. Daphne would have laughed if she wasn't sick with fury right now. Both at this Viktor Dashevsky asswipe and at her brother for allowing Dashevsky to traffic humans into her club. Not to mention the whole missile thing. What the hell was Jackson thinking? Her father always said guns were easy money but missiles drew too much attention.

And he was right, apparently. She hoped her brother's ass got swept up in an FBI raid. It was the least of what he deserved.

"Thank you." Diana slipped the stick into her handbag. "I'll get to work on this immediately. I may need to speak with you again," she said to Daphne.

"You know where to find me."

Diana's gaze slid around the room before resting on

her once more. "Indeed. You are very fortunate in your choice of protectors, Miss Bryant."

Daphne awarded points for using her chosen name instead of her legal one. "I'm a lucky girl to have found the kind of friends who watch out for me."

Kane nudged her leg beneath the table. She nudged back.

They were friends. Always.

But she wanted them to be more.

<h1 style="text-align:center">Chapter Thirty-One</h1>

———

Daphne was sitting on the back porch, a dram of Scotch in hand because Kane had bought her a new bottle, gazing at the sunset when he walked outside and joined her. She smiled at him before turning back to the view.

He'd been watching her from the window as he'd cleaned up the dishes and she'd been staring into space the whole time. Processing a lot, no doubt. Hell, he was still processing too. Her identity, the things she knew, how she made him feel, the way he couldn't quite keep a lid on his emotions when she was near, what he thought it meant. So many fucking things, and he was no closer to an answer. He kept thinking about what Blaze had said about how it took almost losing Emma to make him realize he wanted a life with her.

Kane wasn't ready to say he wanted a life with Daphne, but he wanted her in his life right now. He wanted her safe and whole, and he wanted her father and brother gone for good.

A lot of wants, but he was hopeful.

The guys—and Daphne—had a discussion after

Diana was gone, and they'd agreed that Daphne wouldn't go anywhere alone until this was over. They weren't going to keep her hidden though. It was possible Jackson was waiting to make a move. If she disappeared entirely, then he might go to ground as well. Since the Stinger missile deal was still speculation, they were going with what they knew, which was that Jackson would want to get his hands on Daphne and the information she'd stolen.

It was a safe bet he wanted that anyway. The missile hypothesis might be smoke and mirrors, but Daphne was a real threat the O'Malleys needed to silence.

And Kane was sticking by her side like a burr in a horse's tail because he wasn't letting that happen.

When he sank onto the cushioned loveseat, it was after eight and the sun was already behind the horizon. The pink and purple clouds left in its wake were stunning though. The fields had gone wild where they'd once been planted with corn and cotton, yet they were beautiful with wildflowers and other growing things he didn't recognize. A local farmer would cut it next month for hay, but for now it was wild and free.

"How's the Scotch?"

She turned to him. "Perfect. Thank you for buying it, but you didn't have to."

"You're welcome, and I wanted to."

"Have some with me?"

He held up the empty glass he'd brought. "I'm ready."

She smiled and picked up the bottle, poured some for him. Then she got the small pitcher she'd put water in and, using the straw sitting in the jug, she held her finger over one end and carefully dripped some into the Scotch.

"Why are you doing that again?"

"Because this whisky is cask strength. Anything over

about fifty-five percent can really use that water to open it up. Not a lot, just a few drops. Swirl and try."

He did as she said. "Mmm, that's pretty good."

"Right? Not all whiskies need water, but for the stronger ones, it helps to separate the smokiness from the alcohol and make it more noticeable."

He sipped in silence. It'd never been awkward between them before, not even when he was keeping her at arm's length by thinking of her as a sister, but for some reason it was awkward now. So much had happened in a short amount of time.

"How you feeling about today?" he asked.

She shrugged. "Doesn't matter what I'm feeling, does it? It's out of my hands now. I can only wait and hope what I took is enough to put an end to my family's business." She frowned as she swirled her Scotch, watching the liquid move around the glass. "I didn't know anything about missiles or Viktor Dashevsky. I wondered why Jackson started trafficking people when he did, but I figured he was trying to impress our father with initiative and a new revenue stream."

He wished he could tell her more about The Dashevsky Group, but that was off limits. She already knew more than she should, but Ghost had impressed upon her the sanctity of the information. After what she'd risked to escape her family, he didn't doubt she could be trusted. Despite keeping the truth of her identity from them for so long.

"You don't think your father knows about the missiles either?"

"Nope. It's not the kind of thing he'd deal in. Too many complications, too much uncertainty. He always said the guns were enough to keep the business going. Never deal in the big shit because that's what brought more scrutiny, not to mention it's harder to hide shipments. If that's what Jackson's up to, he's not doing it with our father's approval."

"You didn't seem surprised he wasn't staying at the Wheeler Inn earlier."

"I could have told you he wouldn't be there. O'Malleys only stay in hotels with strong layers of security and only when they want to be seen. He'll have rented a house somewhere, probably not in Sutton's Creek, and it'll be under a random alias. If he's here to sell anything illegal, he won't call attention to himself. Only those closest to him will know where he is. If Nathan is the informant, then he's either lying about knowing where Jackson is or he's not close enough to my brother to know everything. Which means he might not know where the meeting is until it's too late."

"Hopefully, Diana will figure it out and be there to sweep him up. The sooner the better."

"Couldn't agree with you more," she said, lifting the glass.

They clinked softly before taking a drink.

"I've been trying to think of who could have told my father they'd seen me here and when. We've had some new customers in over the past couple of weeks, but nobody stands out to me. A couple of guys shot for a few days and haven't been back, but that's not unusual when people are in the area on business."

It wasn't, but Kane frowned. "Knowing what I know now, it was incredibly dangerous for you to take a job with us. There was always a chance somebody in the business would recognize you."

Her shoulders slumped a fraction. "I know. I wasn't going to take the job, but you guys were so nice and I felt safe. The alternative was leaving town and ending up somewhere else with God knows what kind of job or living quarters. It was winter and I didn't want to go somewhere new, knowing I couldn't afford a place to stay, and I didn't want to clean motel rooms again. And Sutton's Creek is so small and remote in comparison to all the gun ranges and stores in Huntsville that I thought it unlikely anyone who knew my connection to Crescent City Armory would visit. I also thought I'd be gone long before anyone figured it out." She shook her head. "But I got comfortable, and complacent. I didn't want to leave. And now I've put you all in danger."

He sipped the Scotch. "Told you before that's not a consideration. You're safer here with us than you would be anywhere else you might have gone. Promise you that."

"I know." She nibbled her lower lip. "But you don't know Jackson. He has no sympathy, no mercy. If he gets a chance to hurt one of you—or someone you love—he will do it for the kicks, and because it will hurt me."

"Not gonna let him do that, babe." He understood her fear. He just didn't share it. Not that he dismissed the threat, because he wasn't that stupid. But he and his guys were prepared for it. There was something he didn't understand though. "You took the files when you left. Why didn't you take enough money to disappear for good? Or at least enough to live on?"

"I couldn't. I spent my own money getting my ID and the car. What was left I used on the road until I ran out." She leaned back and kicked a foot onto the coffee table. "You have to understand that all the money came through my father. I could spend what I wanted on credit cards, travel, buy designer clothes and handbags. Anything. But cash? That was different. I kept some for emergencies, money I knew wasn't marked in some way, and that's what I used. But taking money from the business? I could never be certain if the money was marked and trackable. Club money was picked up every morning after close of business by one of my father's enforcers. I literally had no access to a cash source I could trust."

"You lived like that for a long time."

Her pretty face was troubled. "It was what I knew, what I expected. I hate that I didn't leave sooner, that I accepted my dad's business and rationalized it in the ways I did. I wish I'd been braver."

He reached for her hand, tugged her to his side. She settled in like she belonged there. She was warm and vibrant and emotion flooded his system for a moment before he got it under control again.

"Think you did the best you could, Sunshine. If you'd left earlier, would you have the files you have? Would you have been prepared to tough it out the way you did before you started work here?"

"The answers are no and I hope so." She tipped her head up to meet his gaze. "I wouldn't blame you for hating me, you know. My family is fundamentally flawed, and I am too. I was complicit for a long time."

He put a finger over her mouth. "Daphne. Think. You knew what your father did, but you didn't make him do it. What do you think Kid Daphne—or Kid Josie—should have done, huh? Call the police? What would you have told them?"

"I know what you're trying to do, but I'm twenty-eight and I've been my father's accountant for six years. There was plenty of time to figure out how to put an end to the business."

He tucked a stray lock of her hair behind her ear. "They make movies about people who work for the mafia, or marry into it, or whatever. Escaping is never easy, and it's definitely not without risks. You were born into your family same as I was born into mine. Difference is when I left, my family wasn't going to hunt me down and drag me back. Or kill me. Would yours have let you go if you said you wanted to leave?"

She shook her head. "I'm an asset to be married off for the sake of alliances. I would never be allowed to leave."

He brushed his mouth against hers. Lightly, sweetly. Made him shudder with need. The idea of her marrying someone he didn't know, of never meeting her or knowing how beautiful she was when she moaned his name, squeezed the breath from his lungs.

He wasn't in control of his reactions as the kiss turned hot. Daphne opened to him, moaning as his tongue slipped between her lips. She tasted of smoky whisky and heat, and he wanted more. She did too, apparently, because her hands went to his waistband, tugged his shirt out of his jeans so that she could slide her palms against his skin.

He groaned as she touched him. His dick went from semi to rock solid in half a second. He wanted to be inside her, surrounded by her, driving them both toward a shattering climax that would rock him to the core.

He broke the kiss and stood, tugging her up with him. She didn't have to ask where they were going as he started for his room. Ethan wasn't home, but that didn't mean he wouldn't show up at an inopportune moment. Kane really wished he lived alone so he could fuck Daphne wherever the mood took him. Kitchen, couch, back porch. Whenever and wherever he wanted.

But that wasn't happening today. He sent her up the stairs in front of him, eyes glued to that gorgeous ass in her body skimming jeans, then pushed her inside his room and kicked the door shut.

She devoured him with a look, neither one moving toward the other now that they could get naked without fear of interruptions. Then she smiled as she dragged her shirt off and dropped it. He wanted to go to her, help her, but it was more fun to watch her strip. She toed off her shoes, pushed her jeans down, and kicked them off until she stood in her panties and bra.

Then she sauntered over to where he stood with his back to the door and reached for his zipper. It wasn't until she dropped to her knees that he had any idea what she was about. She shoved his jeans down his hips and wrapped her hands around his cock.

"Daphne," he said.

She licked him. "Oh no, Candy Kane. I told you I could make you see stars. I plan to prove it."

Chapter Thirty-Two

DAPHNE'S HEART POUNDED WITH EXCITEMENT AS KANE rolled his head back against the door and groaned again.

"Fuck, Daphne, you're killing me here."

"No, you just think I am," she said when she stopped sucking to run her tongue along the underside of his dick before swirling it around the head. A drop of salty pre-cum hit her tongue and she knew he was close. So close.

"I want you to come, Kane. I want to drink you down and hear you say my name."

She thought for sure he was onboard, especially when she started sucking again, but he cupped her head in his hands and stopped her. Then he pulled out and gently lifted her until she was standing.

"What are you doing? You were close!"

"Yeah, trust me, I fucking know," he growled. "Want to be inside you."

Kane was relentless as he walked her backwards to the bed, unsnapping her bra and lifting it off before picking her up and tossing her onto the mattress. He attacked her panties, dragging them off her hips and throwing them over his shoulder. Then he dropped between her legs and licked her from slit to clit as she gasped his name and clutched fistfuls of the sheets.

"How you like that, angel?"

"No fair! I wanted to make you come."

"Mmm," he rumbled as he licked her again. "How about we both come?"

He crawled up her body, licking and kissing and sucking as he went, until she was a mass of nerve endings waiting for the spark. She thought he'd drive into her as soon as he fitted himself between her legs, but instead he took his time and kissed her thoroughly.

And then he slid into her body like he had all the time in the world, until he was deep inside her and they were face to face, breaths mingling in the near darkness.

"You're fucking gorgeous, Sunshine. Inside and out. Need you to know that."

Before she could formulate a reply, he started to move. Everything ceased to exist but this moment. This heat and want and rightness.

They moved together like they'd always done so. Like they were made for each other.

Daphne closed her eyes tight and told herself not to think those thoughts, but they crept in anyway. Kane Fox was the most sensual, gorgeous man she'd ever known. He knew her body almost as well as she did. Knew where and how and when to move to make lightning sizzle. Nobody else had ever touched her like he did.

Sex with him was anything but meaningless for her. It was next level. She thought she could spend a lifetime with him and never grow tired of this dance. But Kane didn't want a lifetime and she needed to remember it instead of building castles in her head.

The fall to the ground would be so much easier when it was over if she didn't do that.

He kissed her and the spark caught, burning into a hot flame, before exploding into a million more sparks that had her crying out and holding tightly to him as her body shook with the force of her pleasure. She'd lasted all of a couple of minutes when she'd wanted more time with him.

But Kane kept moving until he stoked the fires just right. She came again, her body going through the delightful motions of tightening and exploding with sensation once more.

Kane let himself go with a shout, driving her into the mattress as he finished strong, pumping into her until he was spent. Then he rolled to the side and took her with him. Sweat dampened their bodies but the air from the ceiling fan made them cool again as they lay together and just breathed, Kane's fingers tracing a lazy trail up and down her spine.

"I can't think straight when I'm with you," he said, his voice a soft rumble in her ear. "Wasn't always this way, but since you yelled at me in the gym and I saw your tits, I've wanted you naked and in my bed so I could do dirty things to you."

Daphne lifted up on one elbow. "I like the dirty things you do to me. I want you to do more dirty things. Often."

She thought he might laugh or give her one of his grins, but he only looked at her with a serious expression.

"Need you to be careful, babe. No more emerging to confront the Nathan Faders of the world, okay? That wasn't cool, no matter that it turned out to be all right. And if your brother happens to stroll into the range, I'm begging you not to show your face. Let us deal with it."

She gave him a quick kiss. "Careful, Candy Kane, or I'll think you care about me more than you should."

"I care, Daphne. Promise me you won't be reckless, okay?"

She thought about making a joke, trying to lighten the mood, but he looked so serious that she abandoned the plan. "I won't be reckless, Kane. I promise."

"Thank you."

"I don't want you to be reckless either. Just saying."

"I'm never reckless, honey. I always know what I'm doing. Except right now. Got to say I'm at a loss with you."

"Is that such a bad thing?"

"For me? Hell, yeah. I like knowing what I'm doing, where I am, what the plan is. I like being in control. I don't feel in control with you."

"That makes two of us. But maybe we just see where it goes, huh? No pressure, no expectations."

She wanted expectations, but telling him that would put an end to the fun a lot sooner. And she liked being in his bed, having the right to touch him, hearing the sounds he made when he let go and gave himself over to the moment. It was intoxicating.

Kane palmed her ass, squeezed one cheek in his broad hand. "No pressure. But expectations? Sunshine, I expect to do a lot of those dirty things you wanted. Maybe spank this gorgeous ass again. While fucking you from behind, because I really want to watch my cock disappear inside you."

Daphne shivered with longing. "Mmm, sounds delicious. When can we start?"

He moved beneath her and she felt the burgeoning swell of his cock. "Soon. Very soon."

"Insatiable. I love it. Maybe we'll cross those erection pills off the list after all."

He growled as he swatted her ass just hard enough to tingle. "Brat."

She wrapped her hand around him. "Yes, big daddy?"

Kane groaned and laughed at the same time. "You're never forgiving me for the age thing, are you?"

"I dunno. Maybe you need to spank me some more, teach me a lesson."

"Maybe so."

Sooner than she'd have thought possible, Kane was inside her, taking her body to unbelievable heights while her heart ached with all the love she couldn't share.

———

DAPHNE WOKE LATE the next morning. It was Sunday, so she didn't have to be at the range. She stretched, her body aching in all the right places. Kane wasn't beside her, but she hadn't expected to find him there. Especially when she smelled bacon. She sat up, naked as the day she was born beneath Kane's sheets, and smiled to herself.

They had spent the night together, sleeping and making love, whispering hot, sweet words to each other. She'd kept the L-word to herself, of course. Kane had told her how beautiful she was, how sexy, how perfect. He'd said so many wonderful things and she felt good. Better than good.

But she didn't feel completely whole and she probably never would. It was unfair to expect him to love her when she knew what he'd been through with his wife.

Daphne was still angry with the woman, but she was sad for her too. She'd had the love of a good man and she'd thrown it away. Thrown him away. And then she'd paid a price nobody should have to pay for making a stupid mistake.

Daphne found her sweat pants and tank top, her sports bra, and dragged everything on so she could go to the bathroom and brush her teeth before heading downstairs. If Kane lived alone, she'd parade through the house in teeny panties and no bra just to wind him up. Then again, she was still sore from last night so maybe not.

Got to give the coochie time to recover before taking Kane for another spin.

After she brushed her teeth, she dragged her hair into a messy bun and went to the kitchen. Kane was there, cooking breakfast. Her gaze slid over the muscles of his forearms, the way his butt filled his athletic shorts, and desire uncoiled in her belly.

Rawr.

A throat clearing had her turning her head to find Ethan leaning against the counter opposite, cup of coffee in hand. "Morning, Daph."

Heat seeped into her cheeks. "Morning, Ethan. How are you?"

"Pretty good. Had to find my earplugs last night, but once I did that, I slept just fine."

Oh lord.

Kane snorted. "Don't tease her, man. Morning, babe. You sleep okay?"

"Yes. Perfectly. Thank you."

She was still stuck on the idea of Ethan needing earplugs. Had they been that loud? She hoped not.

"Coffee?" Ethan asked since he was standing beside the pot.

"Please."

He poured a cup for her. Daphne had to add her own cream since Ethan didn't know precisely how much. Kane did though. He always fixed her coffee before handing it to her. Yet another thing she enjoyed about being with him. He paid attention and he knew what she liked.

In more ways than one.

When she got close enough to where he stood, he hooked an arm around her waist and dragged her to him, kissing her forehead before letting her go. "Bacon, eggs, and grits this morning. That good?"

"Absolutely."

She wouldn't know how to make grits if her life depended on it. She knew how to cook the bacon, thanks to Kane. Eggs weren't too difficult either so long as she wanted them scrambled. Start poaching or trying to do them over-easy and she was hopeless. Scrambled was a mess, so she could manage that since she'd make a mess anyway.

"I asked around town last night," Ethan began. "Wendy Cochran remembers your brother buying coffee and a slice of banana bread a few days ago at around eight in the morning. There were two other men with him."

Daphne shivered as a current of dread tiptoed down her spine. She'd smelled his blend of vape in her hallway though she'd dismissed it because Jackson wasn't the only person in the world using that blend. She'd thought she was being paranoid. Clearly, she wasn't. He'd been there. Maybe he didn't knock the door down and grab her because he wanted time for his missile bullshit first. Sell his Stingers and then sweep her up on the way out of town. He wouldn't have to stash her then, wouldn't have to deal with people noticing she was gone and looking for her.

"He wouldn't be alone. My father would send men with him—though he might have his own loyalists by now if he's trying to make missile deals and listening to this Dashevsky asshole. No other sightings?"

"He also went to Colleen's shop. She said she didn't like him, that his aura was dark. He bought a leather bracelet with some kind of crystal in it. She babbled a lot about strength and evil, and I checked out after a bit. But I remember she said she smudged her shop when he was gone. And her and Reba performed a cleansing ritual, then drank kombucha and chanted to some goddess or other."

Daphne would have laughed if Colleen wasn't correct about Jackson. Maybe the woman was kooky, but she certainly had her aura reading down if she'd intuited that Jackson's was dark.

Kane brought over a plate piled with eggs, grits, and bacon. "Sit down and eat, Sunshine. Keep your strength up."

Daphne sat and Kane put the plate in front of her, kissing her forehead again before returning to the stove. Ethan didn't bat an eyelash, but then again he'd overhead the bit about spanking yesterday at the range so nothing was going to surprise him now.

"Come and get it, Ethan," Kane told him.

"Oh, I don't get a plate brought to me and a kiss? After the information I got for you?"

"Come get it and I'll kiss you then."

Kane waggled his brows. Daphne laughed.

Ethan shook his head. "On second thought, I'll take the plate without the kiss."

"Thought you might say that."

The three of them sat down to breakfast, eating and talking about the Independence Day celebrations in town tomorrow. Today, they were headed over to Chance and Rory's place for chicken, hamburgers, and hotdogs on the grill. There would be sides like Rory's mac and cheese, Emma's deviled eggs, Callie's pasta salad, and of course cake from Kiss My Grits. There would be other sides too, though Daphne didn't know what. Her contribution was money for ingredients.

The guys would play volleyball, because they were crazy that way. It was predicted to be almost ninety degrees, which meant shirtless volleyball. Daphne didn't mind it, really. She didn't think any of the women did.

Chance had erected a big above ground pool he'd gotten at Walmart that they could cool off in. Rory had been dubious about it with a child on the way, but he'd promised to take it down again once summer was over. Daphne had to admit it was nice to climb into it on a hot afternoon. It was nothing like the pool she'd grown up with, but she probably enjoyed it more because she liked the people more.

After breakfast, she showered and dressed and picked up next month's book club book—this one was about a hockey player and the woman who'd been hired to improve his image, very tame—and retreated to the window seat built into the dormer of Kane's bedroom. She'd gasped with delight when she'd found it, and though he didn't have a cushion there, she'd taken a couple of pillows from the guest room and made a nice reading nook.

The house sat under ancient oak trees, which helped keep it cool along with the AC that had been added at some point in the house's life. From the window, she could see the range in the distance along with rolling fields and trees. It was pretty and peaceful and she leaned back against the wall, book drooping as she yawned.

The stress of yesterday, the night with Kane, the uncertainty of where her brother was and what he was up to made weariness seep into her bones. She was too keyed up for sleep, though. Or so she thought until she opened her eyes to find Kane shaking her awake.

"Time to go, Sunshine."

"Go where?" she asked, her brain still foggy.

"To Chance and Rory's place. Unless you'd rather stay home?"

Home. She liked the way that word sounded. She wanted to ask how he meant it, but she wasn't brave enough.

"No, no. I want to go. I just need a couple of minutes to get ready. How long did I sleep?"

"Couple hours. I thought you needed it so I left you alone."

She palmed his cheek because she could. "Thank you."

He kissed the inside of her wrist. "You're welcome."

I love you. It was on the tip of her tongue. She bit it back and went into the bathroom to pee and brush her teeth, then put her hair into a ponytail since it was hot outside. Her white shorts and navy blue t-shirt were wrinkled but she sprayed them with water from a mister bottle she kept in her overnight bag. Mrs. Donovan had taught her that trick, and it worked. Then she grabbed her tote bag with her book, bathing suit, and sunscreen, and headed downstairs.

When her phone rang, she almost let it go to voicemail. But that wasn't right so she stopped and answered.

"Hey, Warren. I'm sorry I haven't brought your car back yet, but this week has been crazy. I can do it today or tomorrow. When's a good time?"

"Hey Josie. Guess I picked the right guy when I picked this dweeby douche, huh? He so helpfully had your number programmed into his phone. Daphne Bryant. Stupid name."

Daphne stopped on the stairs, her heart in her throat. "Jackson. What have you done to Warren?"

Kane moved toward her, frowning. She locked eyes with him. He joined her on the staircase, wrapped his fingers in hers, and held on.

"Nothing yet. But I will if you don't give me what I want."

"And what's that, pray tell?"

"Like you don't know. Dad wants your copy of the files, and he wants you begging on your knees for him to spare you. Personally, I'd like to put a bullet in your head. But I'll let you live if you give me access to those encrypted accounts you funneled money into."

Daphne's eyes widened. Kane frowned harder. She shook her head.

"What the fuck are you talking about? I don't have any encrypted accounts. I wouldn't be here if I did."

Something clanged in the background. A man yelled in pain, and Daphne's heart constricted.

"Wrong answer, JoJo. You stole a fortune for yourself and I want access to it. Oh, and I'll take the files, too. Bring me the goods or there won't be anything left of your nerd friend for anyone to find."

Of course he'd think she stole money. It's what he would have done if he'd been smart enough. She could keep denying it, but he wouldn't believe her.

"Why? I could leave town. What makes you think I care what you do to him?"

Kane nodded his approval. He understood that she had to play it this way, and she was grateful he didn't automatically think her a soulless monster.

"You care. You've always cared too much about people. You stole Destiny from me. I know it was you." He blew out a breath and she knew he was vaping. " You don't have the stomach, Josie. Never have. Dad tried to toughen you up, but it didn't work. You're weak. If he made you his heir, you'd fuck it all up."

"I don't want the business. You can have it."

"Like I need your permission. It's mine, but I want that money. So you bring me those files and you come prepared to give me access. Maybe you don't care about this jerk off, but I know you care about that barmaid and her brother. The pretty doctor and her parents. Don't want them paying for your negligence, do you?"

Her eyes stung, her heart pounded, and she wanted to reach through the phone and punch him in the nuts. If she had a gun, she'd shoot him between the eyes. "Tell me where and when."

"I'll let you know. You try to run, and so help me God I'll kill all the people you care about in this miserable shit hole. Understood?"

She ground her teeth. "Yes."

"Good. I'll be in touch."

Chapter Thirty-Three

"I DON'T HAVE SECRET ACCOUNTS, ENCRYPTED OR otherwise," Daphne said. She looked furious and worried, but Kane sensed the hint of steel in her spine. She'd been scared when she'd confessed all to Diana Corbin and handed over the files, but she was done with fear now. She was pissed and determined.

After her brother had hung up on her, Kane had messaged his guys and they'd agreed to meet at the range. They'd arrived accompanied by women, a teenager, and a dog, bearing food and patriotic paper goods for piling it onto once it was served. There was a cooler with drinks and somebody'd thought to bring a hose and sprinkler in case anyone wanted to run through it since they weren't going to be in Chance's pool. They had to be ready to act, and the range was the best place to be.

Daphne had apologized for the change in plans, but nobody cared. It was the first time she'd been face to face with her book club besties since her identity had been revealed. He'd thought his heart would break for her as she hung back, apologetic, but they swarmed her and threw their arms around her.

He hadn't heard what they'd said because he'd walked away, a knot in his throat.

Now they sat in one of the meeting rooms, just Daphne and the guys, and discussed the call with her brother.

"Why would he think that?" Ghost asked.

She threw her arms wide. "I don't know! Because it's what he thinks I'd do since I'm an accountant?" She frowned. "It could be speculation on his part, just to see if it's true. It could also be a rumor that's been going around since I left town. To demonstrate the utter depravity of my family, it's also possible our father told him I did so he wouldn't 'accidentally' shoot me on the trip home. Guess Daddy Dearest didn't reckon on Jackson trying to steal the money for himself though. When he figures out I've got nothing, he may kill me anyway."

"We'll make sure you have something," Seth said. "Callie can help. We'll set up fake accounts and layers of security. How much do you think he'd believe you took?"

"Hold on," Kane said. "No way is she meeting with this asshole."

Daphne whirled on him. "We've talked about this, Kane. No telling me what to do. Warren's in danger and it's my fault. I can't let my brother kill him."

Kane's heart thumped. "We're going to find your brother and get Warren back. But you don't need to meet with him. It's dangerous. He has no intention of letting you live, even if you give him access to fake accounts."

He thought she would fight but instead she reached out and caressed his cheek. He loved when she touched him that way. Sweet, simple, not sexual. Though he sure as hell loved it when she touched him in a sexual way, too.

"I know why you're scared. I understand. And I fully

believe you will keep me safe. But we have to plan for a meeting. Jackson's a hothead, but he's not stupid. It's best to be prepared. Because he will be."

Kane could only stare at her, at the fierceness of her expression and the tenderness that was for him alone. Despair twisted inside him, clawing at his skin. He shot to his feet because it was that or explode. Then he paced. He didn't care what his teammates thought, didn't care what they saw. All he cared about was making sure Daphne didn't die.

"I fucking hate this," he growled. "Where the fuck is Diana Corbin, huh? Why hasn't she swept this asshole up yet and taken him off the streets for good?"

Diana wanted to catch him trying to sell the missiles, but waiting was too dangerous. He'd taken Warren Trigg hostage and he was gunning for Daphne. They didn't need to fucking wait. She had the files Daphne had given her. Those should be good enough to put him away.

Nobody said anything. Kane knew why. They weren't going to talk about the Athena Project in front of Daphne. She knew about the missiles and Viktor Dashevsky, separately, but she didn't know the bigger ramifications. Catching Jackson O'Malley making a deal for missiles, especially if he was selling them to Dashevsky's followers in northern Alabama, was pretty fucking important.

Athena wasn't launched yet, and though Ghost Ops had caught the last asshole trying to compromise the project when Callie was the target, they didn't know what Dashevsky's followers planned next. An assault on the laboratory where the command and control system was being tested? That'd be pretty fucking outrageous, but terrorists were terrorists. Even when they were his fellow countrymen and women.

"Let's make the plan," Ghost said. "We can't predict

what Diana will do or when, so let's be fucking prepared to take this asshole down. Seth, make those accounts. Daph, how much money would he believe?"

She shot a glance at Kane. He knew despair was written on his face, but he also knew she believed she had to fix the situation. That she was responsible for her brother and his actions.

"Make it ten-million. He'll believe that."

"Ten mil. Got it," Seth said.

Kane closed his eyes. Everything was spiraling out of control. He'd believed he could protect her, that Jackson wouldn't get anywhere near her, and that the FBI would arrest him before he was ever a threat. But this was a *mission plan.* A plan with an untrained civilian at its heart. A woman he cared about.

A woman he didn't want to lose.

He sat next to Daphne and put a hand on her bare leg beneath the table to ground himself in the moment. She was alive, and here, and he wasn't going to compromise her safety by having a fucking hissy fit. He couldn't afford to focus so much on his own feelings that he missed something important in the planning.

She placed her hand on top of his, her warmth comforting. A wave of emotion crashed against the walls surrounding his heart.

"What about Trigg's phone?" he asked, knowing Seth was thorough but needing to ask anyway. "Any location data?"

"Switched off after the call to Daphne. Last tower pinged was near his house."

"We need to check his place just in case," Blaze said.

"You and Chance head over there," Ghost said. "If you see any movement, call first."

"Copy."

"Ethan, you still got that drone?"

"Yes, sir."

"Take it out to the field north of town near the cross-roads. There are old farms, the defunct cotton mill, and the granary out that way. See if there's anything strange. If I were going to stash somebody close to town for a few hours, that's where I'd do it."

"On it, sir."

Ghost stood. "Okay, we've got people waiting for food, so I'm gonna start the grill. Call me with any updates, and get back here ASAP if you don't spot anything. We need to be prepared to go when Jackson calls. Any thoughts on when that might be, Daph?"

"My brother is a night owl. He hates, and I do mean *hates*, being hot. So he sleeps during the day and works at night when it's cooler. Unless somebody else is calling the shots, which I doubt, he'll keep to the usual nocturnal schedule."

"Huh," Ghost said, looking puzzled for a second. "Who knew you could delay a mission because it's too fucking hot outside? Nobody ever let any of us off the hook because of the potential for swamp ass. Woulda been nice if they did, though."

Amen to that.

The team split to go their own ways and Kane took the opportunity to tug Daphne into the tiny office they'd created for her while they were hiding her from Nathan Fader.

She giggled when he shut the door, then wrapped her arms around his neck. "Oooh, you planning to fuck me in here while all our friends are just a couple of doors away?"

His dick jumped at the idea. "No," he said, gripping her hips and holding her far enough away she couldn't rub against him.

"Party pooper." She stepped back and sat on the makeshift desk, her eyes missing nothing as they studied him. "What's wrong, honey?"

"It's not your fault your brother targeted Trigg. He went after him because he was a soft target. The rest of us are harder."

She broke eye contact, her expression crumbling. "I shouldn't have gone out with him. It *is* my fault. Worse, I let him loan me a car for the past few months. I maintained a friendship with him even after we broke up. I knew what kind of monsters were hunting me, and I let someone as harmless and kind as Warren get close enough to me to be an easy mark."

"Baby, you can't think like that. Your brother threatened Rory and Theo. Emma and her parents. He knows who you care about because he's had you watched. If one of them had been alone this morning, he'd have grabbed them. But Warren lives alone, on property outside of town. He was an easy mark."

"What are you suggesting I do, Kane? Let him die because you don't want me to meet with Jackson?"

He closed his eyes, fisted his hands at his sides. "No."

She sighed and came over to wrap her arms around him, press her cheek to his chest. He hugged her back, dropped his nose to her hair.

"I love that you're worried for me," she said. "Not going to lie, I'm worried too. But I have you—all of you—and I have faith that'll be enough." She tipped her head back to look up at him. Something crossed her face. He didn't have time to wonder what it was before she spoke again. "I'm going to say something else, and you aren't going to like it, but I have to. I would have waited longer, but… well, life's too short and all that."

"Okay."

She stood on tiptoe and kissed him. "I love you, Kane Fox. I have from almost the first moment you stormed into that cold apartment in the Sutton Building and took charge of getting me warm and feeding me. I've wanted you from that day forward but I reconciled myself to the fact you didn't feel the same. And I know you still don't feel what I feel, but I have to say it. Don't worry that I'll be a pain in the ass when you're ready to call it quits. I've always known this was temporary."

His heart swelled with every word she said until he thought it might burst. It hurt so much, and it felt glorious at the same time. Walls crumbled even though he didn't want them to. He felt like he was standing before her naked and vulnerable, his heart on a platter. What if she crushed it the way Hannah had? He would never recover if it happened again. Never.

"It's not temporary," he said roughly.

She arched a brow. "Oh yeah? But it's not permanent either, is it?"

He tugged her tighter to him. "It might be. That a problem?"

"You trying to make up your mind or you don't know?"

"I—" He swore. "I did this once before, and it was brutal."

"Oh, honey," she sighed. "I understand. But I'm not her. You aren't even the same *you* that you were when you were with her. We're different people than those two kids were, okay? I can't promise you anything except I know how I feel, and what I feel is something beautiful and life-changing. I've never met a man I believed in more than you. Never met one as honorable and protective of me as you are. You know me and you think the best of me even when I don't. I won't ever leave you, except if it's out of my control."

He knew what she meant and that was almost worse. Losing someone you loved was brutal, even when you weren't sure you'd ever love them the same way you had before.

"It's okay if you don't love me back. You don't have to say it," she told him. "But I wanted to because, well…" She shrugged. "Life is short and unpredictable sometimes. If something happens, at least I'll know I told you."

"Nothing's happening," he croaked. "Not letting it. We're going to get through this, Daphne. Not letting a fucking prick like your brother take you away from me. Promise you that."

She smiled up at him, and his heart ached. "Aw, does this mean you like me, Candy Kane?"

"Yeah, I like you."

His heart hammered with the truth until he couldn't deny it. But if he said it, there was no turning back. It'd be out there, hanging in the air, ready to gut him for the rest of his life. And yet what would happen if he didn't take the chance?

"I fucking love you, Sunshine. Scares the hell out of me because I didn't want it to happen."

"I'm like that tornado that blew through a few days ago —unexpected and capable of devastating all your plans."

"You've definitely done that. Thought I'd be single the rest of my life and now you've got me thinking about spending all my days with you."

Her smile made his heart sing. "Think we can get Ethan to move next door with Alex?"

"You don't want to go back to your apartment, take me with you?"

"I like my apartment. I love the farmhouse. But I'll go where you want to go."

He kissed the tip of her nose. This was getting easier

the more he talked about it. The more he stopped fighting and just let it sit inside his soul.

"We don't have to decide that yet. We've got time."

"True. So, you want to have a quickie on my desk? Or should we go help with the food?"

He let his gaze slide down her body, back up again. "I want to be inside you. But I think the right thing is to go help. Before they start looking for us."

"Good thinking, babycakes. Let's go be with our friends. Plenty of time for getting busy later."

He sure hoped so. He'd lost one woman he loved and never thought he'd find another.

But he had.

Surely God wasn't so cruel as to take this one from him, too.

Chapter Thirty-Four

JACKSON CALLED AT SEVEN-THIRTY-EIGHT. DAPHNE WAS ready. Blaze and Chance hadn't found anyone at Warren's place. Ethan had nothing to report from the drone flight over old buildings and farms. Not that she'd expected any of them would.

Jackson had spent the past several years doing her father's dirty work. He might not have the tactical know-how of Kane and his friends, but he knew how to hide and how to pick a good defensive location.

"It's time, JoJo. Bring the goods, come alone. None of those fuckers you work for better show their faces or they're dead. I've got eight of my hand-picked men with me and we aren't playing around. You fuck me over, those friends of yours die. I know where they all live, and even if you've warned them, they won't be able to hide for long."

"Yeah, yeah, I hear you. Where am I going?"

"You always were a bitch, you know that?"

"I'm very clear on how you feel about me. It's mutual. What are my guarantees you'll let Warren go?"

"You give me what I want, he's free to go. Word as an O'Malley."

She believed him. He was a bastard, but the O'Malley word was sacred. Her father had drilled that into them as well. They had all kinds of tricks not to give it, but when it was stated that plainly, it was meant.

"And what about me?"

If she didn't ask, he'd be suspicious. But she knew he didn't intend to let her go.

"Same. Give me what I want, you can go with him."

And there it was. The trick. He hadn't said the words, just tried to append her freedom to Warren's. Wasn't the same at all, but she wasn't about to call him on it.

"Dad's people will still be coming after you," he said. "But that's not my problem."

"So you're trying to orchestrate a coup, huh? Good luck."

"Don't know what you're talking about."

"Whatever. There better be internet where you want me to go. Can't magic up a connection to these accounts without it."

He rattled off an address. She wrote it down.

"Twenty minutes, Josie. Or I start cutting off fingers."

"Shit," Kane said when the call was over. "That's an old warehouse on the way to the airport. It's at least a twenty-five minute drive."

"Then there's no time to waste, is there?"

Daphne shouldered the bag with her computer and a copy of the memory stick. She'd changed into a pair of baggy cargo pants and a tank top, all black, and she'd tucked her gun into a holster at her back. Her hair was wound into a tight bun and she had on a ball cap.

Jackson would have her searched and he'd confiscate it,

but he'd expect her to show up armed. It's what O'Malleys did.

She was also wearing a small wire that he hopefully wouldn't find. It was inside her bra, between her breasts, and it was tiny. She'd had to remove the crystal necklace that Colleen had given her because it would make too much noise moving around and clanking the microphone, but she'd stuffed it into her computer bag at the last minute.

Kane had put the mic in place with the seriousness of a monk. He hadn't joked about her assets or tried to caress them or anything. Even now he looked serious and not in the least bit approachable in his black tactical gear bristling with weapons.

But she knew why. He was working to control his fear. Whatever helped him cope was fine with her. She was going to survive this and then she was going to sleep in his arms, secure in the knowledge they'd moved beyond pretending not to want more than a fling. The future was in front of them—provided Diana Corbin held to her end of the bargain and kept Daphne from testifying or getting charged with being an accessory to her family's crimes.

They went outside and Daphne turned to him. "You sure you want me to take your Yukon? It could get damaged."

He gripped her chin in his fingers and tilted her face up, kissed her firmly. "I don't fucking care about the car, Sunshine. I care about *you*."

"Aww," Rory said. "Good answer."

Everyone had gone outside with them. Even Nikki. The women watched her and Kane with a syrupy kind of happiness written on their faces. They weren't worried she wouldn't come back. They'd each been on the receiving end of the kind of help Kane and his teammates specialized in and they believed the outcome would be no different this time.

"I love you all," Daphne said. "Thanks for being my friends, for taking care of me, for giving me a job. I—"

She choked up and couldn't get the words out.

"We love you, too," Emma said. "Now go and kick your brother's ass. We still have cake to eat."

Daphne laughed and climbed into Kane's Yukon as Ethan fired up his truck so the team could follow. He kissed her again. "I love you. We'll be right behind you. Just follow the plan, and we'll take care of the rest."

"I love you, too."

Kane stepped back and closed the door. Daphne sucked back a sob and squeezed the gas. If she never saw any of them again. Never saw Kane again….

But no, she wasn't thinking that way. She ground her jaw, turned on the radio, and pressed play on her phone. Five Finger Death Punch's version of *Bad Company* burst from the Yukon's speakers. She sped along country roads, mindful of time ticking away, and sang the words at the top of her lungs when they got to the chorus.

Jackson had no idea what was about to hit him.

———

DAPHNE DROVE up to the old warehouse with one minute to spare. The building was dingy white with windows up high, some of them broken, and the concrete lot inside the fence was mostly empty. There were a couple of rusty shipping containers, but no movement. She left the Yukon running and got out, shouldering her bag. Then she waited.

A door set into the giant warehouse doors scraped open. Her phone rang.

"Yes?"

"Come inside. Hands up. Try anything and the dweeb loses a finger. Keep trying and he loses his head."

Hatred swirled in her belly. Was it normal to hate your sibling so much? Maybe not, but she didn't think many people had a brother like hers. Or a family like hers.

Seth had tapped her phone so they knew what was being said on both ends. They'd also be able to hear what was said inside the warehouse through the wire she wore. She was supposed to narrate what she saw, as best she could, in order to give them an idea where things were. She knew they would have pulled up a schematic of the building, but who knew how old it was?

Daphne stepped over the metal lip and entered the building. There were a few shipping containers inside, but the building was mostly empty.

A man approached, weapon pointed at her heart.

"Hello, Tim," she said. "Fancy seeing you here."

"Hi, Jos. Need you to hand over the phone. And I gotta check you for weapons."

"Of course."

She gave him the phone and then lifted her arms while he patted her down. Predictably, he found the gun and took it.

"Can't blame me for trying," she said. He kept patting. When he reached her cleavage, she thrust her breasts out. "Go ahead. Feel me up while you've got the chance. Somebody might as well get their jollies."

She didn't want him to feel her up at all, but the words worked the way she hoped. All her father's men had it impressed upon them early on that she was untouchable. John O'Malley didn't care if she had boyfriends outside the organization before he arranged a marriage for her, but his men were required to respect the hierarchy and treat her like the princess she was.

The programming paid off because Tim barely skimmed her breasts. The microphone was safe.

He stepped back and motioned for her to go in front of him. "To the back of the warehouse?" she asked.

"Yes. He's inside the office."

Thank you, Tim.

"Where's everybody else?" she asked, looking around. "I'd like to see who intends to stand with my brother while he takes over the family. Y'all know if he fucks it up you're all dead, right?"

Tim didn't reply, but she hadn't expected he would.

Something clanged overhead and her head snapped up. It was dark in the warehouse, but a glint of light from outside flashed off something metallic. "Wow, Jackson must really think I'm dangerous if he's putting two men on the catwalk to watch me walk across the floor."

"Don't know," Tim said. "I just do what I'm told."

"Like break into my apartment?"

"Wasn't me. Manny did that."

"He wasn't very thorough. Jackson might need to send him for remedial training."

Tim grunted. "Don't know anything about it."

They reached the office at the back of the warehouse and Tim opened the door. Jackson stood, undisguised glee on his face. There were three men with him. One stood behind the chair Warren was seated in. The other two flanked it.

She only knew one of the men. None of them looked very friendly toward her.

Warren's face was bloody and bruised, but his eyes flashed with hope when he saw her. Her stomach curled into itself as guilt shook her to the core.

"Wow, you need three men with you to do your dirty work, Jackson? That's unlike you."

That was six men accounted for. Two must be outside, watching the approach to the warehouse. She hadn't seen them, but she hoped Kane and the guys would. And she hoped her narration had been clear. Should she find a way to say there were six men plus Jackson? Or did they understand?

"It's called delegation, JoJo." His gaze dropped to the computer bag. "You better not be planning a con, baby sis. It won't go well for you."

"Honestly, I don't expect any of this to go well for me."

Tim handed over the Glock she'd been carrying. "She came armed."

Jackson studied the weapon, then placed it on the desk nearby. "Did you think to shoot me, huh?"

"I don't go anywhere unarmed. You know that. Rule number one in our world."

He smirked. "I'd have thought you were slipping if you hadn't had a gun. How the fuck did you end up working at a range anyway? You never wanted to spend time at the armory or help with any of the gun business."

"Would you believe me if I said it was an accident?" She shrugged. "I was working as a hotel maid, but I got fired. The range owners found me squatting in an empty apartment and took me in. I couldn't say no to a job, especially when they offered to pay me better than cleaning did."

"I don't know why you fucking wanted to work at all when you had plenty of money."

"Didn't want to touch it for a few years. Might arouse suspicion."

It was bullshit, but it sounded like something he'd expect her to say.

"Yeah, well, working there got you seen. Should have seen Dad's face when he got the call from one of his suppliers. He's been shitting himself on the regular since you left. Figured you took a copy of everything and planned to use it. But you never did. Why not?"

She scoffed. "Are you kidding? Do you know how many people he's bought in law enforcement. I didn't trust anyone to actually put him away."

Before she knew what was happening, Jackson backhanded her. Her head snapped to the side and her cheek stung. There would be a bruise, but she didn't think he'd broken skin.

"You betrayed the family when you left." He grabbed her gun and put it to her cheek. "Fucking turncoat bitch to even consider going to the law. Why the fuck would you do that? You had everything, Josie."

She didn't answer him because anything she said would just give him another reason to hit her. Plus she didn't think he really wanted an answer.

He wrapped his hand around the back of her neck and shoved her toward the desk. "Show me you've got the files."

Daphne stumbled into the desk, then righted herself and sat in the chair. Warren watched her with fearful eyes, but she couldn't let that distract her. She was supposed to take her time if at all possible and she was doing so.

She took the computer from the bag and opened it up. Seth and Callie had created a banking website that was rudimentary, but it would stand up to scrutiny from people who weren't programmers. Before she went there, however, she took out the memory stick and plugged it into the port. It took a few seconds, but the files populated in the finder. She sat back and pointed.

"All there. Copies of the financials, public and private."

"Open a file."

She moved her finger over the trackpad and double clicked. The file opened. It was a spreadsheet, very detailed because she was detailed, with numbers, names, and dates.

"It's all there. Everything you need to know if you're going to run the family business. Satisfied?"

He nodded and she closed the file. Then she ejected the stick and handed it to him. He slipped it into a pocket and jerked his head toward the screen. "Now the money."

"Need the WiFi password."

Tim placed a piece of paper on the desk and slid it toward her. She typed in the string of characters and the WiFi connected. Time seemed to slow as she typed in the name of the fake bank. The website was blank, the cursor spinning helplessly as it waited.

"Why's it taking so long?" Jackson growled.

"I don't know," she answered in the same voice. "Because your connection is shitty?"

She thought he was about to the end of his patience when the bright yellow website popped up on her screen.

Bank of Grand Cayman

There was no Bank of Grand Cayman, but Jackson didn't know that. She navigated to the login screen, praying that Kane and the guys would arrive any second. She could log into the fake account, the balance would populate, and the transfer screen would appear when Jackson asked for it. But nothing would happen after that. There would be no transfer because there was no money.

She almost wished she *had* stolen a couple million. But no, she didn't want that money because it was earned from other people's misery. War, drugs, prostitution, trafficking. She wanted no part of it anymore. She only wished she'd been brave enough to leave that life sooner.

She *was* a good person. Kane thought so. Her friends

at One Shot Tactical thought so. Warren probably didn't, but if she got him out of here, she wouldn't care. He'd be alive, and that would be what mattered.

"Before I login," she said, looking up at where her brother hovered over her, "What about Warren? You promised to let him go."

"When you give me the money."

The chair creaked as she leaned back and crossed her arms. "You know, if I refuse to do this, you could kill me now—but you won't have my money. At this point, I'm thinking I have nothing left to lose. You let him go, now, or this doesn't happen."

Jackson's face turned mottled, which wasn't flattering with his coloring. She knew the explosion was coming and she braced for it. He planted his fist in her gut and she doubled over, wheezing. She'd prepared herself, hardened her core muscles like Kane had taught her, but it still hurt.

Fuck, it hurt. She dragged in air and tried not to gag as he dropped to her level. He shoved his red face in hers, spittle flying as he growled at her.

"I will motherfucking remove his fingers one by one. Then I'll force them down your throat. Log the fuck in, Josie, and give me that goddamn money."

Chapter Thirty-Five

"Wʜᴀᴛ ᴛʜᴇ ꜰᴜᴄᴋ ɪs sʜᴇ ᴅᴏɪɴɢ?"

It was Ghost's voice on the comm. Kane didn't know, but his heart was in his damned throat. When her brother had hit her the first time, because Kane recognized the sound of flesh connecting with flesh, he'd taken the blow in his soul.

This hit, though. He heard her grunt, heard the whimper of pain, and he wanted to rip Jackson's fucking head off and spit down his throat.

"I don't know," Kane said roughly.

"Targets at ten and two," Ethan said into the comm. "Blaze and Chance neutralizing."

They'd followed a couple of miles behind Daphne. He wasn't sure she knew they were listening when she was belting out *Bad Company*, but he'd gotten a chuckle out of it. They all had. She had attitude and spirit. Still didn't mean he wanted her in there alone, but it'd been the only way.

Ghost had called Agent Corbin when they were a few minutes out, as a courtesy. She'd sworn in a way that'd shocked the hell out of everyone. Diana was usually so unbothered, but this time she was clearly pissed.

"Don't do anything stupid," she'd ordered. "We're on the way."

"Fuck her," Ghost had said when the call went dead. "Stick to the plan."

Which is how they found themselves cutting the fence and breaching the premises. Thanks to Daphne's calm recitation of how many men were with Jackson, they knew that two were unaccounted for—provided he'd been telling the truth about having eight men along for the ride.

The team had found the two inside the fence, stationed so they could presumably watch the perimeter, and now they would be dealt with. Left seven men on the inside, including Jackson.

And two hostages.

"You can't make me," Daphne said, and Kane braced. "Cut his fingers off, cut mine off, but you won't have any money unless you let him fucking go. *Now.*"

Goddamn she was brave. And insane. He was going to shake her and hug her—and shake her some more if she got out of this alive.

Nobody said anything as the Ghost Ops team crept closer. Two men on the catwalk, the rest in the office with Daphne and Warren.

"In position," Blaze said.

"In position," Chance added.

Both men were ready to breach the building through the windows and neutralize the men on the catwalk. Seth had found a schematic of the building and the exits, so they knew where they needed to be for maximum impact.

Sweat dripped down Kane's face. He didn't bother wiping it away. Fucking tactical vests with plated armor were hot.

He worried that Daphne didn't have something protective. But there'd been no way to equip her with anything that wouldn't be obvious. If she'd sauntered into her brother's temporary lair with a ballistic vest, he'd have taken it away.

"Escort the dweeb to the front gate," Jackson said, his voice dripping with contempt.

"No escort," Daphne said. "He walks out of here on his own. He can take my SUV and drive away. Once I know he's gone, I'll give you the money."

There was silence again. And then, "Fuck this shit," Jackson growled. "Ain't no traitor bitch telling me how to run my business. He stays. Don, start with the pinkie."

Warren's voice was muffled, probably because they'd gagged him, but it was clear he was screaming.

"Go!" Ghost cried.

The team swarmed the warehouse, throwing a flash bang to startle and confuse the occupants, and arrowed for the office. Two men burst from the door, pistols in hand. Kane took one out with his Sig while Ethan got the other.

Two more men emerged from a door farther down. They were neutralized just as quick. That left Jackson with Daphne. Kane reached the office first while the team fanned out to make sure the warehouse was truly clear.

If Daphne was dead, there wouldn't be anything left of Jackson to bury. Kane knew Jackson had to be a crack shot like Daphne, but he couldn't waste time hanging around outside the office to assess the situation before he went in.

He burst through the door, weapon at the ready—

And came up short as soon as he cleared the entry. Daphne's head snapped up, the pistol in her hand swinging toward him. Until she realized it was him and her hand dropped to her side.

"Dammit, Candy Kane, you scared the crap out of me."

"Sunshine," he croaked. "What did you do?"

She stood over her brother like an avenging angel. Jackson lay on the floor, curled in on himself, moaning.

Kane recognized that pose. It was the pose of a man who'd had his nads punched into next week.

"Not as much as he deserves," she said in a colder voice than he'd ever heard her use as she seated her weapon in the holster. He'd never thought a woman holstering a gun was sexy before, but *daaaammmn*. She looked like fucking Lara Croft, Tomb Raider.

Warren Trigg made a noise. Daphne gasped and rushed to his side, removing the gag with trembling fingers and then throwing her arms loosely around his shoulders.

"Warren, oh Warren! I'm so sorry! Are you okay? What did they do to you?"

Kane wasn't surprised at the stirring of jealousy, but it went away just as quickly. Daphne was his. She loved *him*. But Warren was her friend, one-time boyfriend, and she felt responsible for him. She was a decent, lovely person and she cared about people. He wouldn't dim her shine for all the money in Fort Knox.

He went to stand over Jackson, who coughed and sputtered and tried to talk but couldn't find the air. Kane dropped to a knee to zip tie the motherfucker's wrists and ankles.

"Kill… Bitch…" Jackson wheezed. "Fucking… Bitch!"

"Careful, dickhead," Kane growled as he stood, "Or I'll let her finish the job and shoot your ass. Much as I'd like to do it for her, I don't think she needs me to."

Jackson glared, his face red, and then coughed so hard Kane thought he was probably trying to make his balls drop again. Fucker.

Ghost and Seth filled the door, took in the scene, and went to administer first aid to Warren. Blaze, Chance, and Ethan arrived soon after. Daphne, freed of the need to tend to Warren's injuries, went to Kane's side, eyes brimming with tears. He opened his arms and she threw herself into them.

"Can we go? I want to go home and shower, then I want to lie in bed with you and not talk to anyone for the next twenty-four hours."

Kane kissed the top of her head. "Not yet, babe. Diana's on the way."

"Oh. Was she mad?"

Kane snorted. "Understatement."

He ushered her over to the desk and set her down on it. Then he tipped her head up to study her face. Her cheek was red, and she winced as he touched it. "He hit me."

"I heard. Killed me to hear that and know I couldn't stop him."

"It's okay. I got revenge." She pointedly looked over at her brother and then at him again. "He punched me in the stomach too. Hurt like hell, but I braced like you taught me. Made it a lot better."

Anger crackled like lightning inside. "We need to get you checked out along with Warren. Make sure nothing's damaged."

"Okay. I don't think it is, though. I can breathe without pain, and the achy feeling isn't quite as bad as it was."

He drew a shaky breath. "What happened, Daph? You went off script."

She sighed. "I was just so angry, and I was afraid you wouldn't get here in time. So I decided to bluff. Without me, he couldn't get the money anyway."

"We heard that. But what did you do to him?"

"When the flash bang went off, he was distracted. They

all were. I closed the computer and then swung it at his head. He didn't see it coming, but he also didn't go down the way he did when we were kids. He reached for me—and since I was still sitting in the chair and he had to get close, I kicked him in the balls. Then I punched him in the gut and brought the computer down on his head again. Think it's broke now," she grumbled.

He hugged her tight and breathed in the warm, sweet scent of her. He'd been scared for her, scared of losing her.

"I never want you to have to defend yourself again, but I'm fucking glad you know how."

"Thanks to you."

The slamming of car doors penetrated the warehouse. A minute later, Diana Corbin and a team of FBI agents swarmed the building. Diana lowered her gun when she stepped into the office and surveyed the scene.

"Dammit," she yelled to no one in particular.

"Might want to check those shipping containers, Agent," Ghost said as he strode toward her. "Could be something interesting."

Her eyes narrowed. "Are you telling me…? How do you know?"

Ghost winked. "Face it, Diana. We're better at this than you are."

Uh-oh, Kane thought.

Ghost had poked the dragon. And the dragon was glaring like she'd just found dinner.

———

EARLY MORNING SUNLIGHT shafted through the blinds and across the sleeping woman at his side. He thought about getting up and making breakfast, but he didn't want to wake her. He would lie there beside her until she woke up, and he would thank God for every moment he could do so.

That she was alive. That she'd knocked down all the walls around his heart and forced him to let love in. He'd forgotten how it felt, that boundless warmth and contentment, and he welcomed it now. Love wasn't perfect, he knew that, but he'd been young and dumb the first time and so had Hannah. They might have weathered the storm, but he would never know.

All he knew was that he'd finally let her go. He wouldn't use her as an excuse anymore to keep his feelings bottled up. He didn't think she'd ever wanted that for him anyway.

It was not only possible to love again, it was miraculous. What a fucking dumbass he'd been to resist. Daphne was his miracle and he'd almost fucked it all up.

The sunlight moved across the bed until it caressed Daphne's face. The red spot on her cheek was turning darker where her brother had hit her. He wished like hell he'd found a reason to put a bullet into Jackson O'Malley, but the dude had stayed curled on the floor, coughing and moaning, until Diana Corbin and her agents arrived. Too late then.

Daphne's eyes fluttered open. Warmth filled their green depths, and his heart squeezed. She loved him despite all he'd done to make sure she didn't. He was a lucky bastard.

"Morning," she said, her voice rusty.

"Morning. How you feeling?"

She frowned as if taking inventory. "Pretty good all things considered. My cheek hurts, and my stomach is still a little sore, but I think I'm fine."

Diana had taken over last night when she arrived, which was good because she didn't have to hide who she was, and she'd called the paramedics. They'd thoroughly checked both Daphne and Warren out. Warren had to go to the hospital for observation. He had a concussion and a couple of cracked ribs. Since they didn't know what else might have happened to him, they'd taken him in.

Daphne was fine, thankfully. If she'd had to spend the night in the hospital, Kane would have been right there in a chair by her bed, holding her hand and watching over her. Instead, he'd gotten to hold her in his bed all night long.

"That's good, though I wish he'd never hit you."

"I know, but it could have been worse."

He didn't want to think about it.

"I love you," he told her. It was easier every time he said it.

"I love you, too. And I'm not sorry I rushed telling you yesterday, though I wasn't planning on it for a while yet."

He pushed a lock of hair behind her ear. "I'm not sorry either. Needed to get my head out of my ass, and you forced me to do it."

She grinned. "Oh, I'm sure your head will still be in your ass sometimes."

"Probably."

"So what do we do now?"

His gaze dropped to her naked breasts. "I can think of a few things."

"Oh, I can too. But I meant about us. I know I kind of teased you about moving in here, but we don't have to move in together if you don't want to. We can date for a while, see how it goes. I know this is a big step for you."

He rolled her to her back as she squeaked, settling between her hips.

"We're not seeing how it goes, Sunshine. You're mine and I'm yours. You can move in here because I know you love it. Ethan already told me last night he's going to stay in the other house with Alex. Can't promise you we can buy it, though. It's part of the shared property. And I know there are things you still don't know about what me and the guys are doing here, so I have to ask you to accept that for now. But if I can give you this house permanently, I will."

She traced his mouth with a finger. "I love the house, but I love you more. If we can't keep it, we'll find another one. Provided Diana keeps me out of whatever goes down with my family."

"I promise you she will." He kissed the tip of her nose. "Need you to know something else, babe. I know I have a bit of a reputation for charming women, and I've deliberately leaned into it, but you don't have to worry that every woman you meet in town is someone I've been with. I took some of them out, yeah, but that's as far as it went."

She blinked. "Wait a minute. Are you telling me that you faked being a man-ho?"

"Yeah, I did. Mostly. Not a monk, but I also didn't fuck around with anyone in this town knowing I had to live here and face them in the Piggly Wiggly or the Dawg from time to time."

Daphne laughed. "Oh my God, you almost sound like a prude. Like you seriously didn't bang anybody because you might see them while shopping for toilet paper or, gasp, condoms?"

He dropped his head to her breast, sucked one beautiful nipple into a tight little point, and she stopped laughing.

"Brat," he murmured against her skin as he moved to the other nipple.

Her fingers curled into his shoulders. "Old man," she gasped as he nudged her wet opening with his cock.

But her legs spread wide and he slid all the way home, groaning with the rightness of it.

He took her over the edge—twice—and then took her to the shower where he did it all again.

Then he made her breakfast, listening to her plans for redoing the kitchen someday, waxing the floors to a shine, and hanging curtains, and knew there was no place else he'd rather be.

Life with Daphne was fucking perfect—and he was going to revel in every moment of it.

Chapter Thirty-Six

"This is what you wanted with the fifty bucks you won? Are you sure?"

Daphne stared at the man she loved as he grinned back at her. "Yup."

"Fifty dollars worth of hot dogs, ice cream, and a red, white, and blue cowboy hat that you intend to wear while we walk around town and enjoy the Independence Day Fest? Are you sure you don't want these star sunglasses too?"

"Good idea," he said, snatching those up and motioning for her to pay the grinning man behind the counter.

She shook her head but shelled out twenty bucks for the hat and glasses. They'd already spent twelve dollars on hot dogs and sodas, and he wanted ice cream. As soon as she was done paying, Kane grabbed her hand and they kept walking to the ice cream booth.

It was a beautiful afternoon in Sutton's Creek. Yes, it was hot, but the humidity was manageable for once. Daphne had put on white shorts and a blue cropped top and she wore a straw sun hat with sunglasses. She was cute and stylish. Kane, meanwhile, looked both ridiculously handsome and ridiculous.

They made their way over to the shady sidewalk in front of the Dawg where they'd set up their chairs for the parade and fireworks later. She'd been surprised that the guys wanted to be there for the fireworks after what Kane had said to her about looking for active shooters, but apparently they'd all decided it was their duty to attend and show support for the town that supported them and their business.

"Good grief, Kane," Rory said when she saw them. "Are you auditioning for the part of Yankee Doodle Dandy or what?"

Kane licked his cone. "I'm spending Daphne's money. She lost a bet, and since she'd never spend it on anything ridiculous for herself, I'm doing it for her."

"You are succeeding, sir," Rory said.

"Thanks. Y'all want anything? I still need to get a necklace with flashing lights before it gets dark. And maybe one of those giant foam fingers."

Daphne rolled her eyes but inside she felt warm and gooey. Kane made her happy. Since he'd admitted he loved her, he had no problem showing it. Holding her hand, putting his arm around her, kissing her forehead randomly when they were with their friends.

Backing her into a dark corner and kissing her senseless when nobody was looking.

She loved being loved by Kane Fox. It'd been worth every moment of the angst and pain she'd had to endure to get to this place in her life.

Diana Corbin had come to the range yesterday and given them an update. The O'Malleys were finished. Her father and many of the people under him had been arrested. Jackson had been caught with the shipment of Stingers and wasn't talking. Diana wanted to know who they were intended for, but Jackson wouldn't roll over. Even if he did, it wouldn't get him freed. Though it might help in his sentencing. Not that he seemed to care since he knew he'd be a dead man walking no matter what.

His human trafficking operation was at an end, too. The people who could be rescued would be. It wasn't perfect, but it was something.

Josephine O'Malley was also in custody, according to Diana, and would be prosecuted with her family. There was always the chance someone from her old life would see her in Sutton's Creek, but she was officially Daphne Alison Bryant and always had been.

Daphne didn't know what magic Diana had worked for that, but the ID Kenny made had somehow been government-approved along with her background. She needed to get new—real—documents, but she was legit. She worried that someone would come looking for her eventually, or that her father would send assassins, but Alex had stepped in to assure her that wasn't happening. Her father's influence was at an end and the remaining crime bosses were dividing the territory between them. Nobody was interested in her. Those who were would be in no position to do anything about it. Ever.

She decided to stop worrying and start living. She would always look over her shoulder, always keep her self-defense and shooting skills up to date, but hopefully she would never have to use them again.

She even thought she might like to teach a class, give women the perspective of another woman who'd had to defend herself using those skills. And of course she was angling for turning the range into an event space as well. Alex had promised to consider it—right after he'd given her a raise and told her she was their official bookkeeper now, if she wanted to be.

She did, and they were looking for someone for the front desk, though she was happy to continue there until they found the right person.

A man limped toward them with a woman by his side. Warren Trigg had been released from the hospital the day after the showdown with Jackson. He had a black eye, but he was smiling. He waved when they got closer.

"Afternoon, y'all."

Daphne and Kane had gone to the hospital to see him. Jackson had threatened to cut off his fingers, but they hadn't succeeded before Kane and the guys stormed the warehouse. Thank God. He was beaten and bruised but he would heal.

Daphne had been devastated by what her brother did, but Warren told her he didn't blame her for it. She had come to save him when she didn't have to, and she'd pushed for his release. Not only that, but God had a reason for everything He did. And then the nurse— Gabby—had smiled at Warren and he'd smiled back. Now she was at his side, holding his hand, and Daphne was happy for him if something good had come from the experience.

"Hey, Warren. How are you feeling?"

He squeezed Gabby's hand. "Better every day. Ribs hurt. Hurts to laugh. But I'm happy."

Gabby stood on tiptoe to kiss his cheek and he blushed.

"Want to sit with us? We have extra chairs."

Warren and Gabby exchanged a look. "That would be lovely. Thank you," she said softly.

"You need anything, buddy?" Kane asked. "Hot dog? Hamburger? Ice cream? Bottle of water? Happy to get it for you."

Warren shook his head. "Thanks, but I'm good. Appreciate it though."

Kane put a hand on Warren's shoulder. He didn't squeeze, because he was too mindful of Warren's condition to do so. "You got it, man. You change your mind, let me know."

Tears pricked the back of her eyes as Kane wrapped an arm around her and leaned in to kiss her cheek. "Love you," he said.

"You're sweet, you know that?" She had to swallow the knot in her throat.

"Not sweet," he said in her ear. "I take care of those I care about. He's in the club now."

"Really?"

"He's a decent guy, like you said. And he could have made you feel worse than you already did for what happened. He knows it wasn't your fault, no matter what you think, and I gotta give the guy his due for not blaming you. He could have made my woman feel like shit but he didn't."

Daphne sniffled. "Are you ready to sit down or do you need to get that necklace? Or maybe head over to Colleen's booth to get your palm read?"

"Let's sit with our friends for a while."

They sank into their chairs and watched kids playing in the fountain in the town square. Paisley Allen was there with her daughter, a cute little girl named Violet, and she waved when she saw them. Violet waved too when Paisley said something to her.

Daphne leaned her head against Kane's shoulder and sighed happily. This was the life she wanted. Small town, with best friends and a man she loved. Maybe one day they'd have their own little girl to play in the park with. Or a little boy.

A boy with Kane's eyes. A girl with her hair. Didn't matter to her which they got. They'd be happy either way.

"Got you something because I knew you wouldn't buy it for yourself," Kane said, jogging her out of her daydreams.

"What's that?"

He pulled two pieces of paper from his shirt pocket and handed them to her. Daphne snorted when she realized what they were.

"The cemetery walk and kombucha tasting tour? Really?"

"Hey, she's an old lady hustling for a living. And we might have fun. Especially if Reba drinks too much kombucha and falls into a grave again."

Daphne threw her head back and laughed. Then she flung her arms around his neck and kissed him.

"You're the best kind of fun, Kane Fox. And you're mine."

He nuzzled her ear and nibbled the lobe. "Always, Sunshine. Gonna marry you one day. Soon as the mission is done. You willing?"

"Yes, I am. Always. My heart is yours."

Kane would guard her heart fiercely. He would protect her. He would love her.

His lips brushed her forehead and then he tucked her into his side again. She sighed.

Belonging. It was the most incredible feeling.

———

ETHAN WATCHED Paisley Allen and her daughter frolic in the fountain. He pretended not to, but he was aware of every move Paisley made. Had been since the first moment he'd seen her in the Dawg when Emma had introduced her as the new librarian.

She'd recognized him, he was certain. But now she pretended like she didn't know him, like she'd never met him before. Like their paths hadn't crossed in the most intimate of ways long before either of them were living in Sutton's Creek.

He wanted to confront her, make her acknowledge him.

And he wanted to stop this awareness in its tracks, go back to the way things were before she showed up and made him question everything he knew.

But that, he feared, was impossible. Change was on the horizon.

Time to buckle up and hold on for the ride.

———

THANK you for reading Kane and Daphne's story! I hope you enjoyed it! Ethan and Paisley are next!

SCAN THE QR code to join my newsletter list! Get information on sales, new books, and free content.

SCAN ME

––––––

The Hostile Operations Team ® Books
Strike Team 1

Book 0: RECKLESS HEAT

Book 1: HOT PURSUIT - Matt & Evie

Book 2: HOT MESS - Sam & Georgie

Book 3: DANGEROUSLY HOT - Kev & Lucky

Book 4: HOT PACKAGE - Billy & Olivia

Book 5: HOT SHOT - Jack & Gina

Book 6: HOT REBEL - Nick & Victoria

Book 7: HOT ICE - Garrett & Grace

Book 8: HOT & BOTHERED - Ryan & Emily

Book 9: HOT PROTECTOR - Chase & Sophie

Book 10: HOT ADDICTION - Dex & Annabelle

Book 11: HOT VALOR - Mendez & Kat

Book 12: A HOT CHRISTMAS MIRACLE - Mendez & Kat

––––––

The HOT SEAL Team Books

Book 1: HOT SEAL - Dane & Ivy

Book 2: HOT SEAL Lover - Remy & Christina

Book 3: HOT SEAL Rescue - Cody & Miranda

Book 4: HOT SEAL BRIDE - Cash & Ella

Book 5: HOT SEAL REDEMPTION - Alex & Bailey

Book 6: HOT SEAL TARGET - Blade & Quinn

Book 7: HOT SEAL HERO - Ryan & Chloe

Book 8: HOT SEAL DEVOTION - Zach & Kayla

———

HOT Heroes for Hire: Mercenaries
Black's Bandits

Book 1: BLACK LIST - Jace & Maddy

Book 2: BLACK TIE - Brett & Tallie

Book 3: BLACK OUT - Colt & Angie

Book 4: BLACK KNIGHT - Jared & Libby

Book 5: BLACK HEART - Ian & Natasha

Book 6: BLACK MAIL - Tyler & Cassie

Book 7: BLACK VELVET - Dax & Roberta

———

The HOT Novella in Liliana Hart's MacKenzie Family Series

HOT WITNESS - Jake & Eva

––––––

7 Brides for 7 Soldiers

WYATT (Book 4) - Wyatt & Paige

7 Brides for 7 Blackthornes

ROSS (Book 3) - Ross & Holly

––––––

About the Author

Lynn Raye Harris is a Southern girl, military wife, wannabe cat lady, and horse lover. She's also the New York Times and USA Today bestselling author of the HOSTILE OPERATIONS TEAM Ⓡ SERIES of military romances, and 20 books about sexy billionaires for Harlequin.

A former finalist for the Romance Writers of America's Golden Heart Award and the National Readers Choice Award, Lynn lives in Alabama with her handsome former-military husband, one fluffy princess of a cat, and a very spoiled American Saddlebred horse who enjoys bucking at random in order to keep Lynn on her toes.

Lynn's books have been called "exceptional and emotional," "intense," and "sizzling" -- and have sold in excess of 4.5 million copies worldwide.

To connect with Lynn online:
www.LynnRayeHarris.com
Lynn@LynnRayeHarris.com

www.ingramcontent.com/pod-product-compliance
Lightning Source LLC
Chambersburg PA
CBHW020242010826
48973CB00006B/1619